Conned In Cleveland

Nelle Lewis

© 2018 by Nelle Lewis. All Rights Reserved.
First Publication Date 04/17/2018
Hooky Life Publishing Company/ Hookyforlife@gmail.com
Cover design by Estella Vukovic/ estella.vukovic@gmail.com
Printed by CreateSpace, An Amazon.com Company
Available from Amazon.com, CreateSpace.com. and other retail outlets
ISBN: 0998358916
ISBN-13: 978-0-9983589-1-8

It's the hard that makes it great. — A *League Of Their Own*

For Melanie and Thom

Chapter One

I smashed my chest into the hedge and widened my stance in the muddy earth below me, bracing my weight against the branches to secure my footing. Squinting through a gap in the hedge, I fingered apart a nest of branches and watched Mark MacGregor as he tongued the blonde woman on the front porch of her McMansion. He worked his way from her earlobe to collarbone and across to the opposite ear, stopping mid-flight to molest her mouth again. I could hear the woman's giggle from my hidey hole across the street. Despite being twenty years too old to carry a giggle with any self-respect, and despite being twenty years senior to the man currently slipping a hand up her silk shirt, I had to give her credit. She seemed to be enjoying the hell out of herself.

I positioned my camera lens into the crevice of branches I'd created for my face, and snapped off a dozen shots of the couple's make-out session before shifting my weight back onto my heels to look down at the camera screen. The shots were clean. My boss would be happy. The client, not so much.

I raised the camera to my prey again and zoomed in on the Beemer parked in the McMansion's driveway. I snapped away, capturing a few good shots of the car and license plate, before panning back to MacGregor. By the sudden droop in the woman's cleavage, and the exaggerated shriek coming from her mouth, it appeared MacGregor had successfully undone the woman's bra. I watched and clicked as the woman fumbled to re-secure her goods while MacGregor took a last go at her neck. The woman shoved him away playfully but with enough intent that MacGregor gave her a final peck and turned toward the driveway.

The woman looked over at her neighbor's empty driveway, then stage whispered to MacGregor. "Have a good day, lover."

Bleh. Originality was a lost art. I'd been doing some basic background and surveillance work for my PI brother after coming home to Cleveland several months prior, and the gig had already exposed to me enough infidelity to make me seriously question the wisdom of marriage. Change the names, change the perfumes, but the words, the giggles, the games were all the same. It was like watching one cheap telenovela over and over again. But I got paid to watch that novella, no matter how bad the acting, so I shot a few more pictures of Mark MacGregor's mistress du jour.

Satisfied, I rested back on my heels again and tilted the camera up to review my booty. Bad move.

My left heel sank into the mud underneath me. I shifted my weight to the right to stop the sinking and my foot slid across the top of the mud pool, sending me into a sideways split. Unfortunately, Gumby I was not. I pushed all my weight back to my left and managed to step out of the shoe that was now submerged in the mud. Freed from my sneaker prison, the force of my shifting weight sent me tumbling forward, face-first into the hedge. I landed on both knees in the mud, and face, hands, and camera stuck in the hedge. I smashed my lips together in an effort not to telegraph my pain. My hidey hole was a solid fifty feet from MacGregor and his secret lover, but it was a quiet morning in a well-to-do neighborhood, and my voice isn't one to be mistaken for the sweet tweet of a morning glory bird.

I gingerly pulled the camera from the tangled vines of the hedge and recapped the lens after a cursory check told me my plunge into the hedge had saved it from hitting the mud. I'd styled my hair that morning in a ponytail in honor of the windy day, but the force of my fall had whipped the tail forward and the ends of my hair clung to the branches. I teased it slowly back and forth from the hedge and heard MacGregor's car start up across the street. Hair still stuck, I palmed my cheek with one hand to protect it and pushed into the hedge with the other, creating a new hole to peek through. The woman had crossed to the Beemer and was leaning into MacGregor's driver side window, taking her turn at his mouth. Relieved that I hadn't betrayed my presence, I worked quickly to untangle my ponytail and raise my camera to capture the woman's goodbye overture. I belatedly remembered to remove the lens cap and caught only a snippet as she turned away from the car and MacGregor's reverse lights blinked white.

I capped the camera again and freed my hair at last. I yanked my head back and felt my socked foot slide underneath me. I couldn't cover the yelp this time as I landed on my ass in the trough of mud.

ΩΩΩ

"We might have to put you on surveillance restriction." My brother stood on the porch of the old Lakewood bungalow that served as his investigation agency's office and watched as I pressed the toes of my left foot into the heel of my right shoe in an effort to pry it off. Freed of my shoes, I stuck a finger in the back of each sock, peeling them and tossing them on top of my Vans. Straightening, I pulled my sweatshirt inside out over my head in an effort to trap the mud inside, tossed it onto the growing pile of clothing on the porch and took the towel Paul offered, wiping my face as I stepped past him into the office.

Paul trailed behind me as I headed to my desk and yanked my spare sweater from the back of my chair to button up over my tee shirt.

"To be fair," I said. "I've only kind of botched two surveillance jobs since I started this gig."

"It's been six months. We should probably talk about what you consider a winning percentage."

Paul squinted at the red sweater that I'd layered over my green tee shirt, then glanced down at my muddy jeans and bare feet.

"Tell me you've got something besides that sweater in one of those desk drawers over there?"

"Negative. I'll finish up today's report and head home to change." I folded the fresh towel Paul had passed me and put it in my chair before I took a seat. "Why?"

"We've got a client interview at 2:00."

"Where?"

Paul grinned.

"Ah, geez," I said.

"You're in luck. We're going to the laundromat."

Twenty minutes later, Paul yanked open the door to Bubbles Abound Laundry and stepped back. I slunk past him and breathed in a heady hit of fabric softener, the steam inside the room heavy on my face. It was like being mauled by the Snuggle bear.

I tugged the hem of my tee down over the back of my jeans, and my sweater down over the tee shirt, keenly aware that I looked like first runner up at an ugly Christmas sweater party.

Paul pointed to the back corner of the room, and we walked past a row of oversized washers and dryers, stopping at a claustrophobic box of an office. A desk was wedged against the wall, perpendicular to the door, leaving an eight-inch gap between the end of the desk and the door. The desk was comprised of two clear, plastic barrels filled with pennies, with an unpainted door secured across the top. Through the predrilled hole for the door lock ran a handful of cables connected to the laptop, printer, and fax machine that were crammed side-by-side on the desk. Bolted underneath was a fire-safe lock box, the length of a manila envelope and deep enough to hold a six-pack of beer.

Three mismatched folding chairs were the only other items of note in the space, one acting as desk chair and two for guests that I suspected had been put there for the sole occasion of our arrival.

"Malik?" Paul asked, stretching his hand out to the man rising to his feet behind the desk.

"Hi, yes," Malik said, smiling broadly at Paul before he turned to me. "And you must be Samantha?"

"Sam." I returned his smile and noted his crisp shirt and slacks. I surreptitiously adjusted my sweater straighter along my hips.

Malik gestured to the folding chairs in front of his desk, and Paul and I wedged ourselves in. Malik slid back into his own chair and pressed his dark forearms into a V on the desk.

I settled into my chair and daintily crossed one leg over the other in an effort to hide the worst of the mud. Malik's eyes took thorough stock of me, but showed no judgment. Maybe he recognized a potential customer. I peeked out the office door at the closest row of washers and sighed with envy.

A fair-haired kid I sized up to be in his early twenties slunk up to the door, cutting into my dirty daydream. I smiled at him and looked at Malik. He caught sight of the kid and smiled wide.

"Hey, man," Malik said. He waved a hand in a circling motion at all of us. "This is Shawn, our assistant on the hunts. This is Paul and Sam. They're going to help us figure out this issue with the clues."

"What's up," Shawn said in a drawl that wasn't so much Southern as it was apathetic.

"What's up," I drawled back. Paul shook his head at me.

Between Paul, Malik, and me, there wasn't enough room left in the office to accommodate a thought, let alone another body.

Shawn didn't bother to try to jam his way in; he instead lounged a shoulder against the door frame and crossed wiry arms around his torso. He had a mix of muscle and lankiness that suggested he may have one more growth spurt left in him. He studied Paul and me from under long eyelashes and a mop of sandy curls that women paid a lot of money to re-create. I couldn't tell if the patchy scruff of hair on his chin was intentional or a sign of laziness.

"Can I get my check?" Shawn asked. He caught me watching him, diverted his eyes to Malik and parted his lips, revealing a sizeable gap between his top two teeth. He pushed his tongue through the gap twice, then rubbed his tongue over the front of the gap.

"Yeah, man, of course." Malik produced a key ring from his pants pocket and unlocked the fire safe underneath the desk. He passed an envelope to Shawn, who folded it twice and stuffed it into a back pocket without looking at the contents.

"Thanks," Shawn said, turning on his heel to go.

"Hey, you mind staying a minute?" Malik asked. "Might help these guys with some of their questions."

Shawn returned to the doorway and nodded mutely as he pushed his tongue further into the gap.

"Thanks for meeting with me on short notice," Malik said to Paul and me. "Like I mentioned on the phone, I've tried to tackle this on my own, but I'm coming up empty, and I don't know how much longer this can go on before I start to lose business."

"No problem at all," Paul said. "If you don't mind, can you take us through what you shared with me on the phone this morning? I'd like Sam to hear this from the horse's mouth."

"Of course," Malik said. His smile remained in place, but I watched as stress lines bloomed around his eyes. He rubbed one hand across a head that I guessed was bald by choice given he couldn't have been much older than my thirty-one years. "I own City Scavengers. Have you heard of it?"

I shook my head.

"It's a scavenger hunt of sorts. A way for tourists and even locals to learn about the city without going through a tedious guided tour, or a string of five museums in a row. We provide clues for the participants to follow throughout certain points in the city. We set up the clues at various landmarks, and the participants have to go landmark to landmark, asking locals for help with the clues, using their phones and whatever else they can."

"So, it's somewhat of a self-assisted tour?" I asked.

"No, only partly. We have a hunt host who meets the participants at each point, gives a bit of a history lesson and stage performance for the participants, makes sure they get started with the first clue that leads to the next point, then he goes off ahead of them and takes a circuitous route to the next landmark so that he can be waiting for them when they arrive. The hunts are done downtown and we encourage the participants to walk or take public transportation, but our host goes in a car. Shawn here is our host assistant who helps with the timing, clue drops, etc."

"That's pretty cool," I said. "I saw something like that on the west coast once, but didn't realize we had it here."

Malik nodded. "It's mostly in major cities at this point, and only a few players are in the game so far. We've got two here in Cleveland and my competitor just branched out to Columbus a few months ago."

"Is Columbus large enough to support both of you?" I asked.

"Not yet, but I don't intend to extend there. My plan is to get the model near to perfect here in Cleveland, then open up in the Carolinas. The history, particularly in South Carolina, will feed well into this set up. I've been prospecting there the last few months and think things will be ready in the next six months, assuming I can get past the trouble here."

"And what exactly is the trouble?"

"Someone is stealing our clues," Malik said.

"I thought your host provided the clues during the hunt?"

"Only the starting clue at each landmark. There are one to

three checkpoints in between landmarks where we drop clues ahead of the hunt, and the participants have to solve those to get to the next big landmark where the host gives his performance."

"How far in advance of the hunt do you drop these off?"

"Depends on the hunt. We hold them at varying times. Also depends on who does the drop. It's usually a combination of the host and Shawn."

"How many hosts do you have?"

"Just one right now. Walker Atwill. His real first name is Ridley, but he thinks Walker has a certain 'panache' that fits better with the character he's playing."

"Panache?"

"That's Walker's lingo. He's spent years traveling the country, following bit roles here and there, searching for his big break. He started doing the hosting when we opened. He was between acting jobs and I was struggling to find a host who knew enough about the city to run the hunt, but who didn't sound like a museum docent doing it. So, I hired Walker as a stop-gap while I kept looking for someone long-term. But Walker's in-between job phase has become semi-permanent and the participants love the show, so I haven't taken steps to replace him yet."

"But if he gets an acting role tomorrow somewhere, you'll be stuck, no?" I asked.

"Not exactly," Malik said, inclining his head toward Shawn. "Shawn has been on the last six months' worth of hunts and he could pinch hit if we really needed him to."

Shawn's eyes darted away toward the clinking dryers, then came back to rest on Malik. The tongue pushing kicked up.

"Only in a pinch, man." Malik grinned at Shawn. "I know you prefer being behind the scenes."

"Do you drop all the clues, or do you and Walker split it up?" I asked Shawn.

"I usually do it." Shawn flicked his eyes up to Malik, who frowned in response.

"Still?" Malik asked.

"Yeah."

"I'll talk to him again."

I glanced back and forth between the two. "Is that a problem?"

Malik frowned. "For a while, Walker was putting it on Shawn to get all the clues set out. I addressed it, but sounds like not much has changed."

I caught the look in Malik's eye and let it go. I took it as a sign he didn't want to talk poorly about Walker in Shawn's presence.

"Are the clues written on paper or physical symbols or what?" I asked.

"They're all written on small index cards with our business insignia," Malik said.

"So how do you know they're being stolen and not just thrown out by someone finding them in the street and thinking they're trash?"

"I don't for sure. The first few times it happened, the clues were gone completely. But on the last hunt, whoever stole the clues didn't just steal them...they replaced them."

"Come again?"

"Our clues were taken and replaced by other notes."

"What did the notes say?"

"The answer to the clue that was taken away."

I couldn't help but laugh and immediately stopped when Shawn frowned at me. "I'm sorry."

Malik smiled. "Don't be. I laughed at first, too. I thought we just had a kid prankster who paid attention in history class. When it kept happening, though, it stopped being funny."

Shawn crinkled the pay envelope in his pocket. "I'm not feeling so great today," Shawn said, rubbing his stomach. "Okay if I go?"

Malik tossed a look at Paul and me. "Anything else for Shawn?"

"Not right now," I said, glancing up at Shawn. "Paul and I are going on the hunt tomorrow. Can we talk more then?"

Shawn shook his head and worked the tooth gap. "I'll set up the clues and be out of there before the group gets to the starting point. I'll stay ahead of the group to see if anyone messes with the clues."

"Let's catch up afterward then."

Shawn shrugged as he pushed off the doorframe and turned for the front door.

"What's the deal with Walker not pulling his weight?" Paul asked when Shawn had gone.

"Man, I think it's an ego thing. In Walker's world, Shawn's the stage hand and Walker's the name on the marquee."

"So, I'm guessing he hasn't found the clue sabotage funny. Somebody's stealing his thunder in a way."

"That's exactly how he sees it. The participants are showing up to the landmarks upset and they take it out on Walker, but what really cranks him is not being able to put on his little show."

I jabbed my thumb in the direction of the front door. "You think Shawn could be behind it?"

"To what end?" Malik asked.

"Maybe to get back at Walker for not helping plant the clues."

"I don't see it. Messing with the clues hurts me as much as it hurts Walker. And I don't think I've given him reason to give me a hard time."

"Maybe Shawn doesn't care about collateral damage."

"Nuh-uh, I don't think so. Shawn's a decent kid. Quiet, comes off a little uptight maybe, but he's not the spiteful kind."

"You said you tried to take care of this yourself," Paul said. "What have you done so far?"

"I planted the clue drops myself for one of the hunts. I did it earlier than usual, then started back at the beginning of the tour path and watched to see who came along to tamper with them, but I didn't see anyone at any of the landmark checkpoints."

"Were any of the clues changed out for answers when Walker

or the scavengers got to them?"

"Not a one."

"Any chance it could be your competitor sabotaging you? Cleveland's not much bigger than Columbus. Maybe there's not room for both of you here either."

"Nah," Malik said, shaking his head. "Janie Nagelson's the owner and we've actually worked together on marketing and increasing our customer base. Plus, her tour is completely self-guided. Her participants get a set of clues off the company's website, then they solve the clues through their smartphone. It's more like a search-engine supported tour."

"Which style is more popular?"

Malik shrugged. "It's apples and oranges. The kids seem to want the self-guided tour seeing as how they're glued to their phones anyway. The older crowd and the families tend to want a live guide and appreciate the show."

"Any one you can think of who'd like to see you fail?"

"Not that I know of. I've been pretty head down, butt up working my businesses." Malik waved a hand toward the sound of the dryers. "I've got the laundromat and the hunt service, and both are still in their early phases. I've got family back home in New York trying to scrape by. My parents are both working minimum wage jobs, my brother is making just barely more than that, and I've got a baby sister who wants to go to law school. And she will go, I will see to that. But that means there's no time for a social life, no time to make enemies."

"So, no girlfriend? No woman who wanted to be a girlfriend and wasn't happy you picked work over her?" Paul asked.

"Nah, no one who was any more invested than I was. I tend to pick women who are as busy as I am." Malik shot me an embarrassed smile. "Saves me being the bad guy, you know?"

"What are the names of the non-invested?"

"Aw, man." Malik sat back in his chair and looked resignedly at Paul. "There's only been one woman recently. She wouldn't have anything to do with this, though."

"Why don't you let me and Sam rule that out for you?"

Malik hesitated and looked over at me. I raised my eyebrows at him. "We'll be discreet."

"Cheryl Perkins." Malik picked up his cell and stroked the screen repeatedly with his thumb, before stopping and reading out a phone number. Paul jotted it down and confirmed the spelling of her name.

"I don't know exactly where she lives, but it's near University Circle."

Paul looked up from his scribbling. I didn't see a speck of judgment on it, but Malik blushed. "Like I said, we weren't that invested."

"Do you keep records of who attends your hunts?" I asked, giving Malik's blush a chance to recede with a change of topic.

"We have liability release forms for everyone who takes the tour. Since they're traipsing through the city, it protects me if someone gets too excited about the answer to a clue and trips off the curb on E. 9th and slams their head into the Free Stamp."

"Charming visual," I said.

"We'll need those release forms," Paul said.

"I'll email them over before the end of the day."

"Can you include a hunt schedule?"

"Of course."

"Who else knows you've brought us on to help?"

"Just Walker, Shawn and me. We'd like to keep this under wraps as much as possible."

Chapter Two

"Check out this one. Ronald McDonald's slow cousin." Paul flipped his laptop screen around on his desk. Our desks sat facing each other a few feet apart, and I peered forward for a better look. I stared into the puffy face of one of the previous scavenger hunters. He did resemble Ronald McDonald, if only for the fiery ringlets shooting from his head, offsetting the pasty white of his skin.

Paul and I were back in the agency office, three hours deep into Malik's participant list from the last dozen scavenger hunts, and had yet to find anyone connected to Malik, his family, or his business dealings. I pushed back in my chair and stretched my arms over my head before reaching over to snatch a Red Vine from the tub on my desk. I wouldn't say my affinity for Red Vines was a fetish, but I may or may not have signed up for a Costco membership for the sole purpose of buying them in bulk.

"I'm more of a Hamburglar gal, myself."

"You're looking more like a Hamburglar, McFries, and McShake kind of girl the past couple weeks."

I looked down at the circular outline the button of my jeans was pressing into my tee shirt.

"It's entirely possible I've been eating my feelings lately." I bit into my Vine as the front door to the office opened and Johnny Rosato walked in. Otherwise known as the reason I was eating my feelings. I felt the candy drop from my hanging lower lip and land with a soft plop on the desktop.

I swiped a tissue from its box and dabbed my lip. "What are you doing here?"

"You know, we'd get on a lot better if you were sweeter to me." Johnny wound his way around my desk and patted the top of my head.

"She's sweet enough. Ix-nay with the getting it on-ay," Paul said without raising his head from his laptop.

Johnny grinned. Paul looked up and grinned. I frowned.

Johnny was Paul's current potential agency partner and my former high school crush. We'd had an oddly close emotional connection for two teenagers, and right about the time my hormones started to give me cute ideas about pressing themselves against Johnny's mouth, he'd left town. I'd call it a Dear John parting, except that it was Dear Sam and I didn't get so much as a sticky note of explanation.

Fast forward to my recent return to Cleveland. Johnny and I had rekindled our crush, and just gotten past the awkwardness phase of our reunion and into a tingly hand-on-ass phase, when Paul popped the question of agency partnership to Johnny. The terms of the deal came with one teensy caveat: no more mouth-to-mouth for me and Big J. Johnny accepted the deal on a trial basis. I wasn't yet sure if the trial was to see if he liked being Paul's partner more than a chance at being mine. We were entering month three of the trial phase, and I wasn't any closer to knowing what I wanted Johnny's choice to be. In the meantime, I'd been eating dumplings at an alarming rate.

"I thought you were stalking someone in North Carolina," I

said.

"Tailing, not stalking. I tailed him right to his ex-girlfriend's house. Game over."

"I know I'm new at this, but wasn't the point of the whole pursuit to find this guy and get him served?"

Johnny leaned his six and a half feet against the edge of Paul's desk and crossed one ankle over the other. "Mr. Bob is currently property of the Charlotte county jail. Consider him served and delivered."

"Congrats."

"Can't take the credit. Mr. Bob's ex practically did the work for me. She wasn't exactly pleased to see her old man and decided to greet him with a full can of hairspray."

"What, she spray his hair into place as punishment?" I asked.

"More like she sprayed it in his face. The fun part was when she flicked a lighter into the spray."

"Holy bells, how bad is he hurt?"

"He might need to borrow Mr. Potato Head's accessories for a while."

"Gee-zuss," I sighed. Not that I was all that upset about Mr. Bob. He'd spawned eight kids with eight different women, lost every job he'd had in less than six months, and had paid exactly zero dollars toward supporting his kids. He'd also broken open his oldest son's piggy bank and stolen every cent, including four Canadian pennies and one nickel pressed into the shape of a penguin from a trip to the zoo. So technically, Mr. Bob was $18.12 in the negative on his child support payments. Mr. Bob was actually named Randy Sorkin, but had earned the name "Mr. Bob" for the bobbing and weaving he'd managed to do to get out of being served over the child support issues.

My sigh was in response to Johnny being back in town. He'd trailed Mr. Bob through three states over the course of a month. One blissful month where I didn't have to manage my feelings - or my hands - where Johnny was concerned. Looked like it was back to playing the avoidance game. Call me Mrs. Bob.

Johnny dipped his hand into the Red Vine bucket and winked a green-gray eye at me. It was ninety percent playful and ten percent as intense as a chemical fire. I breathed deeply through my nose and gave him a tiny smile in return.

"Who's Carrot Top?" Johnny turned his attention to the picture of the Ronald McDonald lookalike that Paul was pulling out of the printer. Paul placed the photo next to Walker's on the desk, and gave Johnny a brief rundown of our chat with Malik and our initial research of the previous hunters.

"What have you got so far?"

I held up both hands and started flashing fingers. "Two felons, three repeat offenders for indecent exposure, one property damage misdemeanor, a whopping seven DUIs, and enough parking tickets to cover Cleveland PD's payroll for the week."

"What are the felonies for?"

"Check kiting, grand theft, and assault. All out of state. Evidently, thugs take vacations, too."

"You going to check out the hunt?" Johnny asked.

"Yeah, tomorrow," Paul said. "Then we're meeting with the owner of Malik's competition Monday morning."

"You want me to take that meeting?" Johnny asked Paul. "I thought you were doing the intake on the McCarron case Monday."

I saw Paul flick a look at me, but I was focused on Johnny's face. His mouth was soft and relaxed, but I saw the challenge turning his hazel eyes a sparkling green. I rubbed the inside of my cheek with my tongue.

"I'll take Johnny," I said. Gauntlet thrown. I'd been using North Carolina as a buffer and now it was test time. God, I hated being that girl. My grown woman brain traded punches with my 14-year-old boy libido.

"You're serious?" Paul asked me.

"Why not?"

Paul narrowed his eyes at first me, then Johnny. "You kids think you can keep it in your pants?"

"Our own?" Johnny asked.

"The whole time?" I asked.

"Why do I have a feeling this trial period is going to run out faster than that bucket of licorice?" Paul rubbed his face from forehead to chin. I knew he was counting.

"Ye of little faith," I said. "It's high time Mr. Rosato and I demonstrate to you how mature and disciplined we are. How infinitely high our level of professionalism is. Our unparalleled dedication to our craft. Our undying commitment to never let you down. Our concrete—."

"Alright already," Paul said.

"I think what she's trying to say is you can trust us," Johnny said.

"I trust both of you implicitly, just not in the same room. It's like one of you is Carol Anne and the other is the light."

Chapter Three

Bright and early Sunday morning, I flung my legs over the edge of my bed and planted my feet into a brand-new pair of unicorn slippers. I'd moved back to Cleveland with no notice and no housing, after Paul called me home to help Mom heal from my dad's passing. Turned out Mom didn't need my help so much as the help of a certain hairy man named Wally who looked like he'd been in line for funnel cake the day God was handing out vertical inches. Between the Wallster's entrance onto the scene, and my deep-rooted desire to get the hell out of the childhood bed that sat twelve feet away from Mom's sleeping head and what I feared would soon be Wally's snoring mouth, I hesitantly and fearfully accepted my Uncle Gino's offer to stay at his old house. Uncle Gino had moved on to a better pad, and I'd scrubbed every surface twice over with industrial cootie-remover, but memories of the remnants he'd left behind still had me religiously slipping a barrier between my feet and his floors. Partly from fear of what I might catch, and partly from fear of slipping and falling to my death in an overlooked spot of lube.

I'd showered, layered up in honor of Cleveland's winter-to-spring-to-winter weather cycle that occurred every twenty-four-hour period in May, and was swallowing the last chunk of my banana bread when Paul coasted into the driveway. I grabbed my bag and hit the door.

"What did you have for breakfast?" Paul asked as I buckled myself in.

"Banana bread. Gluten free. Organic coconut sugar. Vegan."

"I smell chocolate."

"The chocolate chips were organic, too."

Paul shook his head and coasted back out of the driveway. He had a vegetable juicing addiction left over from a former fiancé that may have rivaled my Red Vine addiction. If he dedicated himself a bit harder, he could be some real competition, but I can't say I was all that worried about losing my crown.

"What's our story if any of the other scavengers ask?" I asked as Paul turned down Pearl Road and headed for the freeway.

"How about we say we're brother and sister?"

"Genius."

"I try."

"We could say we're visiting from Detroit on vacation."

Paul glanced over at me. "If you were trying to get away from Detroit, would you really come to Cleveland?"

"That's the best part. People will think we're stupid and won't suspect we're there to investigate anything."

"God help me."

"Just trying to be a rainmaker."

"Hey, here's a novel idea," Paul said. "Why don't we tell people – and only if they ask – that we live here and know squat about our own city. We're just trying to educate ourselves."

"I feel like you're wasting an opportunity with this whole investigating thing. You can be anyone you want to be. Any disguise," I said.

"And I feel like you'll miss important information if you're thinking about your backstory more than what's going on in front of your face."

"This might be an agree-to-disagree moment."

"This might be a stop-annoying-your-brother-and-boss moment."

"But that's my favorite treat."

"Funny, I'd have said it was organic chocolate chips."

"Touché, mofo."

ΩΩΩ

"What do you think?" Paul asked.

"I think your Ronald McDonald description was being kind," I said, cupping my palm around my top lip. I didn't think Mr. McD could hear me, but the couple standing just to my right looked like their attention was actively diverted to anyone but each other.

Paul swept his gaze across the small group of hunt participants while I stared out past the group toward Public Square, at an angle that allowed me to keep Paul's gaze in my peripheral vision. I could tell he was taking in Mr. McD with each casual sweep of his eyes.

Mr. McD, legally known as Ernest Brown, was a repeat scavenger. We'd learned from the hunt's business records that Ernest had participated in twenty-seven hunts in the prior five months. A call to Malik yesterday told us that a couple months after Ernest started attending the hunts, Walker complained to Malik, citing Ernest as a detractor to the hunts. I rolled my eyes at the word "detractor". An actor, indeed. Walker cited two occasions wherein Ernest had suggested to Walker that he could do a better job of making the clues that lead the group to each landmark. Ernest never made these suggestions in front of the other scavengers, but on both occasions he pulled Walker aside at what Walker considered the crescendo of his performance.

After the second encounter, Walker threatened to go to Malik and have Ernest removed from the hunt and permanently blocked from participating in future ones. Ernest in turn quietly told Walker that it would be a shame if he had to post an online review that was less than favorable toward Walker. Ernest further intoned that he could happily use the time he'd otherwise spend at the hunts posting as many negative reviews as his thick fingers could manage.

Walker suggested to Ernest they compromise. Ernest could freely give his feedback to Walker, but never in front of the other scavengers. Ernest obliged, and a truce was formed.

Of the scavengers who had signed up for that morning's hunt, Ernest was the only standout oddity, based on the frequency of his scavenger hunting alone. A third of the group were international tourists, and cursory background checks on the rest of the folks signed up for the day's hunt revealed no obvious connection to Malik or his business, nor anything more criminally obscene than a urination in public charge.

I returned my attention to the group and checked out the couple who seemed to want nothing to do with each other. Plain gold bands told me they were married, and tight lines around both their mouths told me they probably had been for a long time. A sullen kid of about twelve shuffled behind the husband, shoelaces dragging on the sidewalk, black with dirt. He leaned into the base of the monument, fingers stabbing at the ornate detail under the statues. Anger radiated out of his fingers, and I wondered if this family was having one bad day or just one of many.

Seven other scavengers stood among us, peering around the monument. We'd met in the lobby of a hotel adjacent to Public Square and were presented with our first clue card by a baby-faced concierge who looked like he'd rather come on the hunt with us than spend the rest of the day telling hotel guests how to get to Jack Casino. The clue card had told us to *fight, shoot, swim, or row your way across the street, where you'll find honor, but no privacy.* Through smartphones, and common sense, we easily found our way to Public Square and the monument.

The scavengers stood scattered about reading the various plaques, some looking at the buildings surrounding the Square, another off to the side smoking a cigarette, and a bored-looking teenager with his mom who looked like he wanted to bum one of the other guy's smokes. I was tempted to introduce him to the tween boy with the dirty laces.

Two blondes caught my attention. They looked like the DoubleMint twins, with matching gravel voices. From our quick recon of the registration info Malik sent us, and the short round-robin of introductions we made to each other while waiting for our first clue, I knew they were sisters vacationing from Germany.

The sisters were also catching heavy attention from a trio of boys from Detroit. The earlier introductions revealed that they hailed from Detroit, and everything else about their countenance revealed their hipster status. Looking at them, I picked up three critical clues: they were barely old enough to know the definition of hipster let alone affect the moniker, Detroit had a solid selection of thrift stores, and LensCrafters was taking very good advantage of these boys' parents' health coverage. All three pointed their skinny-jean-clad knees and plaid-covered torsos squarely in the sisters' direction, failing in their attempt to act disinterested while they ogled. The sisters, heads bent together over the flower beds surrounding the monument, remained clueless to the maturation process they were causing in the hipster trio.

For our own backstory, Paul and I went with his boring, but effective 'we're ignorant about our own city' sibling routine, which the hipsters ate up. They immediately cut us off to tell us about the value of learning about our roots and how they were here conducting research before they begin filming a documentary that would take them across the country to illustrate the history and the bastardization of wheat and textiles. My eyes glazed over about twelve seconds in, and I could tell from Paul's face that had we not been there on a case, he would have walked these boys right over to the nearest Starbucks and reunited them with the rest of their generation.

While we waited for everyone to check out the plaques and architecture, I scoped out the surrounding plaza, keeping my head tilted back enough to create an illusion that I was checking out the architecture in a manner meant to fill time, but put my peripheral vision to work spotting Shawn. I didn't see him, but hadn't really expected to, knowing he was meant to stay several paces ahead of the group. I did see a handful of homeless lingering near the casino entrance, their entertainment for the morning coming from a fifty-something woman strumming a ukulele from her perch inside a grocery cart. The stuffed parrot sitting atop her Chaka Kahn-esque wig bounced as she strummed. Random detritus of party goers from the previous night surrounded the plaza. The city's efforts at revitalization were commendable, but no public effort could catch every condom, plastic beer cup, or casino chip littered about like confetti.

I noticed the guy I'd seen smoking a few minutes earlier had drifted away from the monument, a good fifty yards toward the Tom Johnson statue across the plaza. I vaguely remembered from high school history class that Johnson was a mayor, but I couldn't remember why it was he rated a statue on the plaza.

During the introductions, the smoking loner introduced himself as Art, but there was no Art on Malik's registration list. While Malik said it wasn't uncommon at all to have people register and no-show the day of the hunt, it was nearly impossible for someone to show up without registering. Either Art was really "Kelly Artuno", a name of the registration list that hadn't yet been attached to a physical body, or Art had attached himself to this random group of obvious tourists on a Sunday morning in downtown Cleveland. Either way, my curiosity was piqued.

I meandered over to the Tom Johnson statue, taking a different route than Art had, working my way around the grass instead of trampling over it. I paused to feign interest in an honorary plaque on a nearby bench before moseying my way to Mr. Johnson's monument. I stopped a dozen feet short of Art and studied Mr. Johnson. Art glanced my way and, in a demonstrated display of casual, glanced over his shoulder at the rest of the group. Not a single face pointed in our direction, but I could tell from the way Paul stood in profile to us, head cocked slightly up, that he had marked my location.

Art turned toward me, eyes on Mr. Johnson's lap. To be fair, the statue was a depiction of the mayor resting a book in his lap. Art studied the cover of the book, but I saw him hunch his shoulders in that way one does before they get up the gumption to do something. I, too, studied the cover of the book, but angled myself toward Art, silently inviting him in. Bait cast, the fish bit.

"Hi, there." Art smiled at me, confident.

"Hi." I flashed a lot of gum in return. "Having a good time so far?"

"A riot. Haven't learned this much since eighth grade."

"Yeah, I was thinking it felt like a senior class trip."

"I didn't make it to senior year."

"Ah." Slick, Sam. Way to engage.

Art cast another look back toward the rest of the group. The hipsters' attention was still buried in blonde, but the bored teen had taken an interest in my and Art's conversation. Art caught the level of interest and put a few feet between us. He focused his attention out to the street beyond the monument, but I saw his shoulders resume their hunch.

"You, uh, you like to cuddle?" Art asked, barely above a whisper.

"I'm sorry. Did you say 'cuddle'?"

"You heard me. You like it?"

I took a quick peek back at Paul, who had now turned his face full-on in my direction. I held one finger upside down on my outer thigh, signaling to him that I was good for the moment. Paul nodded a fraction, acknowledging he caught my signal.

"I, uh. Sure. I mean, who doesn't like to cuddle?"

"You got somebody to do it with?"

This had to be one of the oddest pick-up moves I'd ever been party to. And I was counting the guy who came up to me in a bar in Tampa and offered to tattoo my profile on his belly if I was willing to show him my "lovely lady spot".

And this brought me to a dilemma I'd been facing as a newbie slash wannabe investigator. My nature told me to run like a sugar-fried five-year-old back across the grass to the safety of my big brother and the larger group, but my budding inner PI was screaming at me to say 'yes' to this man and bat one or both of my eyelashes to get what I sought. Problem was, I didn't know if he had what I sought.

My inner PI won the coin flip, but my winking skills are right on par with my sewing skills, so I tipped my head down and looked back up at Art through my eyelids, hoping for smoldering. Art looked confused for a nanosecond, but must have taken it as good enough, because he took a step closer to me.

"How much?"

"I'm sorry?" I kept my head tipped down, and the smoldering turned squinty.

"How much? For the cuddling?"

My budding inner PI briefly wondered if I looked like to this guy like a budding hooker, and I put a hand up as I took a step back. "No, I think you misunderstood. I'm not trying to charge you."

"Oh, I know." Art waved both hands in front of him, apology written on his face.

"Phew, cool."

"I mean, how much would you pay me?"

Now both my inner PI and my inner hooker were confused. Art leaned forward and raised both eyebrows at me. "I'm a professional cuddler. Fifty bucks an hour. But for you, I could do thirty."

"Fifty bucks an hour?" I dropped both the smoldering and the squinting, lifted my head and put my hands on my hips.

"I said I could do thirty."

"No."

"Fine, twenty-five. That's my final offer. I gotta eat, too, you know."

"No, I mean no. Like, no and no. I'm not trying to bargain here. Do people really pay you fifty bucks an hour to cuddle?"

Seeing he'd lost me as a potential client, Art straightened up and looked at me defensively. "Sometimes more."

"Unbelievable."

"I know. You'd be surprised by what they'll pay for. I could tell you stories."

"Please don't."

"Nah, I'm not even talking sexual stuff. I mean like, what they want to hold you with."

God help me, I couldn't resist. "Tell me."

"Oven mitts, loofah gloves, finger puppets, plastic sacks. And not just any sack. Like, I got this one lady who likes me to cover my hands in Target bags and spoon her from behind with my hands wrapped around her chest. Can't be Giant Eagle, can't be the Walmarts. Gotta be Target."

"Okay, I changed my mind. I don't wanna know anymore." I was going to have nightmares about finger puppets for weeks.

"Hey, don't judge it. I'm telling you, if you tell yourself you're just playing a part, it's not a bad side gig."

"You guys, we found it!" Art and I turned at the sound of one of the hipsters yelling at us across the plaza.

Hipster number three, a fair-haired kid named Devin was waving an over-sized index card at us. I beelined over to Paul, Art following at a more leisurely pace behind me.

Devin cleared his throat and read aloud from the card.

Rush your Journey along the gold bricks of E 9th St.
until you found the deep purple house with Doors and
Four Tops, the one that sheltered Eagles, beetles,
birds, Orioles. If you look closely once inside, you
might find a Prince, a Queen, and even the King.
Before you hit the doormat, you shall be welcomed by
the butler.

The group was quick to decipher that we were meant to go to the Rock and Roll Hall of Fame. Ernest suggested to the group that the clue's last line meant Walker would be there to greet us.

We trundled off down Ontario St., the scavengers sorting themselves largely into pairs, trios, and quartets. I noticed Ernest trailing behind the group, red curls bouncing in mesmerizing fashion in the sunlight. As we passed the County Courthouse, Browns Stadium, and eventually the Science Center, I split my time between looking for Shawn and watching Ernest's red head bob up and down. I saw no sign of Shawn nor anyone else along the street paying the least bit of attention to our group.

As we came up on Erieside Avenue and approached the museum, I looked past our huddled group and onto the plaza itself. Two rows of massive replica guitars spanned the distance of the plaza, the vivid colors and designs on their necks climbing nine feet off the ground. I was tempted to leave Paul to work the rest of the hunt on his own, so I could go inside and pay my respects to Prince. And by respects, I mean rub myself up and down on the glass protecting his concert outfits from the likes of me, but the museum didn't open for another two hours.

As the last of the group straggled onto the sidewalk, we all looked around expectantly for Walker. Based on what Malik had described, I was picturing a dramatic entrance, or even for Walker to be front and center to welcome us to the landmark, but all that sat on the plaza were our little motley crew and a group of pigeons, standing with cocked head and hungry beaks, evaluating what our pockets might hold.

Even the streets surrounding the plaza were empty. Sunday morning was a day of rest for some and day of hair-of-the-dog for others. There was no Walker, no Shawn, nor anyone else running up the street to gaily provide us with a nugget of Cleveland history. Five minutes passed and the German sisters started a heated discussion between themselves, about our delay or where they were going to get lunch was anyone's guess. The hipsters had taken enough pictures to fill an art gallery and began to look as if it had just dawned on them the undertaking ahead of them if they planned to "research across the country". Ten minutes passed, and the group started to separate. The smoker hit the curb, the bored teen mindlessly wandered several feet behind him, leaving mom on the sidewalk scouring a tour book. The rest of us climbed the steps to the plaza and went for a closer look at the replica guitars.

The German sisters ceased their argument as they approached a purple guitar, paused to look up at it as if at a church cross, reverent and respectful, before catching each other's eye and resuming their verbal war.

The hipsters moved as a group to the guitar next to the sisters, one reading the explanatory plaque and the other two taking pictures of each other posing in front of it.

Ernest made his way to a bright green guitar in the row closest to the museum entrance. Paul and I trailed a dozen feet behind him and stopped in front of a tie dye affair three doors down, one row up.

"Where is this guy already?" Paul asked. I followed his gaze out across the street and back down toward the Browns stadium. There was zero Sunday morning traffic and even the on-street parking was ample. Malik said Walker came by car, though I had imagined Walker would make a grander appearance than easing up in a Corolla.

The group's patience finally broke. One of our hipster friends griped loud enough to make even the fighting sisters pause. "You think we should go try to find this guy or what?"

"I think I just did." A shaky voice came from across the plaza.

We all swung our heads toward Ernest, who had made his way past the last of the guitars and was standing, hands up as if under arrest at the edge of the plaza. A low wall of concrete bordered an oversized planter that separated the plaza from the sidewalk beyond.

"Ernest?" I called out to him, but he didn't turn around. His hands, still in the air, began to shake. From behind, it looked like he was giving us a very muted version of jazz hands.

Paul cut me a look and we took off at a trot. We wove our way up into Ernest's row, and down the remaining twenty feet to reach him. I misjudged the last step and clipped the back of Ernest's heel. Paul grabbed my arm as I pitched forward on my feet, and saved me from falling over the wall and landing on top of Walker. It looked like he'd been through enough.

Chapter Four

Springtime in Cleveland brings a lot of "firsts". The first green buds sprouting on tree branches, the first car wash that won't be obliterated by road salt five minutes after the dry cycle finishes, and the first of a billion orange barrels lining the construction-ready highways. This Spring surprised me with my first dead body. At least, it was my first fresh one.

In the five months that I'd been learning the ropes as a private investigator, I'd experienced the joy of a couple oatmeal-raising trips to the morgue, but those bodies had been dead for a while. This one was hot out of the oven, fully dressed, and lounging in a flower bed not thirty feet from a national museum attraction. He looked for all the world like a tourist resting for a sun-shaded moment. Except that the side of his head looked a lot like the Play-Doh bust of Abraham Lincoln that I made in third grade. Right after Vinnie nailed it with a baseball.

"Maybe you shouldn't keep staring at him." Paul flicked his eyes alternately between Walker's body and me. We stood shoulder to shoulder on the outside perimeter of the police tape, part of the growing crowd of onlookers.

"I'm good. I got this." I wasn't and I didn't. I forced my head to stay trained in the direction of Walker's body, but I crossed one eye over the other until it became just a blur in the concrete.

"Could have fooled me. You keep rolling your eyes around like that, one's gonna start calling the other one lazy," Paul said.

I closed my eyes and breathed in deep through my nose. "That's helpful."

"Here to serve."

I opened my eyes and turned at the sound of a disruption behind us. Two plainclothes detectives parted the sea of looky-loos, pushed past us, and ducked under the cordoning tape that the first-responding police officers had wound through the display of guitars. One of the detectives leaned over Walker for a close-up while he spoke with head bent to the uniformed officers. After a few moments, one of the officers scanned the crowd, eyes coming to rest on Paul and me. The detective followed the officer's pointed finger and strode toward us. The other stayed with the body and was joined by a woman who I suspected was the M.E.

"Sam Carter?" The detective said to my brother, who shook his head and pointed at me.

"I'm Paul Carter. This is my sister, Samantha."

"Apologies." The detective palmed the shield hooked on a lanyard around his liver-spotted neck in our general direction, and slid the world's tiniest notebook out of his jacket pocket. "Detective Barnes. I'm told you two know the victim."

"Know of him would be more accurate," I said.

"How do you know *of* him?" Barnes asked. His words carried equal parts fatigue and irritation.

"His name is Ridley Atwill, but he goes by Walker," Paul said. "I own a private investigation agency and Walker's employer hired us to find out who has been sabotaging his business," Paul said.

"What kind of business?" Detective Barnes asked. He punctuated each of his questions with a sigh that I quickly determined was probably his pattern in daily life. I imagined it made for fun times at a drive-thru window.

"A guy named Malik Hensen owns a service called City Scavengers," Paul said. "They run a scavenger hunt for tourists and locals who want to learn about the city. The participants have to find pre-planted clues throughout downtown, then they meet up with Walker at landmarks along the way, where he gives a history lesson to the group before they go off to the next clue."

Barnes looked doubtful. "How is that being sabotaged?"

"Someone is stealing and sometimes altering the clues that are planted at sites in between the landmarks," I said. "After the second time it happened, Malik dropped the clues himself before the next hunt, and waited to see what happened, but no one messed with the clues. We can only assume whoever is doing it knows Malik by sight and begged off. So, he hired us to do the legwork."

"You got numbers for him?"

Paul scrolled through his cell and rattled off Malik's info. Barnes copied the numbers onto his pad, his thin fingers gripping low on the pen's tip like a chopstick.

"What have you found out so far from your research?" Barnes asked, flipping to a fresh page and pinning eyes on Paul. His look was hard, bright, and assessing, but it seemed to speak more to his intelligence than to his energy.

"Not much," Paul said. "We just signed on yesterday and wanted to go on a hunt ourselves to see how the whole process works. Who has access, how visible an outsider would be, that kind of thing."

"Anything seem off to you during the hunt? Did this Walker guy seem upset? Nervous?" Barnes asked and sighed.

"You've seen as much of him as we have," I said, jutting my chin in Walker's direction while keeping my eyes on the top of the detective's balding crown. Barnes lifted his head from his notebook.

"I thought you said he waited at each landmark for the

hunters," Barnes said.

"That's how it's supposed to work, but the museum was the first big landmark. We started with a clue card the Renaissance concierge gave us, that took us to Public Square, then to the Hall of Fame. Walker's first history lesson would have happened here."

Barnes turned back toward Walker's body and eyed a group of a half dozen people standing on the far side of the police tape. They stood quietly, not making eye contact with each other. Our fellow hunters. Two officers stood among them. Those same officers had separated Paul and me as soon as they learned we were employed by Malik and had a vested interest in the body in the planter. Barnes studied the others, one by one, then turned back to us.

"Anybody in that group stand out during the hunt?" Barnes asked.

Paul and I both shook our heads.

"Not for any malicious reasons," I said.

"I got thirty years in this game and six months left to retirement. How about you save me both the time and grief, and let me judge what's malicious?"

Paul and I exchanged a look and he shrugged. I gestured with my forehead at the group, and Barnes turned to stand next to me, following them as I moved my gaze from one to the next.

"The older woman in the red coat is here with her son. That's him behind her, the bored-looking one in the grey hoodie. The two blonde women are sisters visiting from Germany. The three guys in the checked plaid are friends on a road trip together. Hipster getaway."

"What about the ginger on the far end?" Barnes asked, nodding toward Ernest. Barnes, Paul, and I watched as Ernest gnawed on his thumb like the defending champ in a cuticle eating contest. He flicked his eyes between Walker's body and the crowd on the other side of the plaza. My gaze traveled to the point in the crowd where he seemed to be staring, but I didn't see anyone or anything that warranted special attention. I slowly scanned the crowd. When I looked back at Ernest, he was staring at me. I caught his eye and he yanked his thumb from his mouth, then calmly rolled his gaze away from me and across the crowd.

I gave Barnes the rundown on Ernest, including his penchant for going on hunts and his spats with Walker. "I know looking at him makes you wonder what meds he might be missing his regular dosage of, but to talk to him he seems relatively with it. Socially inept maybe, but not dumb."

Barnes considered Ernest for a moment, then asked for the agency number and our cell numbers, before flipping his notebook closed and stuffing it back in his pocket. He pressed his shoulders back, smoothed his too-long tie, and tucked the tip into his trousers. "I'll want to see any notes from your conversation with Malik."

"Any chance we can talk to the other hunters?" Paul asked.

Barnes smiled. "Not a one."

ΩΩΩ

Detective Barnes pawned Paul and me off to his partner, who had us walk through our arrival at the hunt, and give an account of the timing. By the time the officer exhausted his list of questions and we made our way out of the plaza, my stomach had returned to happier times, but my mind's eye was still negotiating a way to reject the sight of Walker's body.

Paul called Malik as we drove out of downtown. The police had just finished with him, and he agreed to meet with us if we could come to his office. Paul swung us through Robek's for two orders of green juice with protein powder shots.

I rolled chia seeds around on my tongue, and my stomach fought to understand why I was punishing it for the second time in the same day. I silently promised to reward it with a handful of Red Vines later and sucked up the rest of the juice as we rolled into the lot of Malik's office.

Malik's lithe, dark frame rounded over the desk toward a skinny, pale boy whose head was rolled down nearly onto his chest. Two empty cardboard rolls and several piles of wet, wadded toilet paper took up the half of the small desk not consumed by electronics. Paul rapped one knuckle lightly on the doorframe. Malik lifted his head at the sound, but the boy remained hunched.

"Hi," Malik said. "Come on in."

Malik stood and motioned to me to sit behind his desk, while he pointed Paul into the remaining guest chair. Malik maneuvered around me and rested against the door jam. The boy dragged his head up and I was surprised it was Shawn. His bony frame, red eyes, and snot-laced cheeks made him look closer to ten than twenty. I shot him what I hoped was a calming smile. He looked at me blankly, belatedly registering the musical chairs as if the seating rearrangement hadn't just taken place within four inches of him.

Shawn's hands were clenched in a crisscross around his abdomen, clutching at his elbows. He stared blankly at me before hanging his head back toward his chest.

"I just told him about Walker," Malik said.

I dragged my chair as close to the desk as I could and leaned toward Shawn.

"Shawn, is there anything we can get you? Maybe somebody we can call?" I asked.

Shawn swung his chin back and forth across his chest, creating a scratchy sound as the seedlings of hair clinging to his chin brushed against the thin material of his shirt.

I glanced at Malik. He shook his head and motioned for me to follow him into the main room. I squeezed out from behind the desk, and Paul shifted over to position himself in Shawn's line of sight.

Malik walked me down the length of the laundromat and stopped in front of a row of vending machines. Detergent, fabric softener, soft drinks, and cheap plastic toys competed for quarters.

"How long has he been like that?" I asked.

"Since we told him about Walker, maybe an hour."

"Who's the 'we'?" I asked.

"The cops were already here talking to me about what happened when Shawn came in, and he overheard the cop before I could say stop. Shawn may not have heard the softest version of events."

"The police didn't talk to him at the scene?"

Malik frowned at me in confusion. "No, he came straight here from home. I called him to come in."

"I thought he was ahead of us at the hunt?"

"He was supposed to be, but he called in sick this morning. I think that's part of why he's taking this so hard. He said if he hadn't called off, Walker would still be alive."

"Ah, man. He couldn't know that for sure. Why did he call off?"

"His stomach got worse. Said he barely made it home from talking to us yesterday, before he ended up in the john."

"Damn. I was hoping he may have seen something or someone this morning."

"I hear you."

"I take it Shawn and Walker were close?"

Malik twisted his mouth. "I didn't think so."

I looked back toward the office. "Guy seems pretty destroyed."

"I don't know how much of that is because he's sick and how much is about Walker. When Shawn first started working here, he talked to Walker a lot, asking him questions about life, kind of like an older brother thing. But after the first few months, it seemed more like they just tolerated each other."

"What do you mean by tolerated?"

Malik slipped long fingers into his pockets and gave me an apologetic look. "I hate to speak ill of the dead. Especially like the same day. But Shawn's a pretty simple kid and Walker could be challenging sometimes."

"How? Aside from wanting to be the center of attention?" I asked.

"Walker humored Shawn at first with his questions, but it quickly turned more into Walker's monologues about life more than real two-way conversation."

"Do you think Shawn was jealous? Did he ever talk about wanting to host the hunts?"

"No. You saw how he reacted when I suggested he could be Walker's back-up if Walker quit. My guess is Shawn just felt let down. He came out here from back East six, maybe seven months ago and I don't think he has many friends. Like I said, I think he was hoping for a big brother thing with Walker and saw pretty fast that it wasn't going to happen."

"He have family here?" I asked.

"Mmm, don't think so. His mom and dad are still back east. Jersey, I think."

"Roommates?"

Malik shook his head. "Not that he's ever mentioned. I've got a friend who does grief counseling who I can call. I'm sure he'll help."

"How about you? How are you holding up?"

"Truth? I'll be busy with details for a while and will have the luxury not to think about what happened. I need to talk to Walker's family, find his replacement, deal with any public fallout. I'll be in fixer mode for a while. Hopefully long enough for me to skip the grief piece."

I smiled. "Not a big fan of releasing emotion?"

"Nah, I'm all about releasing it. I just don't need anybody watching while I do it."

Malik stepped back to help a woman with a walker unjam the soap machine. I watched as he fed in her money, then reach into his pocket to add a few more quarters to get her what she needed.

After he got her back to her washer and got her clothes loaded, he came back to me.

"Nice of you," I commented.

"Making friends with karma has got to be better than making enemies with it, way I see things."

"Speaking of enemies, Paul and I have done some digging and you seem to come up clean as far as haters go."

"Told you. I don't interact enough with anyone to give them time to hate me."

I laughed. "Fair point. But Malik, you have to consider the possibility this is all being targeted toward you. Are you one hundred percent sure there's no one you've gotten into it with? If not recently, anything even in the past few years you can think of? Any resentment that someone could be building against you?"

"I've thought about it a thousand times over and keep coming up with zilch. The cops talked to the gal I was seeing and told me right out that she wasn't a factor. I just can't fathom anyone else going to this extent to cause damage to me."

"What about your family? Could someone be trying to bring you down to bring them down? When we first met, it sounded like you provide them with quite a bit of support."

Malik crossed his arms and rocked back on his heels in thought. "I do, but it's not like they'd be homeless without me. I just make sure they have the extras they need, you know?"

"How about Walker's family? Are they local?"

"Nuh-uh. He's got an ex-wife in Pittsburgh, and a grown son by her. Not sure if he still lives at home or not. He's got a sister in Indy. Parents are dead. The cops already notified the ex-wife and sister."

"Did he have a next of kin or emergency contact listed in his personnel file?"

"Yeah, oddly enough. He listed the ex-wife."

"Maybe they parted on good terms."

"Or maybe in Walker's head, they did."

"If you wanna share her number with me, I'll make it a point to find out."

Chapter Five

I nestled a bite of hard-as-rock chicken in my cheek and waited for the conversation to swing to the other end of the table before rolling the bite right back out of my mouth and into my napkin.

Sunday Supper was in full swing and my mother had laid the table with her best inedible recipes. Dad had always been the cook in the family and had passed away the previous year, leaving Mom to pluck willy-nilly from her 1970's cookbooks. Most Sundays, we tried to lobby for take-out, under the premise that we wanted to relieve her burden, but Mom's heart was set harder than the half-baked tortellini I was hockey-pucking around my plate.

Tonight's table was a packed venue. My younger brother Vinnie sat across from Paul and me, eyeballing Mom's new boyfriend, Wally. Mom and Wally had been together for a few months, and while Paul and I were largely resigned and edging toward encouragement, Vinnie was slower to warm up to the idea. I leaned past Paul to catch a glimpse of Wally. He finished chewing a bite of his chicken and sucked at his lower teeth, a sound reminiscent of a defective tracheal tube. Maybe it wasn't the idea of the man so much as the actual man that had Vinnie's shorts in a knot. He was petite enough to count in inches, with the belly of a man you'd count in yards. His hair reminded me of a Black and Tan, but I didn't have the guts to ask Mom which color was store bought and which was homemade. The wisps sloped upward from his ears, and across the top of his head, held in place by what I could only guess was hair oil. Nasal voice with just a hint of a whistle. So light you had to listen intently to make sure it wasn't the microwave timer going off in the other room. It took me weeks to get the whistle while you work song out of my head when I saw him. On the plus side, he complimented Mom every hour on the hour, and had never once complained about her cooking.

"This is good sauce, Marie. Real good," Wally said. Mom preened, blushed, and scanned the crowd at the table. Paul and I showed a lot of tooth in response, while Vinnie put up half of a fake smile and continued to drill his eyes into Wally. Mom daintily laid her fork on the edge of her plate and sent another look around the table, this one nervous. She darted a look at Wally, who had returned his attention to sawing his chicken cutlet.

"Wally," Mom said. Wally looked back up at Mom and she nodded her head a fraction at him. Wally shook his head back at her, one quick flick to each side. Mom pushed her forehead forward and nodded jerkily at him.

Paul met my eyes. "Do you think it's code?" he murmured.

"That or a tableside do-si-do," I whispered back. "Remember how Grandma used to chair dance with only her shoulders?"

"I do," Vinnie said from across the table. "Used to freak me out."

Mom cleared her throat. A flush crawled up Wally's neck and Mom's cheeks fired up a shade.

"Wally's been having some trouble down at his shop," Mom said, looking at Paul and me. "I was thinking maybe you two could help him fix it."

"It's okay if you can't," Wally said, smoothing several strands of tan into the black with one hand. "It's really not a big deal, Marie."

Mom opened her mouth, but Paul cut her off. "What's the problem, Wally?"

"Well, see, some of my inventory's been coming up missing." Wally owned a clothing shop on the edge of Parma, a few miles from Mom's house.

"What kind of inventory?" I asked.

Wally squirmed. "Um, it seems like just some of the, uh, accessories."

"Accessories? Like, ties, belts?"

"Mm hmm, ties, yep. Not belts."

"What else?" I asked.

"I think, well. Let's see, there's, uh, some underwear."

"Could it be just a matter of a wrong shipment or a screwed-up order?"

"I don't think so. See, well. We only order from a few vendors, so we get different items all in one shipment, but…"

"But?" Paul asked.

"Well, I'm not missing whole orders. It's like, just some real specific things." Wally glanced at Mom, then sent a sideways glance at me. I cleared my throat and his eyes popped wide, his glance moving to a spot just north of my right ear.

"What specific things, Wally?" I tried to push the impatience from my voice. "Like, expensive things?"

Wally's eyes bounced up around my hairline and he shot another quick glance at Mom.

"No, not really. More like specific styles."

I was exhausted. It was easier to chew the chicken. I looked down at my plate. On second thought.

"Wally," I said. "Help us help you. What exactly is missing?"

Wally straightened up in his chair, pushing his belly into the table's edge and his shoulders back against the slatted chair. His face stiffened like he was working up the courage to take a tetanus shot.

"Bow ties and underwear." Wally paused. "All the blue bow

ties. And our, uh, Ample Man underwear."

The pink on Mom's cheeks bloomed outward and her eyes widened to the point she looked like one of those cat clocks. I got the feeling Wally hadn't been exactly specific in defining his problem to her.

"All the Ample Man underwear, or just the blue ones?" I asked.

"That's your question?" Paul asked, swinging his head back to stare at me. "Somehow, I think we're missing the bigger picture here."

"Pun intended?" I asked.

"Absolutely not."

I looked back at Wally and he nodded gravely. "Just the blue."

I grinned at Paul. He shrugged one shoulder and smiled back. "You seem pretty in tune to this case already. It's yours."

"Oh, no," I said.

"Oh, yes. Remember who signs your check."

"Remember who hasn't signed a lease here yet."

Paul raised a fist and held it toward me. I balled up my own hand and we shook. One, two, three. I unfurled two fingers into a scissor sign. Paul held up his still-clenched hand and bumped my fingers with his fist.

"Dammit."

Chapter Six

Monday morning, Johnny scooped me up from my front curb, and we tootled over to Garfield Heights to meet up with Janie Nagelson, Malik's competition in the hunt world. Janie didn't have an office to invite us to, but seemed to instead have taken up residence in one corner of a Panera Bread on Rockside Road. Paper cups with tea bag strings hanging limply over their rims littered the workspace around Janie's laptop, which sat partway off the edge of the table, braced against her sternum. The edges of every single tea bag were lightly shredded, as was a stack of napkins to her right. They were piled a half dozen high, and sat unfolded, their middles soft and uniform, their edges ragged. To her left sat a second stack, edges as yet unmolested.

Janie clacked away on her laptop's keyboard and didn't notice us until we were on top of her. Janie stopped clacking, frowned, and reached a hand out to take a fresh napkin from one pile and stack it onto the used pile. Still staring at her laptop screen, she absentmindedly began to drag her thumbnail across one edge of the fresh napkin. She maintained a laser focus on her screen while managing to cut perfectly spaced thumb cuts into the napkin. She must have sensed our presence at last, because her shoulders suddenly pressed back and her thumb stopped and raised, like a bunny's ears at the sound of a critter in the underbrush.

Janie raised her head of lank blonde hair, revealing a concentrated face. She smiled genuinely but not wide.

"Ms. Nagelson?" Johnny asked.

"Mm-hmm. Janie."

"We're from the Carter Agency. I'm Johnny and this is Sam."

We exchanged handshakes, and Johnny and I slid into the booth across from her.

"You guys want something to eat? Drink?" Janie gestured toward the ordering counter.

Johnny and I shook our heads. Johnny pointed a knuckle toward Janie's laptop. "Is this still a good time for you?"

"Yes, of course." Janie continued to rest her fingertips on her keyboard. "Sorry, I just finished my finals and grades come out today. They're supposed to be posted any time."

Johnny and I exchanged surprised looks, and Janie laughed.

"Malik didn't tell you I was a college kid, did he?" Janie asked.

"He sure didn't," I said. "What are you studying?"

"International business, with a minor in Mandarin Chinese."

"Um, wow," I said. "And you have time to run a tourism business?"

"Don't be too impressed. The business started out as a class assignment really. We had to build a business model and my teacher was convinced it was viable, so I thought why not? The start-up cost was next to nothing really, because most of the service is online."

"Is that why you decided to do an online version instead of having a host like Malik does?" Johnny asked.

"Sure, partly." Janie hesitated. "Listen, I like Malik, but I think his concept's a bit old-fashioned. People nowadays like the flexibility of self-service that online services offer. It's so much less commitment."

I smiled inwardly. When I thought of commitment, I thought of marriage, houses, and babies. Not vacation tours.

"Speaking of commitment, what are your goals for the business? Do you think you'll keep expanding?" I asked.

"Sure, but only to the point where I can sell. I'm dating it, not marrying it."

"Do you think you can sell it for a lot?"

Janie looked past us at a toddler sitting in a high chair at the next table. The boy was ripping his mother's straw wrapper into bits and launching them at the sugar canister with a chubby fist. Janie's eyes brightened and her thumb found the edge of her napkin stack as she watched. After a moment long enough to make me think she wouldn't answer, Janie brought her gaze back to me and the thumb went idle.

"We're working on putting together numbers now."

"Who's 'we'?" Johnny asked.

"I have a friend who is something of a partner. We worked on the class assignment together, but he didn't put up any money to get things started, so he's not like a 50/50 partner."

"What's your friend's name?" I asked.

Janie's eyes clouded briefly. "Why do you want to know?"

"We're covering all our bases." Malik had told Janie he'd hired us to look into the stolen clues, but hadn't given her a lot of detail. I wanted to stay as vague as possible.

"His name is Steve. And he wouldn't know anything more about the business than I can answer."

"Is there any possibility of Steve buying the business from you?"

An annoyed look flashed across Janie's face and she smirked as she glanced back at her laptop screen.

"Absolutely not," Janie said. "Steve is only involved because I think he has a teeny crush on me. He doesn't have the money to buy me out, but even if he did, I don't think he has any interest in actually running the business."

"What is he studying?"

"Business, with an emphasis in hospitality and tourism," Janie said. The words came automatically, her surprise catching up a second later. Johnny and I watched her, waiting for the irony to register. Her eyes went wide when it did. "No. I'm telling you, he's not interested."

"What's Steve's last name?"

"Nall."

ΩΩΩ

When I was a kid, I had a mild obsession with Beaker from The Muppets. I don't know if it was his flaming orange hair or his affliction of clumsiness that paralleled my own, but the vibe was strong. As I sat in a hard, plastic chair in an overflowing student cafeteria, I was mesmerized by Steve Nall. He was my Beaker come to life. Spiky orange hair bushed out from his head in all directions, topping bulging eyeballs and a block jaw. My trance was shattered when he opened his mouth. Beaker owned the vocal pipes of Barry White.

Johnny must have sensed my distracted and confused state, because he dominated the conversation. Unfortunately, we'd been with Steve for twenty minutes and had come up with zip. As Janie had suggested, Steve's insight into the scavenger business failed to extend beyond Janie's. Steve answered our questions as if he were saving syllables for a rainy day.

"Janie mentioned that you and she are evaluating the potential sale price for the business," Johnny said. "What's your take on that so far?"

"Don't have one," Steve said.

"Not even a ballpark figure?"

"No."

"How large do you think the business could grow?"

"Don't know."

"Are you interested in buying it?"

"No."

"Why not?"

"Don't want it."

My reverie broke.

"If you don't mind my asking," I said. "Why did you pick hospitality as a major?"

"My dad runs a hotel. He wants me to take over so he can retire."

I sent a prayer to whichever saint looks over pensions that his dad wasn't relying on the hotel profits to put food on his retirement table.

"How long have you known Janie?" I asked.

An apathetic shrug. "Since sophomore year."

"Been friends all that time?"

Steve stared at me a beat. "Friendly."

"The difference?" I took a swing at connecting through mono syllables.

"We've shared classes almost every semester."

"How about outside of school? You guys go to the same parties? Date?"

A hint of amusement slid past Steve's face. "No and no."

"Did Janie say no, or did you?" That netted me a nasty look from the Beekster.

"Neither of us asked." Steve picked up the energy drink resting on the table and drained it.

"If she did ask, would you say no?"

"What difference does it make?"

I could smell the energy drink on his words. It smelled like bleach and berries. I turned my head and took a cleansing breath before I answered.

"Just curious," I said. "Wondering if you two had a connection before you went into business together."

Steve crunched the can in his hand, first in one direction, then the other. "It was just a class assignment. The professor put us together based on last name. We happened to both be N's."

"Do you clear much profit personally?" Johnny asked.

Another crunch of the can. "Some. Nothing to write home about."

"You and Janie split 50/50?"

"More like 70/30. It was her idea."

"The business or the split percentage."

"Both." Steve scraped his chair back and stretched down to pick up a canvas backpack.

"Steve," I said. "Do you think Janie would do ever do anything to sabotage Malik's business?"

Steve stood to his full Beaker height. "I don't think Janie cares enough to try. She's got bigger sights."

"On what?"

"The world."

ΩΩΩ

Johnny swung me past my house to pick up my car. By the time I filled a Thermos with coffee and dashed back out the door, I made it to Pittsburgh just in time for rush hour, a tangle of metal converging in three points of exit out of downtown.

I thrashed my way across the bridge and rolled into Squirrel Hill on the northeast side of the city twenty minutes past the appointed hour. I turned onto Darlington and slowed to a stop in front of a massive red brick home. Mary Abram's electric bill had to be more than my rent.

I climbed the steep set of stairs cutting into the hill holding the house and was proud to be only minimally out of breath when I hit the porch and rang the bell. A mellow gong sounded twice and after a moment, the heavy glassed-in door opened to reveal a petite woman in yoga pants and a canary yellow cardigan.

"Samantha?"

"Hi, Mrs. Abrams. "So sorry I'm late."

Mary Abrams waved me inside the house with one hand and flapped away my apology with the other. "I haven't been on time for anything in the last ten years. And call me Mary."

I smiled my appreciation for being excused and trailed behind her through a heavily wood-paneled foyer into a brightly lit kitchen at the back of the house. Granite and antique washed cabinets dominated the room. I swept my eyes across a counter laden with every appliance ever to have touched a Sears catalog or donned an As Seen on TV label.

"I hope you don't mind my working while we chat," Mary said as she began scraping down the inside of a bowl with a spatula. "Adam will want to eat as soon as he gets in and I've barely started."

"Husband?" I asked.

"Son. My stepson, really, but he feels like mine as much as Scott does," she said, referring to the son she shared with Walker. She lifted her face up to smile before burying her hands into the mixing bowl. She put the spatula aside and began kneading the dough, rolling her small frame up on the balls of her feet and pressing down hard, the taut muscles in her forearms highlighting her effort.

"How old is your stepson?"

"Twenty-three."

"He lives at home?"

Mary heaved the mixing bowl onto one end and dumped the innards onto a marbled section of the kitchen island. I belatedly realized her grimace was due to my question, not the strain of the chore.

"He's not a lazy bird taking advantage of the nest, if that's what you're thinking," Mary said. "He goes to school not far from here. Carnegie Mellon." She paused, seemingly waiting for my applause.

"That's impressive." I took the bait. "What's he studying?"

"Engineering."

"Senior?"

"Junior. He took a year to travel abroad after his sophomore year."

"Ah," I said. Lots of money lying around in Squirrel Hill. "How about Scott? I heard he's a sophomore. Will he be taking a year abroad?"

Mary's smile broadened, but her eyes strained as she began cutting circles into the dough with a copper ring. This thing had a wooden handle, scalloped edges, and came from a drawer where I spied another dozen in a set. My Nonni used the rim of a cracked coffee cup.

"My Scotty goes to Michigan State." Mary smiled indulgently. "He wanted to go away from home, but stayed within driving distance to please me. He's still deciding on whether to take a year to explore. Scott feels it might be a bit indulgent to take that kind of time off. My husband and I have been trying to explain that there really is no better time. He should do it now before life hands him a bunch of responsibility."

"Have you told him about Walker's death?" I asked.

Mary nodded as she slid a thin-bladed spatula under each circle of dough and eased them onto two baking sheets. "We spoke this morning."

"How's he doing?"

"He's taking it in stride. Scott is a practical boy, always has been. He feels bad about the loss of a life, but not the loss of Walker as his dad. Harry - my husband - has been his dad for near eight years."

"And how about you? Are you taking it in stride?" I asked.

Mary stacked the baking sheets into the oven and set a timer. She crossed to the sink, rinsed her hands, and dried them thoroughly on a hand towel hanging from a bronze rod before turning to face me with wet eyes.

"Walker was very special to me. He gave me Scott, of course, and he was a playful partner at a time when I hadn't grown up myself. He was my Peter Pan before I realized there needed to be a time stamp on that sort of life. Our relationship didn't end well, and it took some time to get past the hurt, both for Scott and me. But we moved on. There's a piece of me that will always love Walker, but I can't mourn a loss that I already mourned long ago."

"Had you and Walker kept in touch?" I asked.

"From time to time." Mary hesitated. "My husband doesn't know about that."

"When was the last time you two spoke?"

"Maybe a year ago." Mary shrugged and leaned back against the edge of the counter.

"Did you see him in person?"

"No, no. We talked over the phone. Just a few times over a couple weeks."

"What did you talk about?"

Mary twisted the hand towel. A pattern of doves marched across the fabric and I watched as Mary's twisted the doves' necks. "Not much. Mostly his work."

"His work with the scavenger service?"

"No, his acting. He was up for a part that he didn't get, and was frustrated about it."

"How long had it been before that?" I asked.

"How long before what?"

"How long before that time did you two talk?"

"I'm not sure why that matters." Mary snapped the hand towel out straight, then carefully wound it back through its holder.

"It may not, but anything we can learn about what was going on in his life leading up to his death could be helpful. Did Walker seem worried to you? Mention any conflict in his life?"

"Walker's conflict was never with other people."

"What do you mean?"

"Walker's life view was mostly internal. He always focused on how good his acting was, how it could be better, what other people thought about him and his performances."

"Anyone he was competing with for a role?"

Mary frowned. "Not that he said, but I really can't see anyone being so competitive as to hurt him. And, well this is going to sound horrible—."

"What is it?"

"Walker wasn't that great an actor," Mary said softly. "I can't imagine anyone feeling he was a real threat."

"Mary, it's okay."

"I sound awful."

"No, you sound truthful. And that doesn't lessen the love you had for him." I paused, but Mary didn't look convinced. "Are you planning to come out for the funeral?"

Mary cast her eyes toward the front hall at the sound of the front door opening and closing. She shook her head and swiped at her eyes with the hem of her cardigan. "I can't. I'm sorry, you'll have to go."

Chapter Seven

I was knee-deep in the files on each of the scavengers Tuesday morning. The hipsters came back unsurprisingly clean. All I found in their brief back stories were three sets of indulgent parents who must have been footing the documentary building phase of their youngsters' lives, and I wondered if this was the new version of backpacking abroad. Not that I had back-packed as far as Cincinnati, let alone abroad. For starters, I didn't finish college, but even if I had I was more likely to be selling backpacks than trekking across France with one. I grew up in a neighborhood where we went straight from high school to work, and if there was college slipped in there somewhere, it was financed by the job we'd had since we were legal to work. Or even earlier for those of us scrappy enough to find an under-the-table gig.

I had just crossed the last hunter off my list and uncrossed my eyeballs when the office phone rang.

"Carter and Rosato. How may I help you?" I answered.

"Have I told you how much I like hearing you say my name?" Johnny asked.

I blushed and sent thanks to whichever saint watches over conflicted women.

"What can I do for you, Giovanni Anthony?"

"Well, I don't like it when you say it like that."

"Hey, I used both your names. Not doubling your pleasure, huh?"

"I feel like I'm in Sunday school."

"When did you ever go to Sunday school?" I countered. Johnny had come to live with his aunt in Cleveland as a teen, after his parents were killed in a car accident. Aunt Jeanine was not exactly what one would call devout after her brother's and sister-in-law's deaths. She'd be more likely to take Johnny to a brothel than shuttle him off to Sunday school.

"Let's just say it makes me feel dirty."

"I thought you liked dirty."

"Yeah, the good kind."

"Did you have a real question for me anywhere in this call?" I tapped my pen on the edge of the phone.

"Yes, what are you wearing?"

"I'm hanging up now," I said.

"I called because I've got a few hours open. You got time for the gun range?"

"I'm gonna take a big Pasadena on that one," I said.

"Come on, you gotta break the seal someday."

"Today is not that day."

"Have you had lunch yet?" Johnny asked. I could hear the smile in his voice.

"You can't bribe me. I'm having a clean eating day today."

"Why?"

"Because."

Johnny waited me out.

"It's been a while."

"How long's a while?"

"What month is this?"

"Come on," Johnny said. "There's a Mr. Hero next to the range."

"Nuh-uh."

"There's a DQ down the street."

"Not even slightly tempting."

I heard Johnny's breathing slow. "Dimitri's."

"Now, that's playing dirty."

"Mmm," Johnny purred. "I knew I'd get you back to dirty one way or another."

ΩΩΩ

"Gee-zuss!" I hopped backwards and threw my body forward from the hips, forcing my arms to stay in a tight V in front of me. My chest burned from the heat of the fifth casing to pummel it, but I kept my hands locked around the gun and managed not to turn around and pistol whip Johnny. I took a breath, took my last two shots, and carefully flipped on the safety lever.

Johnny stepped up behind me, slipped his arm past my shoulder and gave me a thumbs-up before relieving me of the gun. I stepped backward out of the box and rubbed my smarting chest while I watched Johnny shoot tight circle patterns into the target's forehead and heart. Show off.

He replaced the gun in its case and motioned me to the door separating the shooting area from the retail portion of the range. I pushed through the hallway connecting to the second door and tugged my ear guards from my head as I went.

As soon as Johnny cleared the second door, I turned around. He ran straight into me, bouncing against my chest, and took a small step back in surprise.

"That's why you asked what I was wearing, isn't it?" I asked.

"I told you to tuck your shirt in. It would have helped keep the fabric tight to your skin."

"I thought you were pulling my leg when you said that. I thought you just wanted to scope out the landscape."

Johnny began to smile but stopped when I raised my hand to rub my chest some more.

"Is it really that bad?" He hooked a finger in the V of my tee and pulled it toward him. I slipped my forefinger under his and used my middle one to brace it against the back of his, pulling hard.

"Shit, okay! I see we're going to need to work on some of your trust issues."

"I don't think they're so much my trust issues as they are your motive issues."

"Samantha." Johnny slipped his good hand under my hair and gently squeezed the back of my neck. "I think I've made my motives quite clear."

"I didn't mean clarifying them. I meant controlling them," I said.

"Trust me when I say there is a lot of control going on here."

I took a step back and Johnny laughed. "Come on, let's turn in this gear."

We collected our IDs and headed to the parking lot. I checked out my chest in the visor mirror and Johnny leaned over to take a look.

"They'll go away by tomorrow, I promise," he said. "But take out the fact that we can play connect the dots on your chest. How'd it feel?"

"What, shooting?" I flipped the visor down and adjusted my shirt up a couple inches by pulling the hem down in the back.

"Yeah."

I looked through the windshield at the range building. "I could do that all day."

Johnny turned wide eyes on me. "You've been fighting me

and Paul on doing this for months."

"I'm not saying I'd want to shoot out here in the open." I waved my hands. "Not like, at someone."

"Let's pray you never have to."

"Amen."

"Does this mean you don't want your tuna melt reward?" Johnny turned the ignition in his truck, and I put a hand over his as he went to move the gearshift into Drive.

"I kind of had something else in mind."

"And what exactly is that?" Johnny looked down at my hand on his, then lifted his eyes to mine. His were darkening to charcoal by the millisecond. Ruh-roh. I eased my hand away.

"Wally," I said slowly.

"Sam, I'm not saying I wouldn't be into a trio type of situation in our future, but I was kind of hoping the third person would be less, you know..."

"Male?"

"Hairy."

"What I find amazing here is that you and I haven't even been a *pair* yet, and you're hopes are already up for a trio."

"My hopes aren't the only thing."

"Calm down. I'm talking about Wally. Doll house sized, hair for days, always a little bit damp Wally. If your 'hopes' can stay up through that visual, we need to get you professional help."

Johnny held his hands up in front of him. "What did you have in mind for little Wally?"

"He's suffering some losses down at his shop and wants Paul and I to help figure out what's going on."

"What kind of losses?"

"Inventory."

"Internal problem, or external?"

"He's not sure. That's where Paul and I come in."

"What kind of shop?"

I smiled and put some sweetness into it.

"Samantha."

My smile deepened, and I laid some innocence on top of the sweetness.

"What kind of shop? I might be in the mood to make a few purchases."

I draped my hand back over his, tucked my fingers up under his palm, and squeezed. "Oh, Giovanni Anthony. I can guarantee there will be nothing there for you."

ΩΩΩ

"He sells clothes. What's the big deal?" Johnny looked past me out the truck window, toward the plate glass front of Wally's shop.

"I wouldn't say it's a 'big' deal," I said, snitching a fry from the bag in his lap.

Johnny watched my mouth as I chewed. "I thought today was a clean eating day?"

"One fry won't destroy all my good work."

"That's your fourth."

"You're supposed to be monitoring the shop, not my fry intake."

"I am monitoring," Johnny said. "Exactly three people have gone in and three have come out. None of them carrying a bag large enough to hold more than a couple shirts."

I slid one more fry out of the bag and looked out the window at the storefront. Dudek's Clothiers. Assorted outfits were pinned to a display board, sans mannequins. They ranged from golfing get-ups to blazers, to coordinated jeans and polos. A fairly conservative line-up…in miniature.

"I turned my head away from the shop window and looked at Johnny. "Do you seriously not notice anything different about the window displays?"

Johnny turned down his mouth in thought and I tried not to focus on the fullness of his lower lip. I shoved two more fries in my mouth.

"What am I supposed to be seeing here?" he asked. "Other than some of those get-ups are little high falutin' for Parma, I don't get it."

"They don't look sort of small to you?"

Johnny shrugged and playfully smacked my hand when I reached for another fry. He smiled but kept his eyes trained on the shop window. I retrieved my hand and looked back at the shop window.

"They're samples, right? They make 'em smaller for the displays."

"Try again."

"They're really mature kids' clothes."

"Go the other way."

"I give, I don't—. Holy shit."

"There ya' go."

"This place is for little people?"

"Well, technically, I think it's for all petite guys, not just little people."

I turned and caught Johnny's appraising face bobbing up and down. "Genius."

"Mmm-hmm. Wally might be more on the ball than we thought."

"Speaking of balls…"

A slow smile spread across Johnny's face, and I smacked his hand. "God, guys are so easy."

"You say that like it's a bad thing."

I gave him the lowdown on the undies and bowties that had been disappearing. His smile widened until it became a deep laugh. The laugh petered out and a swipe of confusion crossed Johnny's face.

"Wait, if they're called Ample Man, but these guys are smaller than average—."

"Let's not try to do the math."

Johnny's face scrunched up.

"Told you," I laughed. "So, Paul and I think it's likely to be an inside job given how much product has jetted, but because it's only a couple types of accessories, we can't rule out that it was a delivery problem. We're tracking the paperwork backward, but I thought it'd be worth scoping out the foot traffic."

Johnny looked at me thoughtfully.

"You're still trying to do the math, aren't you?" I asked.

"No, I'm trying to figure out why you wanted me here for this."

"You're licensed."

"You don't need a licensed PI to watch a window."

"You do when you're trying to get the two thousand supervisor hours it takes to get your own license." I pointed a finger at my chest and smiled. "Sorry to use you like this, but…"

Johnny studied my mouth, a smile playing at the corner of his.

"If you're going to use me, there are much more fun ways."

"Which are still on hold until you and Paul figure out this partnership situation. Until then, I'll be using you for my professional needs only."

"But who's going to help you get your other needs met?"

The muscles in my cheek flinched and Johnny's smile broke wide.

"One at a time," I said. Heaven help me.

Chapter Eight

"What's wrong?" I asked as I fingered my way through a rack of dresses.

"Why does something have to be wrong?" Vinnie asked. My younger brother by three years, Vinnie was never one to dress-shop with me, and I said as much.

"I hired a new manager, so I got a night off. What's wrong with wanting to hang out with my sister for a minute?"

I stopped my hand on a see-through number that would have made Johnny's partnership decision an easy one, but wouldn't exactly please the priest at Walker's funeral.

"Vin, it's Dress Barn," I said, waving my hand in the air above my head. "You're single, you finally have help at the pizza shop, and you're free for the first time in months. No offense, but I don't know that you'd be my first choice of playdate if I was in your shoes."

"I've barely seen you since you got back into town."

"We barely saw each other before I left town. Dude, what's going on?"

Vinnie flicked his fingers across the dress rack and picked out a royal blue chiffon dress with a sequined butterfly collar and an open back. He held it up to me.

"Not even if it was Elton John's funeral," I said. He shrugged and absentmindedly flitted through the rest of the rack.

"Why don't you just wear what you wore to dad's funeral?"

"I burned that as soon as I got back to Florida. You might not be the only one with a hang-up about Dad being gone."

"You think this thing with Mom and Wally is going to last?" Vinnie asked.

"Heck if I know. You still freaked out about it?"

"I'm not freaked out." Vinnie's mouth formed a soft pout and I smothered a laugh. Vinnie sported two full sleeves of tattoos under a polo shirt that stretched taut across oversized traps. He'd need a lot more than a pout to pull off the victim look.

"You didn't talk to Mom for two weeks after you found out about Wally, and you bitched to me and Paul that entire time. That, my friend, is freaking out."

"She almost sold our childhood home!"

"Oh, poo. She had it on the market for a few days and changed her mind. And it's not our house anymore. It's her choice." I stopped digging through the rack and turned to face Vinnie full on. "I know it's weird, but Dad's gone. Letting Mom be happy with this guy isn't the end of the world."

"It's different for you."

"How?"

"You haven't been here for like a decade. You come on holidays and sometimes not even then. Paul was off with the ex most of the time. I was the one with Mom and Dad all the time. Even after Dad turned the pizza shop over to me to run, he was still in there all the time. Now with Wally here, it's like all of a sudden, they're kind of both gone."

I put down the cream suit I was holding and turned to face Vinnie. "Are you saying you're lonely?"

"Too busy to be lonely."

"You can be busy and lonely at the same time, Vin. Trust me."

Vinnie shook his head and frowned at me.

"Do you miss having someone to go to for advice? You know Paul's there for you if you need something, right?"

Vinnie shrugged. "Nah. Me and him aren't like you and him. You guys speak a different language sometimes."

I didn't have a response to that, but Vinnie didn't seem to expect one.

"Besides," he continued. "I'm not looking for a dad. I was kind of thinking like I could maybe help someone who doesn't have one."

"Really?"

"Don't sound so surprised."

"Shit, Vin. Not 'cause I don't think you wouldn't be a great dad, I just didn't think that was something on your radar."

"I'm not trying to have a kid. Hell, I forget to feed myself half the time. I was thinking, like, you know. Maybe that big brother group they got."

"Like Big Brothers Big Sisters?"

"Yeah." Vinnie stared down at the dress rack. I lowered my head toward his, but he wouldn't meet my eye.

"I think that would be fantastic, Vin."

"Aww, get that grin off your face. It's just something I'm thinking about. I didn't say I was gonna do it."

I squeezed my eyes shut, fanned my hands in front of my face, and made a big show of fake sniffling. "Our little boy's growing up."

I heard nothing but silence and opened my eyes to see Vinnie's back retreating out the front door.

ΩΩΩ

Paul and Johnny both had dates in court Wednesday morning, which left me short a plus one for Walker's funeral. I thought four eyes would be better than two and recruited my friend Angie to meet me at the cemetery. We'd been best friends in high school and picked up like peas and carrots upon my return to Cleveland. Well, sort of. Angie had a coupon book of payback IOUs for me for deserting her, which required me to tag along with her to every whack-job, new-fangled exercise class that popped up. But she was the first to swipe on black face paint and crawl through wet lawns on her elbows and knees to TP an ex-boyfriend's house if I asked for help. Which I may or may not have asked her to do. Twice.

I turned my Jetta into a vacant lot across from Holy Cross Cemetery where a line of cars piled in ahead of me. There'd been no church service for Walker, but his sister had arranged instead for a short graveside affair. I hadn't attended a funeral since my dad had passed, and the fact that I had never met Walker somehow didn't quell the uneasy feeling in my stomach. I gave myself a quick pep talk, hauled myself out of the car, and traipsed across the street to the cemetery entrance. To one side of a twenty-foot tall angel statue stood Angie. I laughed to myself at the irony. To the outside observer, Angie was an angel of a mother, wife, and girl's girl. To those of us lucky enough to call her a friend, she was all of that wrapped around a loyal heathen core.

The heathen was currently fending off the attention of two men in suits. One came with a wife who was throwing Angie enough side eye to filet a carp.

I felt bad for the wife, but Angie couldn't help it. She was dressed neck to ankle in a black pantsuit, zero skin in sight spare her face, but she couldn't hide her Betty Boop figure.

Angie caught my eye, smiled sweetly at her suitors, and brushed demurely past them. She wore a wide-brimmed hat with an abbreviated mourning net rimming the front. When she reached me, we kept walking right through the gate and headed in the direction of the other mourners.

"Quite the hat, Ange," I said as we strolled. "Are we channeling Faye Dunaway this morning?"

Angie managed a tiny curtsy mid-stride. "And will you be catching up on your woodworking chores or making cheese this afternoon?"

I peeked down at my dress. Three stores after the Dress Barn, Vinnie had tapped out and I had settled for a grey shift dress with a white bibbed front. I was two strategically placed darts and a ruffle away from being mistaken for an Amish teen embarking on Rumspringa.

I ran a finger down my pleated bib. "I have to say I'm looking forward to having a life that's not so makeshift anymore. Makeshift house, makeshift job, makeshift dress." I still didn't know if my pit stop in Cleveland would turn into something long term and I hadn't installed anything more permanent than a new paper towel holder since I'd arrived.

"On the plus side, that makeshift job comes with a wicked hot makeshift boyfriend," Angie said.

"Johnny's not a boyfriend, makeshift or otherwise."

"He could be." Angie reached out and ran her finger down my pleated bib. "Unless you keep this up."

"We've been down this road. I'm not doing that to Paul."

"Paul will get over it. He'll see you two can work together, and it'll be fine."

"What if we can't?"

Angie peered over at me, tilting her head to near paralysis point to accommodate the hat. "Afraid Johnny won't be able to keep it in his pants?"

"I'm afraid I won't try to stop him."

"That's just your dry spell talking. Take a few weeks to get that out of your system and you'll be able to work with him without even noticing he's there."

"Spoken like a woman married forever with her fourteen kids."

Angie held her fingers up in a trident. "Three. And Tony's different."

"How's that?"

"He's never stopped chasing me. Keeps it fresh."

I stopped in front of a plot with a marker as high as my head. "You think Johnny will stop chasing me?"

"He will if you never let him get close enough to feel like he's got a shot at catching you. Look," she said, pointing to tents set up on two different parts of the lawn. One had dozens of mourners splayed out behind the rows of seats near the casket. The other group was barely large enough to warrant the back room at a Macaroni Grill. "Which one is us?"

I scanned both groups and my eyes caught on a flash of fiery red curls sticking out above the smaller of the two crowds. Ernest. I pointed Angie's hat in his direction and we moved closer.

As we approached, I counted heads and came up just shy of two dozen. Weddings and funerals often reminded me of high school. Cliques could be found everywhere. Jocks, nerds, drama geeks. Groom's side, bride's side, family, co-workers. Walker's memorial was no exception. Malik and Shawn huddled together, a woman I assumed to be Walker's sister solely by how the minister was deferring to her, a small child clutched to her hand, two older women hanging close to them. A half-dozen women dressed either for a Shakespeare in the park performance, or channeling Stevie Nicks and sorely missing the mark, loitered to one side.

The only fringe exceptions were Ernest standing on the edge of the plot, away from everyone, and a brown-jacketed man I recognized as Detective Barnes' partner. He must have recognized me as well because he gave me the smallest of nods when I caught his eye. I smiled back and let my eyes wander over to Malik and Shawn.

Shawn looked much calmer than the last time I'd seen him.

Malik, looking much more strung out than last I saw him, was talking with head bent to Shawn. He occasionally patted Shawn's shoulder as he spoke. Shawn shook his head at something Malik said and they walked away from the group by a few feet. In their wake, I caught a glimpse of the couple who'd been standing behind them. Steve Nall and Janie Nagelson.

I was surprised to see the pair, but not as surprised as I was to see Steve's palm crossing the plane of Janie's ass. I made a mental note in my Blue's Clues notebook and took in the faces of the rest of the mourners, doing my worker-bee best to avoid looking at the casket. I swung my head back in the detective's direction and watched him watch the group. He caught my gaze and studied me for a moment, emotionless. I smiled and moved my gaze past him. No need to antagonize the hand that might feed me some needed information later. Barnes may have shut Paul and me down hard, but there were other wheels to be greased.

"Who's that you're making googly eyes at?" Angie tilted her mammoth hat back a fraction and squinted up at me.

"One of the detectives investigating Walker's death."

"Then keep ogling. Maybe if you make nice, he will, too."

I turned and looked down at her. "How 1950's of you."

"There's a skill to knowing how to use what God gave you and not being taken advantage of for it."

"And here I thought you were a feminist."

"Sweetie, that is my definition of feminism."

I'd have laughed if we hadn't been at a funeral. Location, location, location. As if he could smell Angie and I on the brink of inappropriateness, the minister stepped up to his platform under the tent and cleared his throat. The group of mourners made a display of shuffling to attention and the minister began speaking in that generic way that tells you he's never met the dearly deceased.

ΩΩΩ

Fortunately, the minister's ministering was as short as the crowd was small. As he made his final blessing, I caught a snatch of canary yellow and turned to see Mary Abrams moving up to the edge of the crowd. She had donned a tailored black pants suit for the occasion, severe in every detail except for the yellow scarf that wrapped around her neck and trailed out behind her.

Mary seemed off in her own world, unseeing to anything but the casket. Her face, from as far away as I was, appeared dry, but strained.

I watched her for another moment, scanning either side for her sons, but it looked to be just her. The minister gave the wrap-up sign by stepping away from the platform and, as soon as it was polite to do so, the majority of the group broke away from the tent and lingered in the grass nearby. The three women remained near Walker's casket, the priest hovering close. Mary turned and beelined for the front entrance of the cemetery. I quickly introduced Angie and Malik, leaving them to kibitz while I scuttled after Mary. The grass was still soft from recent rain and I hiked the skirt of my dress up a few inches to aide my effort, calling out to Mary when I was a few feet away.

Mary turned and frowned at me, whether because of the sun in her eyes or my pursuit, I couldn't tell.

"Hi," I said. "I thought you weren't coming?"

"I wasn't. But I couldn't stop thinking about what you said yesterday. About how my talking bad about his acting didn't lessen my love for him."

"I'm sorry, I don't follow."

Mary shook her head. "It doesn't follow, really. I just started thinking that maybe I owed it to Walker to say goodbye."

Mary looked past me, at the tent, and pointed. "And I realized I owed it to Walker's sister."

I followed her gaze. "Did you get to talk to her?"

When she didn't answer, I turned and was startled to see her stricken face. I looked back toward the tent, half expecting to see the casket open and Walker sitting up. I reached out and put a hand under her elbow. "You okay?"

Mary jerked her head up and down and peeled her arm from my hand. "I'm fine. It's—. I just need to sit. This is too much."

"Why don't we find you a drink and a chair."

"No. I don't drink."

"I was thinking more like some juice. Mary, you're shaking. Did you eat this morning?"

Mary drew her eyes away from the tent and focused on me. Surprise and fear flared across her features before her eyes cleared and she took a step away from me.

I turned again toward the tent and caught sight of Ernest. He was talking with Malik, or rather, Malik was talking to him. Angie stood behind them, one arm wrapped around Shawn, who was now crying with head bowed like I had last seen him at the laundromat.

I looked at Mary and pointed toward Ernest. "Do you know him?"

Mary shook her head, the skin around her eyes drawn tight. "No. I shouldn't have come. I can't—. I can't see this. Oh my God, I can't see this."

"Mary, wait—," I said, but she backed away from me.

"Don't. Leave me alone." She turned and bolted on a low-heeled boot, and I knew there was no way I could catch her again. I watched her as she hustled across the grass to her car, then headed back to rescue Angie. Angie's kids were all booger-aged and I felt bad that she escaped the house for a few hours only to deal with Shawn's snot.

Angie shook me off when I attempted to cut in, so I made my way over to Ernest, who had disentangled from Malik and was standing on the far side of the casket, away from the three women.

"Hi, Ernest. Do you remember me?"

Ernest kept his eyes forward but nodded his acknowledgment.

I followed his eyes toward the casket and picked a spot just past it to focus on. "Did you know Walker well?"

"I helped him with the hunts."

"How so?"

"I told him how to do the clues."

"I heard he was quite the performer."

Ernest shifted his chin toward me while his eyes still hovered on the casket.

"He couldn't do it without me."

"Did he tell you that?"

"He didn't have to."

"Must have been hard on you to find him like that."

He lifted his head and the sun caught the red tendrils leaping from his forehead. "That's the way it should have been."

"What makes you say that?"

"Nothing." Ernest's face hardened as the woman with the little girl stepped forward and rubbed one hand across the top of the casket.

"Do you know who that is?" I nodded toward the woman.

"Walker's sister." I studied his face, the harshness of his words startling.

"Have you met her before?"

Ernest shook his curls side to side. "I heard the minister tell her he was sorry about her brother."

I looked across the tent to where Malik, Shawn, and Angie were standing. Malik raised his eyebrows at me. I gave him a half smile and watched as Angie murmured into Shawn's ear, one arm still wrapped around his shoulders. Barely squeaking in at five feet, she was easily a half foot shorter than he, but it appeared as if she was cradling him. I turned back toward Ernest.

"Will you still go on hunts? Help whoever the owner gets to replace Walker?"

Ernest looked at me sharply. It was the first eye contact he had granted me. "They won't replace Walker."

I chose my words carefully. "I think they'll have to."

"No one can replace Walker."

"I just meant that the owner will find someone to take on the hosting duties."

"Who?"

"I don't know. I'd imagine Shawn will help until the owner finds someone."

Ernest jerked his eyes away from me and sought out Shawn.

"He's no good."

"Maybe you can help him the way you helped Walker."

"I won't help him."

"Why not?"

"He ruined everything."

"How did Shawn ruin everything?"

"Not Shawn. Walker."

"What do you mean?"

He looked back at me and shook his curls vehemently, then turned and strode away from the tent, across the far side of the lawn and onto a stone path that led deeper into the cemetery.

I turned back toward Malik. He watched as Ernest receded. Shawn watched warily for a moment, too, before lifting his dress shirt covered arm and swiping it in a long arc under his dripping nose.

Chapter Nine

Angie and I parted ways at the cemetery gates. Her glass slipper had cracked and her grand carriage was rapidly turning back into a pale blue Impala. Time to return to rug rat mania.

I accepted Malik's offer to grab a cup of coffee. He convinced Shawn to let him drop him off instead of taking the bus back home. Shawn relented to a ride to the RTA station.

I had settled into a booth at Luna's Deli and was stirring cream into my steaming mug of coffee when Malik pushed through the door. The waitress flipped over Malik's mug, filled it, and dropped three creamers onto the tabletop before pivoting to the next table.

Luna's was a haven for locals, tourists, lunch breakers, and those seeking a cure to their Sunday morning hangover. All were welcome and the people watching was divine. I did just that while Malik jockeyed around with his coffee.

"What did Ernest have to say?" Malik thumped three packets of sugar against his thumb, ripped the tops, and poured them into his mug.

"Well, he seems to think he was 50/50 partners with Walker."

"For real?"

"This guy was as sincere as a shy girl at the Sadie Hawkins dance."

"You have an interesting way with words, you know that?"

"In my experience, 'interesting' doesn't exactly translate to a compliment."

Malik grinned. "And it won't today, either."

"I gotta admit, I like your honesty. But seriously, Ernest is convinced. When I suggested that you'd be finding a replacement for Walker, he talked like it couldn't and wouldn't happen."

"That definitely adds to the vibe I'm getting off him."

"Which is?"

Malik looked past me and considered for a moment. "There's something creepy there, I just can't put my finger on it."

"Did you get that impression from talking to him this morning? I saw you chatting him up."

Malik sipped his coffee, then blew on it in spurts as he answered. "That was part of it. All I said was how sorry I was and that I know how important a hobby the hunts are to him. He snapped at me. Said the hunts weren't his hobby, they were his work."

"That's a little kooky."

"I certainly thought so."

"Where's the other part of the creep factor coming from?"

Malik tried his coffee again. "One of the detectives was at the funeral. Did you see the man in the brown jacket?"

I nodded. "I met him at the Rock and Roll Hall of Fame. I played eyeball footsie with him this morning and he didn't seem to appreciate it."

"Is that a single girl thing?"

"Forget it."

"Forgotten. The detective said his team went to Ernest's apartment, but he wouldn't let them in. He just stood between the door and doorjamb. The detective is taller by a lot, but all he could see above Ernest's head was a wall completely covered in brown cloth."

"Cloth?"

"Like some kind of fabric or canvas or something. The detective said he couldn't be sure. I got the feeling he was holding back on what he was telling me. He said they'd done some background on Ernest, too. Found a couple misdemeanors for destroying property and for repeatedly going to one of those private nudie peep show joints down on Brookpark Road."

"But that's not illegal here."

"It is when you, ah, make yourself happy on your side of the window."

"Glad I decided against having the eggs." I pushed my coffee cup away as I tried to simultaneously push the image away. "What property did he destroy?"

"A public pool."

"How do you destroy a pool?"

"He dumped a couple gallons of chemicals into it. I can't remember what the detective called the chemical, but evidently it reacted with the chlorine levels in a pool and created a toxic state to the point where the whole pool had to be drained and refilled. And we're talking a community pool. Not something you can throw a hose into and fill back up in an hour."

I wrinkled my nose. "I can't believe that's only a misdemeanor."

"It's not. Barnes's partner said they're looking into it. Said it's likely there was some kind of plea bargain attached. Ernest picked up community service and a year of mandated counseling."

"Do they think Ernest killed Walker?"

"Barnes told me the day it happened that he thought it was

significant that Ernest was the one who found Walker, but he didn't straight out say he thought Ernest was involved."

"Did Barnes say whether they're talking to Ernest's family?"

"They already did. The little that's left, anyway. He had an older brother who died when he was a teen, and his dad passed away just a few years after the brother. Mom lives out in Mentor, some assisted living retirement village. Ernest is only forty-three, but Barnes said he was a late-in-life baby and his mom's in her eighties."

"How'd the brother die?"

"Some kind of flu that got out of control. Surprise to everyone."

"That's awful."

Malik murmured agreement and looked around for the waitress.

"Did Barnes ask the mom about the pool incident?"

"Nah, didn't get that far. He said Mrs. Brown has all her faculties and then some. He wasn't three sentences into his spiel before she was defending Ernest. Barnes said she was dismissive more than defensive. Like she wouldn't even conceive the possibility that he'd done something wrong."

"How so?"

The waitress stopped to top off our coffee mugs and I waited while Malik went through his sugar packet routine again.

"Before Barnes could even ask if she thought Ernest would be involved in such a thing, she said he couldn't have gotten into any trouble because he was with her most of the week. Then Barnes asked which days and nights, and Mrs. Brown asked which ones he wanted to know about. They went back and forth for a bit before Barnes let it go."

I shrugged. "I struggle to see it myself. Ernest definitely wants to feel special, there's no doubt, but why would he kill Walker? If anything, he loses his 'job' creating the hunt clues."

"Maybe in his mind, if he gets rid of Walker, he gets to take over as the starring role."

"I still don't see it. You said when we first talked that Ernest agreed to share his ideas with Walker on the side instead of in front of the other hunters, right?"

"So?"

"So, he's not a make-a-scene person. He doesn't interact with the other hunters much, he doesn't fight with Walker publicly, and he's been on two dozen or more hunts? If he wanted to take over, don't you think he'd have made a different play by now? And why start with murder? Why not just make a complaint to you, try to get Walker fired? It seems extreme."

"Maybe for you and me. But you have to admit, this guy's a taco short of a combination plate. Who knows what extreme is to him?"

I chewed my lip and watched an elderly couple approach the front of the deli through the window. "If his mother lives in a retirement home, there must be visiting hours. And records that would show if and when Ernest was really there that night."

"It's not a true assisted living facility. Residents are allowed to come and go, and all the units are independent of each other, so there's no restriction on guests."

"Sounds like the place my Nonni lives in. Sometimes I think it's more like an all-inclusive resort than assisted living."

"Doesn't sound half bad actually." Malik pushed his coffee mug away and rubbed his eyes.

"You hanging in?" I asked.

"Yeah, there's just a lot going on. I've spent a bunch of time with these cops, and I'm trying to revise the hunt schedule. I cancelled the tours through today, but we pick back up tomorrow morning. I thought I could use Shawn for the short term, but he still seems to be in rough shape. And he's not a sparkling personality to start with."

"He did seem pretty beat up still at the funeral."

Malik nodded. "He is. Still feeling guilty, I think. That's the other reason I need to find a replacement fast. I won't be surprised in Shawn cancels for tomorrow. I'm afraid he'll feel even worse trying to fill Walker's shoes."

"Did you ever find out if he's got family or friends to help him out?"

"Nuh-uh. I asked him again about any roommates or friends, but he just shrugged me off."

"You think he'd be open to a surrogate big brother?"

Malik looked at me thoughtfully. "Who did you have in mind?"

"My brother Vinnie. He's been toying with the idea of getting involved with Big Brothers Big Sisters."

"Mid-life self-exploration?"

I laughed. "He's only twenty-seven. We lost our dad last year and I think he's trying to find meaning, you know? We're not the most religious family ever and a connection to something bigger than him might be helpful. Maybe lending Shawn a shoulder will help them both."

"It's worth a shot." Malik dug out his cell. "I'll text you his number. You might want to make the introduction to grease the wheels first."

"I'll grab the Crisco."

Malik stared at me for a beat, grinned, and raised his hand for the check.

Chapter Ten

I came home from the funeral, stripped out of my birth control dress and shoved my limbs into a pair of faded jeans and a tank top. I dumped a can of soup into a bowl and called my cousin Leo while I waited for the microwave to do its thing.

Leo was my Uncle Gino's stepson. While he'd grown up around Gino and had enough kink to him to answer the nature versus nurture question for good, his lack of blood relation brought my comfort level with being near him into a quasi-normal range. Besides that, he was the only man I knew who came close to looking like a kosher shopper at Dudek's. Leo had the inseam of a squirrel.

Leo answered on the first ring and told me he'd meet me at the Save A Lot next to Dudek's, but he had to do it right away in order to make it to work on time. Leo was a supervisor at what he described as a telemarketing office, and what the rest of the family described as a bookie's back room. I spooned up half my soup, shoved a fistful of Red Vines into a baggie to round out my lunch calories, and motored out.

I rolled into the Save A Lot parking lot and found Leo right away. He drove a Mary Kay-pink Jag with rosewood trim and a rose gold bra. He was kind of into pink. The way Boy George is kind of into eyeliner.

Leo hopped out of the Jag and I grinned. He was sporting navy blue pants with a crease that could slice cheese, a green button-down shirt with extended lapels, a striped vest, and a magenta tie replete with a tie pin and chain. He couldn't spell makeover better if he'd been a fourth-grade spelling bee finalist.

"Oh, Leo, I so owe you. You're playing the part to a tee."

"What part?"

The laugh died in my throat as I looked into his earnest eyes.

"I just meant that you look like a savvy shopper. Hiding in plain sight." I pointed across the rows of cars to the Save A Lot building. "Wow, is that bakery next door new?"

Leo cut me a suspicious look. "If by 'new' you mean it's been there since you were five, then sure."

I smiled brightly and tapped my temple with a forefinger. "The ole memory bank, huh?"

"Whatever. So, you want me to stroll in there and straight up ask for these blue panties, or what?"

I cringed at the word 'panties'. I was barely okay with looking 'underpants' in the eye.

"Not exactly. I was thinking you could check out the clothes while I look around the store. I want to get a sense of the layout and watch the employees. We've looked through all the receiving shipment paperwork and it looks like the same employee has signed for every shipment that included either the bowties or the, uh, panties." I controlled my internal gag. "Her name's Erin and she's working today, along with a guy named Niko."

Leo worked his head up and down and bounced on the balls of his feet. "Got it. You want me to try some stuff on?"

"Let's play it by ear."

"I don't like to buy unless I try on."

I eyed him for a beat. "You looking for something in particular?"

"Depends on your budget."

"Leo, we're not here to buy. This is just recon." Leo stared up at me. "You know, like a favor."

"Who said compensation and favors can't go hand in hand?"

"Well, actually, that's kind of what a favor implies. You know, doing something just to help someone else out? Without getting something in return?"

"I'm more familiar with the 'you scratch my back, I scratch yours' style of favor. You know, kind of like my dad did for you letting you use his house."

"I pay Uncle Gino rent."

"Market value?"

I sucked in a slow breath and counted to five. Leo took the time to smooth his lapels over his vest. He finished smoothing and looked up at me with a calm smile. All the time in the world for negotiation.

"One shirt. Thirty bucks, max," I said.

"Full outfit. Hundred bucks, not including tax."

I counted to ten. "One shirt and one tie. Seventy-five bucks." I smiled back. "Including tax."

"Eighty, not including tax."

I blew out a sigh. "Fine. Eighty, not including tax. And you never say the word 'panties' in my presence again."

Leo stuck out his tiny hand. I shook it wordlessly and we took off toward Dudek's.

ΩΩΩ

Walking into Dudek's was like walking into one of those backyard dollhouses you see in the richer areas of town. All the display tables were a good six inches shorter than normal, the mirrors reflected me back from my neck down, and the mannequins' chins came up to my chest.

Leo, who had all of his clothes tailored, was immediately lost in a candy land of ready to wear duds. Every sixty seconds he'd hold a hanger up toward me and raise a thumb up in the air. I mouthed 'eighty' to him the first couple times, shook my head the third, and ignored him after that.

I skirted the perimeter of the shop, stopping occasionally to finger a garment. The entire right side of the shop was brick wall covered with bars bolted into it to support rack after rack of dress shirts, jackets, and polos. The left was a mirror image with the exception of a wood door recessed into the wall about two thirds of the way back, where the cashier's counter stood. Behind the register stood another wall that ran parallel to the back of the shop, with five feet of open space on either side. I knew from talking to Wally that one opening was the entrance to the dressing rooms and the other to the receiving room and employee's breakroom. Wally said the breakroom included a bathroom, and I pressed my acting skills into action.

I had spotted Erin at the cashier counter as soon as we walked in. As I perused the racks, I made the universal motions of responding to a bladder in need. After frowning at Leo when he held up a tangerine shirt next to a lime-green tie, I made my way to the counter and put on what I hoped was a pained smile.

"Hi, there," I said to Erin. "Any chance you have a restroom I could use?"

Erin shot me an apologetic smile. "I'm sorry, our restrooms are only for employees."

I eyed the iced coffee propped on the counter next to Erin's elbow. I pointed to it. "I completely understand. I wouldn't normally ask, but I just had one of those and, well, you know how that goes."

Erin hesitated and darted her eyes to Niko, who was engrossed with a customer near the front window. "Yeah, okay, go for it."

"I'll be quick like a bunny, promise," I said, and ran around the counter.

Once behind the wall, I quickly scoped out the area. To the right was a short hallway that connected to what I assumed was an exterior door based on the fire exit and emergency handle. A sticker on the door forewarned of a sound that would pierce your soul if you opened it without approval and a key. Along the wall rested three hooks holding clipboards that tracked weekly inventory, delivery schedules, and shipment receipts. Written on the wall beneath the clipboards was a reminder that all deliveries must be stocked on the same day of delivery. I flipped through the half dozen receipts. Three for trash removal, two for recycling pick up, and one showing that the store's sole fire extinguisher had been inspected and refilled the week prior. Along the floor of the hallway, colored tape outlined three squares and a purple marker had been employed to distinguish the squares with "UPS-Monday", "FedEx-Monday", and "Germaine's-Friday". All three squares were empty.

The space opposite the hallway led to a tiny breakroom, which was just an inventory closet full of boxes on one wall, and a battered four-foot folding table pushed up against the other. A single folding chair was shoved under the table and a cheap printer stand stood in the corner, the top shelf supporting a microwave, with a mini refrigerator crammed into the space beneath.

The top row of boxes had been opened and I hurriedly popped open the flaps. Two were packed tight with handled bags for customer purchases, and the third was partially filled with packs of tissue paper. I slipped one hand underneath the layers of paper and came up with nothing more than a minor paper cut on my pinkie. I sucked on my finger while I used elbow and free hand to wrestle the box flaps back into place. The remaining boxes were all sealed with original tape and I passed those by in favor of rifling through the one cupboard and two drawers that were drilled into the back wall. Plastic cutlery, straws, and toilet paper cluttered the cupboard, while the usual flotsam of mustard packets, splintered chopsticks, and Chinese takeout menus littered the drawers.

I quietly closed the last drawer and slipped through the adjacent doorway into the restroom. I'd seen roomier bathrooms on those tiny house shows. Meager rifling opportunity here. Toilet, hand sink bolted into the wall, and a metal paper towel holder reminiscent of those in my elementary school. Scratched into one side of the holder was a heart and two sets of initials. Over top of the carving was a lopsided rendering of a skull and cross bones inked in purple marker. The only other item in the room was a trash can that was twice the size of the toilet. I popped off the lid and peered inside. Two paper towels rested in the bottom of the liner. I peeled the liner out of the can and peered underneath. Nothing. I replaced the liner, flushed the toilet in case the plumbing could be heard on the other side of the wall, washed my hands, and added two more paper towels to the trash can's contents. I opened the door to find Erin standing in the hallway, face pinched into a frown.

"Sorry," I said. "For a minute there I thought it might be more than the coffee." I'd learned early in life that any reference to any kind of bowel movement hastened the listener to quickly excuse me. Erin was no exception. She waved a hand past her, indicating I should go ahead of her. She followed closely on my heels back into the front of the store.

I scanned the sales floor and spotted Leo coming out of the dressing room in the orange shirt and a navy-blue silk tie. He checked himself out in the wall mirror. Erin looked for Niko, and seeing him helping another customer, slid past me to Leo.

"Those look great on you, sir."

Leo smiled his thanks but pasted on a doubtful expression. "I don't know. There's something about the scale of it."

I bit my lip.

"It's an awful lot of blue," Leo continued, placing hands on hips and twisting to and fro in front of the mirror.

"Oh, but orange and blue are complementary colors," Erin said. She stood just behind Leo's right shoulder and I eyed them both in the mirror.

Leo frowned and cocked his head. "Mmm, I don't know. Less blue still, I think." Leo met Erin's eyes in the mirror. "Maybe a bow tie instead. I didn't see any on your table. Would you have blue in the back?"

Erin's eyes registered surprise, then uncertainty. Leo gave her a disarming smile. Erin turned her head, again seeking out Niko. Niko was stepping up into the front window of the store, pulling a suit jacket from a mannequin for his waiting customer.

Erin turned back to Leo and met his eyes in the mirror. "Are—. Are you a part of the group?" She kept her voice low.

Leo smiled and raised one manicured eyebrow. "You have to ask?"

Uncertainty returned to Erin's face and she lifted her eyes to mine. I gave her my most innocent smile, but I could tell I wasn't winning her over. Maybe my quick-turned-marathon trip to the restroom hadn't cemented a trust relationship.

Erin stepped away from Leo and faced him head on. "I don't have any in blue right now. But, um, maybe I could take your number and find you one."

"What do you think, babe?" Leo looked at me.

"Yeah, that'd be great," I said.

Leo beamed at me and looked back at Erin. "In the meantime, we'll take the shirt."

I reached out two fingers and caught the price tag dangling at Leo's wrist. My quarterly car insurance cost less, but I caught sight of Erin pulling paper and pen from her pocket to write down Leo's number and decided to kept my trap shut.

"Thanks, love bug." Leo showed me a mouthful of teeth and I gritted mine in return.

"Anytime, sweet cheeks."

Chapter Eleven

I parted ways with Leo back in the Save A Lot parking lot and assessed my options for the evening. Best friend unavailable. No boyfriend. That left hanging out with Mom and Wally or sitting alone in the dark with Netflix.

Hoping for some good new releases, I turned my Jetta toward home and swung into Dazio's pizza shop on the way. It was close, fast, and my family happens to own it. Dazio's had been my dad's baby and namesake, and he passed on the day-to-day management to Vinnie not long before he passed away. Paul and I helped here and there with the more technical side of the business, but Vinnie's sweat and tears lay all over the place. He was the face of the business liked Jared was the face of Subway. Minus the kiddie porn.

I navigated my car into one of two remaining spots in the strip mall and trotted up the sidewalk. Music pounded out of the bar two doors down. I spied a Ladies' Night sign on the heavy wooden door and wrinkled my nose at the thought of how bad the smell of desperation must be beyond the threshold to the joint.

I found Vinnie standing at the front counter, nodding and pointing to the screen on the register terminal as a young woman next to him poked at it. They both looked up as I cleared the front door. The woman's cheeks folded into dimples that were each punctuated with a tiny steel ball. I stretched my return smile wide and hoped my eyes didn't betray the "ow" running through my head.

"Hey," Vinnie said. "Sam, this is Jade, our new assistant manager. Jade, my sister, Sam."

Jade's smile deepened and the metal balls rose closer to her eyes. She side-stepped the register and extended a hand over the counter. I shook it and caught an eyeful of the sleeve of tattoos running up her outstretched arm, and the strings of tattoos smattered along the other. I took in the rest of her. Petite, toned, dark head of curls, and big chocolatey eyes. I looked over at Vinnie and grinned. My brother had hired his female mini-me.

"Nice to meet you," I said.

"Likewise."

"You still training?" I nodded toward the register.

"Yeah, Vinnie was just showing me how the inventory reports work."

"You like it so far?"

Jade bobbed her head and slid back behind the register. "It's a little less stressful than my last job up in Buffalo."

"What was that?"

"Roller derby."

"I'm sorry?"

Jade laughed. "Are you familiar with it?"

"Um, like fake wrestling, but on skates?"

"Not even close. Way back in the day, there was choreography and scripting, but now it's a full-on sport."

"Why was it stressful?"

"Well, you kind of get beat up a lot. But I also had to manage all our events and get people in the door. Plus, some of the women on the team were constantly fighting, and I had to sort that out. When the team isn't working as one, it's not just a matter of losing. It isn't safe."

"Why'd you move here?"

"I couldn't afford to stay, and my boyfriend and I were just about over, plus my sister's been on me for ages to come live with her. She's got a place over in Middleburg."

"I'm doing the starting over thing myself, so let me know if I can help."

Jade nodded and popped a dimple at me in thanks. I gave her my "any time" smile and crooked an eyebrow at Vinnie. "You got a minute?"

"Yeah," he said, waving me behind the counter. "Jade, you want to try running the report for last month?"

Jade nodded, already tapping again at the screen, a thoughtful frown on her face.

Vinnie and I cruised to the back of the shop and crammed into the small back office, me in his chair and Vinnie on a filing cabinet.

"So listen," I said. "If you still wanna do a Big Brother Big Sister kind of thing, I might know a kid who needs your help."

"What kind of help?"

"He's just gone through some bad stuff and is having a hard time dealing with it. He could use some companionship."

"What happened?"

"One of his co-workers got killed."

"Co-workers? How old is this kid?"

"Mmm, twenty-one, twenty-two. Ish."

"I don't know. I was thinking I'd help a little kid, you know? Somebody who doesn't have a dad or brothers of their own."

"Well, this guy kind of qualifies on that score. He's not close to his parents and doesn't have any friends."

Vinnie chewed his lip and thought about it.

"Vin, I really think you could do him some good. I feel bad for this guy. He's connected to a case Paul and I are working and he doesn't have anyone local."

"He's not that much younger than I am."

"That's why it's perfect. He might trust you more."

"Does he like video games?"

ΩΩΩ

"For future reference, telling me I'm your second choice is not the way to get a second date with me," Johnny said.

"For current reference, this isn't a date, it's a job. And you were actually my third choice. I was trying not to hurt your feelings."

"I'm happy we're back to the level of intimacy where you consider my feelings."

"Do I need to remind you we promised Paul we'd do our jobs without any conflict of interest?"

"But I like conflicting your interest."

"You do it well."

I could hear Johnny's grin through the phone line. Punk.

"Can you go or not?"

"I'll be on your curb in twenty."

I hung up the phone and consoled myself with the thought that this was Paul's fault. We were supposed to go on today's hunt together, but he bailed at the last second to meet with a new client. I had immediately dialed up Angie, but she couldn't call off from mom duty, an unusual occurrence. Between Angie and her husband Tony, there were always a couple dozen grandparents, aunts, uncles, and cousins seemingly at the ready to take on Angie's sometimes sticky but mostly well-behaved brood.

That left me with Johnny, who sidled up to the curb exactly twenty minutes later. He unfolded himself from his truck and trotted around to open the passenger door as I crossed the lawn.

"Just 'cause you're holding open the door for me, doesn't make this a date." I slipped past him and boosted myself up into the seat.

"A man can try."

We made good time heading downtown and found only one other person waiting at the appointed starting location for the hunt. Ernest Brown. He was not thrilled to see me.

"Hey, Ernest," I said, waving a hand at Johnny. "This is Johnny."

Johnny proffered a mitt. Ernest crossed his arms and tucked them into his armpits.

"What are you doing here?" Ernest said, addressing the ground.

"I didn't get to finish the hunt last time. Thought I'd see the rest."

Ernest grunted. "Do you know who's going to host?"

"I think they're using Shawn today."

A patch of red crawled up one side of Ernest's face. "He was supposed to be here that day."

"The day Walker died?"

"It should have been him."

"Ernest, come on. Shawn could have been hurt or killed, too. Where's the sense in that?"

Another grunt. Dismissive at best. Happy with my suggestion at worst.

A family of four, decked out in Cleveland sweatshirts that still had creases silently proclaiming their recent purchase from a hotel gift shop, moved toward us from across the street. Ernest pulled his coat tighter around his middle and strolled down the sidewalk, stopping in front of the gates of the Indians' baseball stadium. They'd changed the name in the years I was gone, going the way of commercial sponsorship, but it would always be The Jake to me.

Soon another half dozen hunters had joined the group,

including three eager and partially annoyed young women who clamored around what quickly appeared to be Bridezilla of the year. 'Zilla wore a "Bride" sash and cheap crystal crown, both of which she subconsciously touched every three seconds.

Johnny rolled his eyes at me and I tipped my imaginary crown to him before yanking a thumb in the opposite direction. We drifted toward Ernest, who frowned at us and walked away. Two other newcomers joined the group and when it was apparent they were the last, we divvied up the space in front of the stadium and started scavenging for clue cards. Propped in the frame of a closed ticket window, one of the bridesmaids-to-be squealed her discovery of an envelope containing the first clue that would direct us to the next stop, which turned out to be Gray's Armory. We made our way down Ontario Street to Huron, catching a glimpse of the Q and its shrine to Lebron, before heading down 7th St to Bolivar.

The Armory was touted by both the clue card and Google to be one of the oldest standing buildings in Cleveland, not surprising given the forbidding girth of the main turret anchoring the building. As we approached the main steps, I stooped to pick up two white plastic bubble tubes that must have been holdovers from a wedding. The Armory was a popular spot for social galas and creative brides.

Tied with black ribbon to one of the ornate iron bars covering a lower window, we found a card detailing the history of the Armory, and a second card boasting the clue to our next destination.

While one of the hunters, a young woman named Annie who had positioned herself as queen bee as soon as the hunt started, read the history card aloud to the rest of the group, I let my eyes wander down both directions of the street. There was scant foot traffic in either direction. Bolivar cut through two main downtown arteries and housed the back doors of restaurants and businesses whose fronts sat on the main thoroughfare. Rush hour had passed and lunch breaks were still a distant thought for the many office workers situated on neighboring streets.

The hunters broke circle after the history card was read and spread out to take pictures. Johnny strolled down to the corner and disappeared down 14th Street. I turned in the opposite direction and strolled toward the building next door, past the pay lot attached to the armory, checking out the opposite side of the street. I didn't spy a stray cat, let alone a saboteur hanging around to see the result of his handiwork. I headed back toward the main entrance and asked Annie if I could look at the clue card. She frowned at me and resignedly handed it over only after I reassured her I wasn't trying to steal her thunder. The clue read:

> *If you could head around back and straight on through*
> *Of the beds of the dead, you would have a view*
> *But around the corner to Eerie instead you must go*
> *To reach the final home of visitors departed long ago*

At the bottom of the card was the notation ".2", which we'd been told in our instructional pamphlet referred to the mileage from our current location to the next landmark. I flipped the card over, but it was blank. No obvious or hinted-at answers of any kind, and to my eye, the card was untampered with. I handed it back to Annie, who testily folded it and tucked it in her pocket. The other hunters had begun to mosey back toward the front steps and half were lazily taking selfies while they waited for the show to kick back up again. I watched as a teenaged brother and sister duo worked to line their camera phones up to the building's turret, to make it appear as if the boy was wearing the top of the turret as a crown.

Johnny reappeared from around the corner, hands shoved in his pockets, long legs eating up the distance in short order. He met my eyes and gave me a brief shake of his head. I caught sight of Ernest over his shoulder, walking toward us, a hard look on his face. He caught me watching him and petulance momentarily colored his expression.

I walked toward Johnny and met him at the outer ring of the group as they formed a semi-circle around Annie, who had brandished the clue card from her pocket and was looking from face to face of the hunters, expectantly awaiting their full attention.

"I checked out the clue card and there's nothing there that shouldn't be," I said under my breath to Johnny. He nodded and kept his eyes trained on Annie. I swept my gaze back over to Ernest, who looked marginally less pissy than before, though not what I'd describe as overjoyed.

"Any idea what the next landmark is?" Johnny asked.

"It's got to be Lake Street Cemetery. The clue talked about the dead in their beds behind the Armory."

Annie read the clue card aloud to the group, who all promptly dug out smartphones and started Googling their way through the clue. Ernest look disinterested, standing with arms crossed on the periphery of the crowd. His hard look had evolved to a sad mask. He made no attempt to contribute his thoughts on the clue to the rest of the group.

After a couple minutes of the group debating whether we were meant to head to the cemetery or the Winking Lizard bar – this last suggestion based on one hunter's allegation that the bar served a beer called "Beds of the Dead" as part of its world beer tour – we all toddled up the street and turned onto E. 9th St. We circled around to the other side of The Jake from where we started, and I spied the statues of Bob Feller and Larry Doby as we approached the cemetery from the other side of the street.

The cemetery was fronted by a massive stone archway that marked the start of a wide gravel path, swaths of grass and headstones flanking either side. About a third of the way in, I saw Shawn standing to the right of the path. As we approached, I could see he'd cleaned up some since I saw him at the funeral. Shaven, crisp cargo pants and a pressed polo hanging from his slight frame, but his face was gray and his hands shook. The piece of paper he was holding rattled between his fingers.

Johnny came up on my right while I watched Ernest to the left. The flush from earlier was creeping back up his neck, mottling the underside of his jowls a rusty purple. The rest of the group gathered round, the bridesmaid crew clicking away, taking pictures of Shawn and the headstones sunken into the earth behind him. Shawn blinked several times at the group, then raised the paper clutched in his shaking hand and used the other to steady it.

"Welcome, hunters," Shawn started. His voice cracked and he cleared his throat, his Adam's apple bobbing with nerves. He continued to read from his script. "Congratulations on making it to this point in your journey. The crowd around us is not in the position to clap or cheer, but I am sure they are equally impressed that you are here."

Johnny and I exchanged raised eyebrows, and I wondered who had written the script. If it was Walker, I could see why Ernest thought he needed help. If it was Malik, he needed a host replacement faster than he thought. No sooner than his name crossed my mind, Malik's number popped up on the screen of my vibrating cell phone. I backtracked three steps away from the group and turned toward the cemetery entrance.

"You got a minute?" Malik cut off my greeting.

"I'm at the hunt."

"I know, that's why I wanted to catch you. Detective Barnes called me with some info that I thought you and Paul should know."

"What is it?"

"The cops found a note tucked inside Walker's shirt."

"What did it say?" I put another three feet of distance between me and the group. I could hear Shawn stuttering along behind me.

"It said 'I tried to warn you.'"

"You have any idea what that means?"

"No, but it was written on one of our company cards."

"And the other sabotaged clues were on plain index cards," I mused out loud.

"That crossed my mind as well."

"Was there a clue on the card?"

"No, it was the card Walker would have used to guide his presentation at the Hall of Fame."

I spun in a slow circle, scanning the perimeter of the cemetery. I still wasn't at all sure whether the clue sabotage was connected to Walker's murder, but my heebie-jeeb meter set up a ding-fest. I took another rotation and stopped when my eyes caught on Ernest.

He cleared his throat, a sound between a hum and a choking victim that caused half the hunters to turn and look. The purple flush wound higher up his jawline into his temples and he clenched his fists at his sides. He looked like I imagined a bull right before he busts from the holding pen. Shawn's continuing dissertation on the cemetery's history waved like a red cape in front of Ernest's eyes.

I looked at Shawn, who was explaining in a monotone that the city's first permanent settler and first mayor were both buried on the grounds. He looked up as he took a breath between sentences, and I watched as his eyes grew round in fear. Before I could crane my head around to see the source of his angst, a blur of curly red hair darted past me on the path, crossed into the grass, and rammed Shawn backward into a four-foot-tall headstone.

Chapter Twelve

"Gee-zuss."

"What?" Malik asked.

"Call the police for me. Ernest just took Shawn out at the knees. Erie Street Cemetery." Shawn's eyes were closed and he wasn't pushing Ernest off. "Tell them to send an ambulance."

Johnny sprinted across the path and grabbed the back of Ernest's jacket with two hands, hauling him up before tossing him flat on his back onto the ground. Shawn lay where he fell, and it seemed had Johnny not pulled Ernest away, Shawn would have let himself be pummeled. He slowly rolled onto his side and curled his knees into his chest, not seeming to notice the blood running from temple to earlobe. I shoved my phone in my pocket and motioned to the other hunters to stay back while I ran to Shawn's side, getting a closer look at his face. His left cheek was badly scraped and the blood seemed to originate from a small gash in his hairline, presumably from where his face must have grazed the side of the headstone. I glanced briefly at the headstone and wondered if poor Allen Shlecton, born 1817 and died 1866, could have imagined two men would get into a fight over him a hundred and fifty years later. I wondered, too, why the hell I wonder such things.

One of the hunters, a fifty-something blonde woman named Helen, approached and said she was a nurse. I leaned back to give her more access to Shawn, who still lay curled in a ball, breathing in hiccups, eyes staring vacantly into the grass. I patted his shoulder and crossed to where Johnny had one knee in the grass, one in the small of Ernest's back, and was bent over talking into Ernest's ear.

The last of the fight drained out of him and Ernest began crying into the earth, three quarters of his face mashed into the ground not from Johnny's weight.

I squatted down next to them.

"Ernest," Johnny said, his face stone, voice firm and soothing, the way I imagine Dog the Bounty Hunter would sing Itsy Bitsy Spider. "Here's what we're going to do. I'm going to pull you to your knees, then you're going to stand up and we're both going to walk straight down the path toward the entrance. Do you understand?"

Ernest buried his forehead further into the dirt, large chunks of ground seeping their way into his nest of hair.

"I know you hear me, Ernest, and you want to do what I say. I'm going to help you."

Ernest's sobs subsided, his shoulders pressed into the earth, and he cocked his head in the mud toward Johnny's voice.

"Ready on three." Johnny moved his knee off Ernest and pushed back, bracing into a deep lunge. When Johnny hit "three", Ernest pushed back while Johnny pulled his wrists from behind. The effort was too much for Ernest and he sat back on his haunches, breathing hard. Mud crusted the upper half of his face and slid down over and around his nose. I pulled the hem of my long-sleeved shirt down over my hand and leaned over him, rubbing off the worst of the mud so he could breathe. Johnny waited until I was done, then in one motion pulled Ernest up onto his feet and pivoted him onto the gravel path. The first wails of a siren sounded in the distance. I watched as Johnny propelled

Ernest toward the front of the cemetery. Ernest's mop of muddy, fiery curls hung heavily from his bowed head, his pace slow and weaving slightly despite Johnny's hold.

The nurse was still bent over Shawn, encouraging him not to move any more until the paramedics could come brace his neck. No point taking chances, she told him, but his eyes were still trained blankly into the distance and I doubt he heard.

The crowd of hunters grew restless, aside from the few who garishly continued to take pictures of Shawn and then, moving in closer, of the headstone he'd been plowed into. I shooed them away by standing in their lens' line of sight and was relieved to see two police officers and a pair of EMTs approaching out of the corner of my eye.

Clue card-controlling Annie bounded toward them, already relaying the scene before she got within twenty feet of them. The nurse murmured something into Shawn's ear and backed away to stand next to me, deferring to the medics.

"What's wrong with him?"

I looked at her, confused. She smiled and tipped her head forward a few inches.

"Besides having just lost a fight against a headstone. I mean, there's something else wrong with him, isn't there?"

I looked down at Shawn. The medics had wrapped a stabilizing collar around his neck and were transferring him onto a board.

"What's your name?" I asked.

"Norma."

"Sam." I extended my hand. "Why do you think something's wrong with him?"

"I work ER. I see a lot of trauma." Norma gestured faintly in Shawn's direction. "That boy's had trauma."

"He has. His co-worker was just killed and he thinks he's responsible because he wasn't where he was supposed to be when it happened."

Norma lifted her eyes from Shawn and gave me a pointed look. "No, honey."

"I'm sorry?"

"It can't be just that. I'd bet my bingo allowance that boy's had a lifetime of trauma."

We both watched as the medics transferred Shawn and his board onto a stretcher. I smiled, hoping Shawn would lift his eyes to mine and feel some kind of reassurance, but he continued to stare unseeing somewhere beyond the edge of the stretcher. I made a mental note to call Vinnie on the way to the hospital. I was already worried Shawn wouldn't be receptive to Vinnie's friendship, but now I feared he wouldn't be responsive to anyone at all.

Johnny appeared at my side. "What's the good word?"

I nodded a smile of thanks at Norma and walked Johnny off the grass and onto the main path.

"Where's Ernest?"

Johnny gestured back toward the front gates. "In care of the city's finest. How's Shawn?"

"In the care of the city's first responders." I shared Norma's opinion about Shawn. "I'm going to call Vinnie and see if he can meet me at the hospital."

"Why Vinnie?"

"I sort of offered him up to help Shawn."

"And Shawn agreed to that?"

"He doesn't know yet. I made the offer to Malik."

Johnny smiled down at me. "Are you mother-henning?"

"Something like that. I just feel bad for him. I wouldn't be surprised if what Norma suspects is true."

Johnny shoved his hands in his pockets and shook his head in frustration. "Man, where is this kid's family?"

"They're in Jersey. Malik's tried to get Shawn to call them, but he refuses. Says he's fine. Malik's impression is Shawn wouldn't look to them for help even if he did admit needing it."

"Maybe that's where the trauma came from."

ΩΩΩ

Johnny dropped me at the hospital and took off to help his cousin move into a new apartment. I called Malik from outside the hospital lobby and brought him up to speed on the shenanigans at the cemetery. Barnes had already reached out to Malik, urging him to make sure Shawn would press charges. Barnes made it clear that the events of the day confirmed for him that Ernest was responsible for sending Walker to the scavenger host afterlife. Malik promised he'd get over to the hospital to see Shawn as soon as he could.

I hung up with Malik and dialed Vinnie, and by the time Shawn had been transferred from the ER to a room for overnight observation, Vinnie had appeared in the ER waiting room holding a brown carryout bag from Dazio's. My stomach growled its reminder that I'd skipped lunch.

"Tell me that's lasagna and tell me there's enough for me."

Vinnie unfolded the top of the bag and I bent over to peek inside. "A Gameboy?"

"You said the kid's not talking. I figured we could ease into things."

"Good idea."

"Even a deaf squirrel can get a nut, right?"

I smiled and refolded the bag. "Yeah, Vin, something like that. Thanks for doing this. I know it isn't exactly what you had in mind."

"If he's as bad off as you said, I probably can't make it worse, right?"

"You should write inspirational posters."

We followed the orange footsteps along the hospital corridors until we found Shawn's room. We hovered in the doorway, watching a beleaguered-looking doctor writing in a folder. She finished scrawling and clipped the folder to a hook near the door.

"How is he?" I asked when she looked up.

"He should be fine," she said, using two fingers to tuck a stray piece of gray bang behind her ear. "He lost a good chunk of skin from his head, but nothing the stitches won't put back together. I heard he took a serious header into a gravestone and I want to keep him here for the night just in case. He apparently he went from not talking at all to the medics to being pretty agitated by the time he rolled into the ER. We gave him a mild sedative and he's a bit looser, but it still concerns me."

"I think the agitation may have more to do with the events of his life this past week, not so much taking that hit."

"What's happened to him?" The doctor unclipped her pen from her pocket and clicked the top.

"One of his co-workers was killed and he thinks he could have stopped it."

The doctor tossed a glance back at Shawn, then motioned Vinnie and me out into the hall. "Could he have stopped it?"

I shook my head. "No. He called off sick from work the day of the murder."

"Murder?"

"Yeah, but we don't know for sure if it was random or targeted. Either way, I don't think it would have mattered if Shawn was there."

The doctor nodded and replaced her pen. "We have counseling support here at the hospital. I'll have the nurses get the information to Shawn."

I thanked the doctor and she headed two doors down, disappearing into a room we had passed on our way in. The door had been wide open, revealing a young woman covered neck to wrist with bandages on her left side. From the glimpse I'd gotten of her face, she looked higher than Keith Richards on tour.

I patted Vinnie on the shoulder and he followed me into Shawn's room. Shawn was covered to the top of his chest in a blanket, arms hidden beneath, his face turned toward the curtained window. I walked around to the far side of his bed and Vinnie hovered just inside the door.

"Hey, Shawn." I patted the bedsheet where I thought his hand was and connected with his forearm. Shawn blinked and slowly raised his eyes to mine. He mumbled what I took for a "hi".

"Can I get you anything?"

"Nuh-uh."

I pulled two straight-backed chairs from under the window and placed them side-by-side at the foot of the bed. I motioned to Vinnie to come sit while I watched Shawn take him in.

"Shawn, this is my brother Vinnie. He's not as scary as he looks."

Vinnie ignored my usual introduction and raised a hand toward Shawn. "Hey, man. Sorry you're laid up."

"It's alright," Shawn said. To me, he said "How many brothers you got?"

"Just the two. How about you?"

"I'm an only. My mom couldn't have any more after me."

"That sucks."

Shawn shrugged and winced from the movement. "Not really. She shouldn't have even had me."

"Why do you say that?"

Shawn chewed his lower lip and I could see now the effects of the sedative as he curled his lower lip up and bit down on it in slow motion. He dragged his top teeth across his lip, then paused to suck on it. He stayed away from the gap in his teeth entirely.

"You got any family here?" Vinnie asked after it became obvious Shawn wasn't going to answer my question.

"Nah."

"How 'bout a girl?"

Shawn shook his head and groaned. "No."

"You want me to see if I can get you some more med or something?"

"No, I feel queasy as it is."

Vinnie leaned back in his chair and tossed a glance at me.

"Shawn, has anyone told you that Ernest was arrested?" I asked.

"For what he did to me?"

"Yeah."

Shawn looked down at the bedsheet for a long moment. "You think he blames me for Walker?"

"I think he's having a hard time with losing Walker."

"Why would he care?" Anger flashed across Shawn's face. "That dude was always trying to make Walker look bad. At least, until Walker started acting like Ernest was helping him."

I leaned forward. "I don't think it's just about losing Walker. I think Ernest felt like he was important when he was a part of the hunt. Now that Walker's gone, he doesn't really have a place in all this."

"Does he think slamming me into the ground is going to make room for him?"

I worked to contain my smile. Seeing Shawn angry was a welcome relief from seeing him withdrawn. Maybe I could piss him off right into the next stage of the grief cycle before the night was through.

"Shawn, do you think there's any chance that Ernest could be the one sabotaging the clues?"

Shawn's tongue dipped thickly across his lower lip, then flashed its underside at me as it traveled up to push through the gap in his upper teeth.

"Do the police think he is?" Shawn countered.

"I'm not sure. The police aren't sharing their innermost thoughts with me right now. But you were the closest to seeing what was going on between Walker and Ernest. Malik said there was somewhat of a truce between those two. Do you think it could have gone south?"

Shawn plugged at his tooth gap while he thought. He flicked a glance at Vinnie, then the open doorway. Either he was afraid or his meds were starting to wear off.

"Shawn, it's okay. You'll be out of here before Ernest gets out of jail. The police can help you if you know something."

Shawn rolled his head in a semi-circle, which I took to be less brain rattling than shaking it.

"I don't know anything."

"What are you afraid of?"

"I'm not. I didn't say I was afraid."

"Okay." I lifted one hand in submission. I looked at Vinnie as Shawn dragged his blanket closer to his chin. "Did the doctor tell you'll be here overnight?"

"Yeah."

"You got a ride home tomorrow?"

"Nah. I'll Uber or something."

"I don't think they'll release you without someone here to watch over you for the first 24 hours." I had no idea if that was true, and I swallowed my relief when Shawn didn't call bullshit. "I need to keep working the case for Malik, but Vinnie's off tomorrow and could help you out."

Shawn's eyes flitted to Vinnie, a curtain of distrust dropping over his pupils. "Why?"

Vinnie leaned forward and braced thick forearms on his thighs. "There's no 'why', man. You ain't got anyone local, and I don't mind helping out."

"You don't even know me."

Vinnie glanced at me, and I smiled encouragement.

"True," Vinnie said. "But Sam does and seems to think you're a chill guy."

Shawn darted a shy look at me.

"Dude," Vinnie said. "I got an extra bedroom and Xbox."

"And a cupboard full of kids' cereal," I said.

Vinnie and Shawn both swung their heads toward me.

"What?" I asked. "It'd be a draw for me."

Tough crowd.

ΩΩΩ

I left Vinnie at the hospital to continue his male bonding with Shawn. I suspected that would last only until Shawn succumbed to a drug-induced nap, at which point Vinnie would transfer his bonding efforts to the young blonde nurse who came in to check on Shawn right before I bailed.

I sat in the hospital's parking garage and used the moment to think about the clue card tucked into Walker's shirt. Malik said the police seemed confident that the clues and the murder were related, but what if they weren't? What if it was simply opportunity? The card was there and the murderer decided to leave a note to deflect suspicion. After all, it was a pretty random statement that could mean anything. On the other hand, who kills someone and then rummages in their pocket for pen and paper? For that matter, whose pen? I made a mental note to ask Shawn and Malik if Walker would have been carrying a pen.

I flipped all the pieces around in my head while I dug through my console for my emergency stash of Red Vines. I unleashed a Vine and nibbled the tip. If the clue sabotage and the murder were connected, why? I came back to the short list of people who'd want to hurt Malik or Walker. The list was not only short, it was seriously lacking motive.

Paul and I had come up empty on Malik's background. No old business partners, no ex-wives, no long-lost cousins claiming Malik stole the idea for the business. Not that the latter would matter, since the business was still new and barely supporting the overhead and the little extra that Malik was planning to invest in the second location.

The police had dismissed Malik's sole-mentioned kind-of girlfriend and I struggled to get worked up about her myself. On the other hand, I only had Malik's word for it. And who knows if the police even told him the truth. I needed to run that down. I'd seen enough cases now to know that half the time, the tiniest detail ignored led to the eventual break in the case.

There was also still the issue of Steve playing grab-ass with Janie at the funeral to contend with. Could Janie be making that much out of the business that she'd want to try to shut Malik down? Not likely, but the grab-ass needed to be answered for. I'd hunt Janie and the ex-girlfriend down tomorrow. In the meantime, I had smaller fish to fry. I knocked my noggin against the headrest and sucked in a deep breath. Time for Dudek duty.

Chapter Thirteen

I rolled into the alley backing up to the strip mall housing Dudek's Clothiers and tucked my Jetta into a corner slot. The lot was divvied up between the strip mall and a squat, brick apartment building that sat at the back edge of the mall. The landlords of both lots must have assumed lighting the corner fell on the other's dime, which conveniently left me with a perfect square of pitch-black in which to hide, settled in between a maroon pick-up truck and an Omni. I eyeballed the Omni, impressed that there was one still on the road, let alone in a rust-free state like this one. I spied a row of cars parked diagonally against the side of the retail building, where Dudek's rested on the end, and felt reasonable sure I was hiding among vehicles belonging to the apartment tenants, not the shop employees.

I threw the gearshift into park, cracked my window a couple inches, pushed back my seat, and unwrapped my tuna melt courtesy of Mr. Hero. In concession to my arteries as much as my waist, I neatly polished off half and tucked the other back into its wax wrap.

Dudek's was scheduled to close in an hour, and I watched as the neighboring retailers began to shutter, one by one. Shop owners appeared at back doors like synchronized swimmers, tossing garbage bags into shared dumpsters. The delivery door to the Thai house to the south of Dudek's opened, and I watched a young man tumble a steaming vat of liquid into a drainage hole beneath the cement loading ledge. My windows were closed, but the scent of lemongrass leaked through my vents and mingled unappetizingly with the lingering smell of tuna.

I twisted around in my seat and checked out the block of apartments. I counted eight units, only two with lit up rooms. Judging from the position of the patios, the lit rooms were bedrooms, with the fronts of the apartments facing away from the strip mall. Through the back windshield, I could just make out half of the sign in the front of the apartment building. Turns out the units were weekly motel rentals, fashioned from what must have been an old apartment building.

At the sound of metal scraping cement, I turned back toward the strip mall. The back door to Dudek's widened and Erin's braided head popped into the triangle of light spilling out from the back room. She'd traded in her work uniform for a denim jumper and fat wedged sandals. She leaned her torso past the edge of the door and looked toward the Thai restaurant. The young man ditching his lemongrass had long since returned inside. Erin stepped all the way out onto the landing ledge, revealing two hands full of assorted trash bags. She crossed the half dozen steps to the communal dumpster set between Dudek's and the Thai joint, and one by one tossed in three small bags like the kind I would expect from the wastepaper baskets at the counter, bath and breakroom. From my previous potty visit, I pictured the small, matching woven baskets. My surprise at Wally having chosen such a classy detail had cemented the memory. Erin tucked back inside the building but didn't pull the door closed behind her. She reappeared moments later lugging a much larger bag with both hands. Well, what do we have here? The squares on the floor I'd spied in the shop's back hallway clearly outlined that deliveries only occurred on Mondays and Fridays. Today was Thursday. The clipboard showed that all orders were processed within twenty-four hours, and the delivery squares on the floor had been empty during my potty trip the day before, so what had generated so much trash? Erin squatted awkwardly and heaved her garbage bag into the dumpster, then leaned over the edge and pushed the bag into a corner. She straightened and snuck another look toward the neighboring back doors before darting back inside Dudek's. She pulled the door closed, turning at the last minute to peek back through to the alley. I sat still, knowing she couldn't see me in the dark, but not wanting to risk even a moving shadow. Squirrels, raccoons, and other critters frequented these alleys and I didn't want to blow my cover if Erin was eyes-out for rabies. She seemed on edge as it was. I would, too, if I sat abutted against a motel renting by the week.

I peeked at my cell phone, holding it by my thigh to cover the light of the screen. It was ten past the hour. I had no idea how long it would take to shut down the shop, but I couldn't imagine it'd be long.

No sooner than I'd extinguished the light on my phone, I saw Niko stroll around the side of the building from the front and unlock a brand new, orange Fiat. Nice car for a guy in clothing sales.

I was mentally doing the division on how many blue bowties you'd have to sell to make that monthly payment when Erin and the young man from the Thai shop appeared around the side of the building. They waved at Niko as they passed the Fiat and stopped two spaces down. Erin fiddled inside her handbag and the headlights flashed on a cobalt blue Cavalier that had seen better days. Between the Omni and the Cavalier, I was starting to feel like Cleveland had experienced a time warp while I was gone.

Niko's car eased out of the lot and Erin and the young man, a whippet thin guy with a dark mop of hair that begged to be trimmed, climbed into the Cavalier. I watched as their heads bent together and became one gelatinous shadow long enough that even I could taste yesterday's Listerine. After a few minutes, I began to wonder if they were going to come up for air. I felt nine-tenths embarrassed for being an unwitting Peeping Tom, and one-tenth jealous. When did we stop making out? I blew out a reminiscent sigh as the symbiotic shadow morphed back into two heads. They joined again for a split second, then Erin fired up the Cavalier and puttered out of the lot and onto Pearl Road.

I jotted down a few case notes in the journal I'd picked up as insurance for my aging memory bank, and waited another ten minutes, but no one else from the strip mall shops appeared. I slipped out of my car and trotted down the side of the darkened building to the sidewalk facing Pearl Road. All four shops making up the strip were shuttered. At the far end sat an empty bus stop bench, and on the near end rested a vacant lot where they'd torn down an auto repair place when I was in high school and had yet to replace it all these years later. I walked back around the side of the building and past the communal dumpster sitting between Dudek's and the Thai shop.

I glanced back toward the motel. Two more units had lit up since I took my jaunt to the front of the strip, but the rear balconies were still deserted. I wanted to take a good look at the bag Erin had tossed into the dumpster and I didn't want any witnesses who thought it might be cute to call the cops for transiency. Erin may have simply been unloading the shop's dustbins, but in my previous visit, I didn't see anything that it would take two hands and a hardy heave-ho to get into the dumpster. The way Erin bent at her knees, I'd guess that bag held three tissues and a pony.

I had just reached the dumpster when I saw lights approach at the far end of the alley. I scuttled around the side and wedged myself into the foot of space between the loading ledge wall and the dumpster. My shirt caught on the rough brick wall, sliding up and exposing my lower back. I arched in attempt to save my skin and succeeded in kneeing the side of the dumpster, but my cry of pain caught in my throat as I caught sight of the nose of Erin's Cavalier as it eased to a stop parallel to the dumpster.

I heard the car door open, a brief silence, then a second door open. A pair of shoes scuffed against the asphalt, the sound coming dangerously close to my hiding place. I glimpsed a slice of slender leg cross the opening to my hiding space. I held my breath, waiting for a face to appear, but then the sandal attached to the leg lifted and slid into the metal sleeve that the dumpster picker-upper truck would insert its metal arm into.

Erin boosted herself up and I felt the dumpster shift slightly under her weight. Unfortunately, it shifted into the few measly inches that created my hidey hole and mashed against my boobs, forcing me to press my already scratched-up back harder into the brick wall. I turned my cheek and met a wet spot on the side of the dumpster. The stench of mustard layered with motor oil and something unidentifiable burned my eyes and produced an immediate and heavy snot response in my nose. I couldn't lift either arm anywhere near my face and I didn't dare try to suck the snot back in. Erin was grunting above me as she rooted around, but I didn't want to press my luck on her hearing me snuffle.

I breathed softly in and out through my mouth and wiggled my upper lip to keep a line of mucus from dripping through the alien paste on my cheek and into my mouth.

Erin's weight shifted heavily and the dumpster rolled a merciful few inches away from me, leaving my left arm still pinned to the wall, but my right one free. I took a fast swipe at my cheek and nose, glomming my sleeve across the whole sticky mess. A loud thump came from my right and I caught a corner of trash bag on the cement. I bent my head toward the entry of my hiding spot but whipped it back as my field of vision filled again with Erin's jumper. I held still, but she wasn't wasting any time. The corner of the trash bag disappeared and the sound of Erin's car door shutting with a soft click met my ears. Erin's full body filled my view as she ran on tiptoes around the front of her car and I soon heard a second door click shut. Blue streamed past as Erin's car slid down the opposite end of the building and the sound of her engine was gone within seconds.

I gingerly tested my fingers against the side of the dumpster and, finding two seemingly dry spots, pushed to widen my exit. I pulled the hem of my shirt down in the back and sidled out without any further damage to my back. I peered around the dumpster, then ran to the side of the building where Erin's car had disappeared. I saw her taillights burning red at the end of the alley. I hauled ass across the thirty feet to my car and drove to the front exit of the strip mall. I knew the alley bled into a residential side street and chances were Erin would turn left to hit the main street. The question was which direction would she go from there. My question was answered when Erin's car passed me. I'd kept my headlights off as I drove to the exit, but I still ducked down and prayed she didn't notice my car idling at the exit. While I was down there, I may have also prayed that the tuna smell would leave my car sometime in the next millennium.

ΩΩΩ

I bumped over the strip mall curb out onto the street and rolled slowly but thoroughly through a yellow light. In this part of town people regularly cruised through on orange, not out of maliciousness as much as people tended to live around here for lifetimes and they knew almost by feel versus sight how to get where they needed to go and where everyone else was around them.

I needn't have worried about running the light. Erin kept her speed at the level of a fifteen-year-old whose driver's permit was still bleeding ink onto her fingers. I fell further behind and let two more cars angle in between us, bringing the count up to four. As if she'd picked me out an extra early birthday present from the novice PI gift catalog, Erin also had a cracked taillight. The bulb hiding within still glowed a bright white, a happy little beacon that made me feel more comfortable with the lag between us.

We toodled along Pearl Road for several miles until we crossed into Middleburg Heights. I knew from Erin's personnel info that Wally had given me that Erin lived on the edge of Middleburg, so I was surprised when she turned down Bagley Road and we soon found ourselves in Berea. Along the way, my four-car buffer had dwindled back down to one, but as we approached Baldwin-Wallace College, traffic picked back up. Erin turned left onto Beech St, the white glow of her turn signal a tiny flicker, but still sufficient warning. I eased my foot off the gas, but didn't make the turn behind her. As soon as I cleared the intersection, I stepped on the gas and tried to turn left at the next side street, seeing at the last second that it was one-way. I hustled to the next corner and swung left, flooring it down Front St. Slowing, I saw lights to my left when I passed Liberty and punched the gas again. I hit the next intersection and turned left on Spring St., hoping to cut back behind Erin onto Beech. I didn't account for the possibility that Erin could turn onto the same street. I saw the Cavalier turn onto Spring St. from the other end and pick up speed, leaving me no choice but to pass her. I let up on the gas after I passed and watched in my rearview as Erin slowed and turned into the parking lot of the Methodist church at the corner.

I swung into a stretch of curb shared between two driveways and threw the car into park. I snatched my Indians ballcap from the backseat and stuffed my curls up into it the best I could while I ran around to the sidewalk. The street was tree-lined, providing some cover as I trotted down the sidewalk, but I still hugged the lawn lines to stay away from the streetlights. It was only two blocks back to the church and when I hit the lot, Erin was still sitting in her car. I slowed to a walk and snuck up into a stand of trees on the opposite corner. Erin opened her car door at the same time as the driver's door opened on the Buick Riviera that she'd parked next to. I spotted a shaggy head of dark hair on top of an ill-fitting tee shirt hanging low over a pair of skinny jeans step out of the Riviera. I couldn't tell the guy's age from that distance. He carried his body like a grown man, but the skinny jeans suggested his mom might still be buying his clothes.

The man-boy slunk around to his trunk and keyed the lid with one hand while he pounded once on it with the other. The lid released, screaming for WD-40, and its owner left it ajar while he went to meet Erin. She fiddled with her own trunk and as she raised the lid, man-boy put one hand over hers and held the lid up while he wrapped his other hand behind Erin's neck and lowered his face to hers. Erin pushed her body into his for a split second before pulling back. He still had her neck in hand and kept her face to his as she tried to push his torso away. Oh, crap. I stepped out of the trees, but before I could yell at him to stop, man-boy released Erin with a laugh. She hit him on his arm and he slapped her butt in return. What the hell?

Erin gestured to the trunk, then rammed her hands in her back pockets. Man-boy raised the trunk lid all the way and leaned in. I stepped away from the trees and crossed the lawn to the edge of the lot, drawing myself another thirty feet closer to the action. I could just see the top of the trash bag and watched as man-boy undid the ties and buried both hands into the bag. He dug around inside, his elbow bouncing up and down in a way that suggested to me he was counting as he fingered his way through. His elbow stopped bouncing, he tied up the bag, and hefted the whole thing out of the trunk and into his own. By squinting one eye, I could make out most of the plate number on the Riviera. I typed it into my cell with one hand.

Business done, man-boy shut his trunk and followed Erin to her driver's side door, placing them both directly under a parking lot light. I could see now he was more man than boy. I'd guess he and Erin were on opposite ends of their twenties, give or take.

Erin's expression clouded as the guy dove in for another round on her face. She was smiling but shaking her head, and her shoulders hunched up into her neck. She reminded me of a woman about to tolerate a goodnight kiss at the end of a bad first date. Was she nervous about lip-locking with the man-boy, or colluding in theft with him? It took some serious cajones to transfer stolen goods in a church parking lot.

The man released Erin, spun her around while he opened her door, and smacked her hard again on the rear. Erin jumped but didn't pause in her effort to get into her car. Man-boy laughed again and walked away, leaving Erin to close her door, which she did with a slam loud enough to wake the angels.

Erin hustled out of the lot before the man made it back to his car. She turned in the opposite direction and I hurried back into the trees using the sound of her car for cover, then took off at a run when I hit the corner. I made it to my car and hooked a U-turn, all the while keeping my eyes peeled for the man's headlights in the church lot. I kept my own headlights off and coasted along the street. No lights from the church lot. How could I have missed this guy? I kept rolling, stopping completely when I got back to the corner lot next to the church. The church lot was empty. Two streets ahead, I caught a flicker of taillights come on just before they disappeared around a corner. Gee-zuss, I was an idiot. Erin had made a grand exit of noise when she left, but man-boy was smart enough to douse his lights until he was well on his way. I flicked on my lights and gave the Jetta some gas, but by the time I hit the intersection, the Riviera had disappeared. I gunned it back up to Bagley Road and looked both ways, but there was too much traffic and too many side streets to take even an educated guess.

I idled at the intersection and peeked at my dash clock. 9:45. I called Paul to see if he was up for a late-night staff meeting.

Chapter Fourteen

Paul was already bellied up to the bar when I walked into the Islander Grille. The pool tables to the left of the horseshoe shaped bar were all in play, commandeered by what appeared to be a co-ed softball team celebrating an inebriated win. The bar itself was two-thirds full, probably due to the Indians game running on the mounted TVs. I spied a handful of happy hour goers still dressed in delivery truck and restaurant uniforms, who probably rolled in after their shift and made their Blue Moons and Eliot Nesses stretch into dinner. Their attire made me marginally less self-conscious of the mystery dumpster sauce drying on my sleeve.

I ordered my own Eliot Ness with a cheese fry chaser, much to Paul's amusement.

"Skipped dinner, I assume?"

"Nope, but I only ate half my sandwich."

Paul cut his eyes at me over the rim of his beer glass. "What kind?"

"Tuna."

"Lemme guess. Dry, with sprouts?"

"Wet with mayo. About a fifty-fifty ratio to tuna."

"Thy pride be misplaced."

The bartender arrived with my beer. I clinked it against Paul's glass. "Pride goeth before the fall."

"That's nowhere even close to an applicable cliché," he said.

"We'd let Vinnie get away with it."

"Vinnie doesn't know better. We don't have a choice."

"Good point." I sipped my beer. "How'd things go with the Merryman case?" Paul had been tracking a man who had allegedly been cheating on his wife. The kicker was the other woman also happened to be his wife.

Paul snorted. "Well, now wife number one knows about wife number two. Wife number two is having a hissy fit because she insists she was number one. Mr. Merryman, having truly struck the dumb-ass lottery, ended the debate by pointing out that neither of them were the first."

"Don't tell me."

"Oh, yes. There's a third Mrs. Merryman. A very legal Mrs. Merryman to boot."

"You should make them all sit down and watch a season of Sister Wives. That should give them enough perspective to stop bitching."

Paul clinked his beer to mine. "And now you see why I like to investigate, not mediate. Sometimes seeing this garbage makes me happy that Erica and I didn't work out."

I grinned. "You and I don't have the best pickers in the world, you know that?"

"I don't think your picker sucks as much as maybe your timing does."

I wrinkled my nose at him. "Picker, shmicker."

"So, what happened with Wally? You said on the phone you're stuck."

"Yeah, a bit." The bartender reappeared with my fries and I pushed the plate toward Paul. He forked up fried potato while I dished out napkins and filled him in on the night's escapades.

"Did you get a plate number off the Riviera?"

"Most of it, but I couldn't get close enough to get it all without blowing my cover. The church's parking lot wasn't exactly lit up."

"I doubt a church thinks they'll have enough shady business happening in their parking lot to warrant lighting it up."

"True. I did get a decent look at the guy's face, though. I'd recognize him again, at least."

"Did you call Roman to find out if he can run the plate?"

Roman Stavros was a cop friend of Johnny's whom we met on my first case. He became friendly with Paul, and had been trying to become even friendlier with me. I'd held that idea at bay until I could figure out where Johnny and I stood. Months later, Roman was being patient, but I didn't know if he was waiting it out alone or with other female company to hold him over. I thought Johnny's return would bring me clarity, but all I had gained was a recurring case of heartburn. To be fair, it could be my cheese fry consumption. On top of the tuna salad. And the Red Vines. Good lord, I needed to reassess. In the meantime, I dug my fork through the fries to spear just the right balance of cheese to potato.

"I figured I'd call him in the morning," I answered through a mouthful of fry. "He's on early shifts right now."

"You know his sleep schedule?" Paul asked with a grin.

"More like his work schedule, smart ass. The rest I deduced all on my no-I'm-not-sleeping-with-Roman self."

"Damn, might help us more with our cases if you did."

I put my fork down. "You want me to whore myself out in exchange for arrest record info?"

"Of course not."

"I didn't think so."

"We can get that info on our own. I was hoping more for like details from other jurisdictions."

I flung a limp fry at his beer glass and missed.

"Back to the tiny little matter at hand," I said.

"Everything's a tiny little matter where Wally's concerned."

I covered my face with my hands. "Please, dear sweet baby Jesus. Don't ever let Mom confirm that with us either way."

Paul crossed himself and I raised two fingers at the bartender for another round.

"What do you think you should do next?" Paul wiped his fingers on a napkin and dug a pen from his coat pocket, then slid a clean napkin in front of his plate and started jotting down notes.

"Oh, how I love your PI pop quizzes."

"Come on, talk me through it."

"Well, I think Wally should take a true inventory to see what he's missing. Maybe the numbers will be a clue in some way."

"Mmm-hmm, what else?"

"If Roman can help me find out who owns the Riviera, it'll get me closer to finding out who man-boy is and what his story is. And I'd like to take a crack at the boy from the Thai restaurant. See if he knows what his girl was involved in that night."

"Likely nothing considering how fast they split up. She must have dropped him somewhere close by."

"Yeah, maybe. I'll chase that down," I said. "Whaddaya think of having Wally order an extra shipment of the stuff he's missing? We can have him throw in some other product so it doesn't seem too obvious. See if Erin hijacks it."

"I like it. Ask him what's most popular and have him order that."

I cringed. "I will, but if he says anything from the Ample Man collection, I can't guarantee I won't gag a little."

Paul looked at me and I watched as a smile slowly broke across his face.

"Oh, gee-zuss, I just heard it."

ΩΩΩ

I woke up Friday morning to a steady rain drumming against the windows, which I had left open the night before. I'd called Florida home for the two years prior to answering my brother's call to come back to Cleveland and it had been a long time since I could sleep with the windows open in May. Springtime in Florida is already hot enough to bake bread on the blacktop, and the smell of the fresh air streaming through my window was delicious. I rolled over and opened my eyes in time to see water spattering through the window onto the interior sill. Not so delicious. I detangled myself from my blankets, closed the windows, mopped up and hopped in the shower.

Twenty minutes later, I was dressed, ponytailed, and screwing the top on my coffee thermos when Roman called.

"I was just thinking about you," I said by way of greeting.

"About time."

"I meant for investigative purposes."

"Sam, has anyone ever told you you're a tease?"

"Not since my first co-ed sleep over, and I like to think that was because I was a respectable and scared twelve-year-old."

Silence from the other end.

"Hello?" I tapped the case of my cell phone and leaned back against my kitchen counter.

"Has anyone ever told you that you have an interesting way with words?"

"You're the second person this week."

"Now I'm afraid to ask, but why were you thinking about me?"

"Can you run a plate for me? It's only a partial, but I have most of it and there aren't going to be a lot of this make and model left on the road."

"Give it to me." I heard rustling in the background.

I read out the plate on the Riviera.

"Got it. That it?"

"Yep, thanks." I switched the phone to my other ear. "Your turn. To what do I owe the pleasure of your call?"

"I heard a rumor and need confirmation."

"Shoot."

"I heard Johnny's back in town."

"Confirmed," I said. Silence on the other end. "But you didn't need me to confirm that."

"No, I didn't."

"What do you really want to know?"

"Is he just back in town or is he back with you?"

"We're still in a no-fly zone as long as he's working with Paul." Roman was aware of the probationary hands-off agreement.

"What's the likelihood this trial partnership's going to turn into two names on the agency name plaque?"

"Too early to tell."

"Are you and I still in a no-fly zone until there's a decision either way?"

"Are you sure you still want to fly in my zone?"

"Would I be calling otherwise?"

"Even knowing I might not have the clearest heart or head right now?"

"Especially knowing that. I'm pretty confident if I get into the zone, I'll clear your heart, head, and any other confusion you have right up."

My chi-chi jumped straight into my left lung and I sucked in a sharp breath.

"Sam?"

"I'm here. I'm thinking."

"Help me out here. Tell me what's running around in that head."

"It would probably scare and excite you all at the same time."

"Scary can be exciting in the right context. Give it to me."

"Argh."

"Let's start simple. Are you into me at all, or is this a one-way attraction?"

A visual of Roman's hands flashed through my head. "Two-way. Definitely two-way. I just don't want to start anything I can't finish."

"That's usually the guy's line."

"Sometimes I feel more like a straight man than the guys I date."

"Then you're definitely dating the wrong men."

I laughed. "I meant that I don't deal with feelings well."

"Who said anything about feelings? I'm talking about a date. A burger and a beer. Why don't we start there and we can figure out feelings if and when one or both of us starts to have some?"

"A date."

"One harmless little date. On which I promise to keep my hands to myself."

I pictured Roman's hands again.

"Did you just moan?"

I felt my blush burn up my neck and thanked the saints Roman couldn't see me.

"Are you absolutely sure you don't want to go after someone with a little less baggage?" I asked.

"I've been online dating for a year. Trust me, you could be undecided about bopping *five* other guys, and you'd still win the less baggage contest."

Chapter Fifteen

"We weren't playing grab-ass."

"Janie, Steve's hand was literally on your ass."

"It's not what you think," Steve said.

The three of us were crammed into a small booth at Panera. I'd hit the jackpot when I went searching for Janie. Not only had I found her holding court in her makeshift office when I'd walked in, but I'd caught Steve Nall bent over the table, spending quality time inside Janie's mouth. I passed on a similar greeting and instead plopped my butt across from Janie and waggled three fingers at Steve, who grudgingly slid in next to Janie.

"What I think is that you two are bonking each other's brains out and both lied to me about it."

"Okay, it is what you think, but it has nothing to do with Malik's problem."

"Malik's problem?" I echoed. "A man being murdered is a 'problem'?"

Janie at least had the decency to blush, but Steve sat pouting. He looked like a six-year-old freshly relegated to his time-out chair.

"Fine, I didn't choose the right words, but we really have nothing to do with Walker's death."

"Why did you hide whatever this is from me?" I waggled a finger between the two of them.

Janie reached out the hand not holding Steve's under the table and dragged a napkin toward her from the center of the table. She spun the napkin lengthwise to the edge of the table, squinted at her thumb nail, and dug in. She had the short edge perfectly shredded before she spoke again.

"Steve's dad doesn't know we're together, and we don't want him to know."

"And you think I'd tell him?"

Janie shrugged with one shoulder, intent on working her thumb back and forth in a perfectly symmetrical pattern across her napkin.

"I panicked and told Steve to shut up in case you came to talk to him. I don't need the police talking to us any more, or it coming out indirectly that we're together."

Steve had bristled at Janie's 'shut up' remark, but stayed silent. I studied them and wondered how much of a show Janie's initial description of Steve having a crush on her was. She obviously had interest, but looked at him as if he should be worshipping her. I'd seen that look before. Either their relationship would be over inside of three months, or Steve was looking at the front-end of a miserable thirty-year-marriage.

"What's the big deal about your dad knowing you two are together?"

Steve frowned and looked across the restaurant. His frown was dismissive, his eyes thoughtful. After a moment, he looked back at me. "Dad won't hand off the business to me if I get married."

"You're what? Twenty-one? Two?"

"Twenty-six." Steve watched my face, but I kept it neutral. Frankly, I didn't care if this kid stayed in school until he was forty.

I was fairly certain after spending all of an hour with him that he would bankrupt his family's hotel before the engraving was done on daddy's retirement watch.

"Are you planning on getting married?" I directed the question to Steve, but cut one eye to Janie's face. She was studying an imperfection in her napkin cuts, her face colored with confusion. I wasn't sure she even heard the question, and I was surprised when she answered first.

"No. Oh, I don't know."

I was as bored with the conversation as she appeared to be. "And you can't think of any reason anyone would want to sabotage Malik's business?"

Two heads shook in unison.

"Humor me," I said to Janie. "If someone wanted to hurt your business, how could they go about doing it?"

Janie stopped shredding and put her hand in her lap. She leaned back into the booth and seemed to give the question real thought. "Reviews could make or break me. I've gotten good reviews overall. A few bad ones, mainly from foreigners who can't read the language well enough to understand the clues." Janie paused and frowned. "Frankly, they'd be better off getting the live treatment from Malik's guys."

I was beginning to hate this girl.

"But a handful of really bad reviews could hurt me," she continued.

"Would that be enough to send customers over to Malik's?"

"No, I'd think they'd pick a different experience altogether, but who knows." Janie looked at Steve, for consensus or dissent I wasn't sure, but Steve's face remained passive.

"Besides reviews, what else?"

Janie considered. "The only other way would be to mess with my content, but they'd have to hack my site. Which doesn't apply to Malik. Walker was his site."

Steve raised his head from the steady stare he'd trained on the table. "And he sure got hacked, didn't he?"

ΩΩΩ

I left Panera with a tropical iced tea, a headache, and a bagful of frustration. I climbed into my Jetta, rummaged in the console for my ibuprofen bottle and chased two tablets down with the tea. I was getting a whole lot of nowhere fast. On paper, there was no one and no reason to mess with Malik or his business. This had to be a direct hit to Walker. But why?

My brain screamed at me to follow the Ernest trail, but I couldn't help but think that Ernest had attacked Shawn out of pain over losing Walker. Couldn't hurt to go see Mrs. Brown and I made a mental note to add it to my painfully short list of remaining leads. Ernest, Janie and Steve, Malik's ex-girlfriend, the unknown factor. I eeny-meeny-miny-moed the trails in my head and landed on the unknown factor. There had to be something or someone else in Walker's past or present that connected to his murder. I'd learned that violent acts are almost always tied to money, love, or jealousy. I knew Walker's cash flow wasn't a gushing geyser, but maybe he had been lucky in love and then turned unlucky. Neither Paul or I had found any current love, or lust, interests in Walker's circle.

I thought back to my conversation with Walker's ex-wife. I wondered if she knew any of the women who came after her. It was a place to start. I dialed Mary's number.

A baritone voice vibrated through the line and I glanced at my phone to check that I'd dialed the right number.

"Hi, may I speak to Mary?"

"She's not available. Who's calling?"

"Um. I'm sorry, I thought this was her cell number?"

"It is." The baritone turned wary. "Who's calling?"

"My name is Samantha. Is this Mr. Abrams?"

"Yes."

"Mr. Abrams, I'm with a private investigations team that is looking into the death of your wife's ex-husband."

"The police have already spoken to Mary. She was with me when Walker died and they've corroborated her alibi. Why do you need to talk to her?"

"Yes, I'm aware of all that. I was actually calling with a few other questions, related to Walker's past. She may be able to help us help the police." I cringed as I said it, knowing somewhere Detective Barnes was highly irritated and not sure why.

"I highly doubt that. Mary hasn't spoken to Walker in years." Ruh-roh. Tread lightly, Nancy Drew.

"I understand. But she may know patterns, traits, prior relationships that could help us piece some things together."

"Be that as it may, Mary's not home. She's visiting our son at school."

"Which son?"

"Scott. And I don't see how it's your business to ask."

"I don't mean to be rude, Mr. Abrams, but she went to Michigan without her phone?"

"She forgot it. She's picked up a pre-paid, so we're in touch. And I don't appreciate the insinuation."

"No insinuation here, just surprise." I needed to pacify this man. "May I have that number?"

"No, you may not. Mary doesn't need the aggravation and I'm sure our son doesn't. He's having a hard enough time processing Walker's death." That didn't match up to the "sensible" boy Mary described to me, but I wasn't going to press my luck with this man.

"I can appreciate that and I by no means want to add to their grief. When is Mary due home?"

"I'll tell her you called."

My phone beeped the disconnected call alert before I could get out a thank you, let alone try one more time to wheedle the info out of the man.

ΩΩΩ

The sound of basketballs flying across three courts barreled at me as I elbowed my way through the double doors of the rec center. The stench of pre-teen boy and muskier men mingled together, hitting my nostrils at the same time. I stood just inside the doors and scanned the courts for Vinnie and Shawn. I spotted Shawn right away, not because he stood out, but because he was one of only a few people in the room who weren't playing. I made my way down the right side of the courts and climbed halfway up the bleachers to where he sat. He looked up and motioned with his head for me to sit, a smile flirting on one corner of his mouth. It was the first time Shawn had come near to smiling at me and I opened my mouth to remark on it, but changed my mind. I wasn't sure if we were at a point in our relationship where he'd recognize my flippant mouth for the affection that it was meant to be. I instead perched next to him and followed his eyes to the courts, where they tracked Vinnie as he roved up and down the middle court.

Vinnie's short but muscular frame showed surprising agility as he played duck-and-weave between the other players. He wore a white tee shirt with the sleeves ripped out at the shoulder seams, sweat weighing down the neckband.

I peeked at Shawn and watched him as he watched Vinnie, his stare both studious and blank at the same time. I wondered for the umpteenth time since the nurse at the cemetery commented about Shawn having seen trauma, if she was right and that was the reason for Shawn's demeanor. I hoped I hadn't bitten off more for Vinnie than he could chew. I didn't want to set up either of them for disappointment.

"Doc say whether you could play?"

Shawn tapped a healthy-sized lump on the side of his forehead. "I did for a while, but this thing started thumping."

I gestured toward the court. "I can take you home if Vinnie's not ready to leave yet."

"Nah, he offered to take me. I'm cool watching him play. Beats being at home right now."

"I could see that. How are you doing with everything?"

"I'm okay." Shawn leaned back and shoved his hands into the pockets of his hoodie, then pulled them back out before jamming them back in again. His hands pushed with enough force for me to see the outline of his knuckles stretching against the pocket seams. I watched him twitch around out of the corner of my eye for a moment, his birdlike legs sticking from his basketball shorts, heels tapping on the bleacher floor.

I smiled softly. "I didn't mean to agitate you. Are you're getting asked that a lot?"

"Yeah, nah. I mean, I don't know." Shawn's heels stilled, and he turned toward me. "Why are you trying to help me?"

I met his eyes in surprise. "What do you mean 'why'?"

"Coming to the hospital, showing up here. Asking Vinnie to babysit me." The last said without malice, but the question was clear.

I spread my hands in front of me. "I didn't see it as babysitting. I just thought you could use a friend right now, and Vinnie's close to your age. Malik said he didn't think you had a ton of support here in town."

Shawn chewed on his lip and absentmindedly fingered the bump on his forehead.

"He's pretty good," Shawn said. I followed his eyes back to the court and watched Vinnie weave up the lane. "Especially for being as short as he is."

I nodded. "Yeah. My dad was on the shorter side, too, and showed Vinnie how to play low, as he liked to call it. Basketball was kind of their thing when Vinnie was little."

"What was your thing? With your dad?"

"Hmmm, you know, I don't think we had one. He played ball

with Vinnie, and taught him how to run our family pizza shop. He and Paul butted heads a lot. That was their thing. I kind of just settled into the gap, I guess. I left home right after I finished school, and wasn't around enough for us to ever have a thing."

"Did you love him?" Shawn looked back at me and I saw genuine curiosity.

"Of course I loved him. I just didn't really play a role. See, with my dad, it was kind of like it was his movie and we all played parts in it. My mom included."

"He sounds like he was selfish."

"Not selfish. He was generous and lively and funny. It's more like he was just the center of every room. I don't think he tried to be that way, or intentionally went after the attention, it was just a natural force that no one could control, including him."

Shawn nodded hard. "My dad was like that. But he did want the attention. A lot of it."

"He 'was'? I thought your parents were still alive?"

"I think he is. He just hasn't been interested in my life for a long time."

"Malik told me they lived in Jersey. I assumed they were married."

Shawn shrugged, and I watched his pocket seams strain under a renewed push from his knuckles. "It's easier just to tell people they're together. I don't share a whole lot if I don't have to."

"You're sharing with me." I grinned. "Am I easy to talk to?"

"No, you're pushy. With you, I think it's easier to give you a little something to shut you up."

I stretched my face into mock shock and nudged his shoulder with mine. "Punk."

Shawn smiled and ducked his head.

"How is it being an only child?"

Shawn's smile faltered. "Like I said at the hospital, it's probably good that I was."

"Can I ask why?"

"My mom suffered from the same attention-needy disease that my dad did."

"They compete with each other?"

"For a while, yeah. Then Mom called it quits, and my dad was in and out of our lives after that. When he left the last time, she just told me to let it go. Like it was a freaking rubber ball I'd lost or something." Shawn's heel-tapping kicked back up and his tongue worked the gap in his front teeth.

"I'm sorry, man, I didn't mean to upset you."

"Doesn't matter. It's over."

I'd seen people less upset at being mugged. "Is it?"

"What's that supposed to mean?"

I braced my feet up on the bleacher in front of me and propped my elbows on my knees. "Malik said he thought maybe you looked at Walker as a brother-figure."

Shawn watched me carefully. "So?"

"So, I'm wondering if maybe you were looking for more of a dad figure. Maybe it's not as over as you think."

"Nah, it wasn't like that. Walker would have made a terrible dad. All he cared about was himself."

"Did you know he had a son?"

Shawn shook his head slowly, tears welling in his eyes. He opened and closed his mouth, looking down at the courts. Tears streamed down his face, and he propped his feet up next to mine, wrapping his arms around his knees. I scooted a few inches closer and put my arm around his narrow shoulders. His frame shook as he silently cried into the folds of his sweatshirt. I cradled his head into the crook of my neck, as much to hide the wetness in my own eyes as to give him comfort.

I looked down the court at Vinnie and thought about our dad. Vinnie was looking for a little brother, Ernest and Shawn seemed to be looking for a big one, and I was suddenly feeling extra grateful for both of mine.

Chapter Sixteen

After Shawn had pulled himself together, and I'd left him in Vinnie's care, I called Angie for some much needed sounding board time. She invited me to her trapeze class that night and I asked if she had any lower-to-the-ground openings available. She said if I could meet her for midday errand running, I could have all the ears and shoulders I wanted. By noon, I'd given her the rundown on Roman's offer and filled her cart with approximately seventeen pounds of organic vegetables.

"If by burger and a beer he means a thorough hay rolling, I say go for it."

"Ange."

"Hand me a carton of that coconut milk." She pointed at a green and white carton above my head. "Not that one. It's got carrageenan."

"What the hell is carrageenan?" I put the carton back in the case.

"It's a filler. And not the good kind that you can stab into your wrinkles." Angie slipped past me, opened the door to the refrigerated case, and pulled out a new carton.

I studied her face.

"Ange, you have exactly zero wrinkles."

"That's because I don't drink fillers. Or eat those." She narrowed one eye at the nacho chips in my cart.

"But I dip them in hummus. That's healthy, right?"

"Sure. If you consider dipping Oreos in antiseptic healthy."

I picked the hummus out of the cart and put it back in the refrigerated case. When I got back to the cart, Angie eyeballed me, then the bag of Doritos. I eyeballed her back. She frowned and pushed the cart into the next aisle. Grocery shopping with Angie was a lesson in organics and dietary guilt, but it was the only time she had without the kids, and I currently needed her to make my life choices for me.

I caught up to her as she tossed a bag of sprouted thirty-grain bread into the cart.

"Back to the burger and beer. What should I do?"

"Take condoms. Have a good time."

"Ange, come on. I'm serious."

"So am I," she said, reading the back label of a pickle jar. "See, it says right here. Guaranteed to be a good time."

I took the jar from her and put it back on the shelf. "Hard hee har."

"When did you turn into such a prude? Go out with this man, have some fun."

"What if we don't like each other? He's a good contact to have, and I don't want to ruin that."

"He's a grown man. I'm pretty sure he'll be able to handle it if you two don't hit it off."

"I don't know." I added a jar of mustard to the cart and turned back to peruse the forty-something rows of salad dressing.

"Don't know what? Whether you really like this guy, or whether you like him more than Johnny?"

"It's not that simple."

"Sure it is." She moved past me and picked through the spice bottles. "We're not in high school anymore. If Johnny wants you in any meaningful way, he's going to come for you. Partnership or not."

I stared at her. "So you're saying I should wait for him?"

"No. I'm saying you should go out and have some dirty, unmeaningful sex with this Roman guy, play some putt-putt, get that burger he wants to give you. Maybe Johnny will come for you, maybe he won't. But maybe you'll like Roman so much, it won't matter what Johnny does." Angie pushed me away and took the cart handle in both hands.

"Wait a minute. Didn't you just tell me like two days ago that I should let Johnny catch me?"

"What I said was you should let him think he has a chance at catching you," Angie called over her shoulder as she turned into the next aisle. "But that doesn't mean you have to drown in your celibacy while he's figuring out what he wants. Go do Roman."

"Doesn't that make me sound like kind of a whore?" I called after her, startling an old woman who came around the corner at the same time.

"No. It makes you sound like a man." Angie turned around to face me. "What are you doing?"

I finished dialing and held my cell up to my ear. "Ordering myself a burger."

"Attagirl."

ΩΩΩ

I flopped onto my sofa, covered in three layers of my Nonni's quilts. The quilts created a physical buffer between my thighs and Uncle Gino's pleatherette furniture, and a mental buffer between my brain and his intimate activities.

I patted my hand around, feeling for the remote, before finding it sandwiched between two layers of quilt. My phone vibrated on the side table and I hit the mute button on the remote. I answered the phone with one hand while initiating my channel-surfing with the other.

"Samantha?" I heard a tentative and familiar voice, but couldn't place it.

"This is she."

"Hi. It's Mary Abrams."

"Oh, hi, Mary. Thanks for calling back."

"Calling back?"

"I left a message with your husband. Isn't that why you're calling?"

"Oh. No, I wanted to check in to see what the police are doing with Walker's case. The police won't tell me anything."

"Could I come back out to see you? I can catch you up, and I have a few more questions for you."

"I'm not at home." She sounded rattled, and I wondered if her husband found out she'd been chatting up Walker.

"Harry mentioned you were out of town. He thought you'd be home soon?" I fudged. And was met with silence.

"I'm not sure. I'm with Scott and really don't want to leave him right now."

"Harry said Scott's having a hard time."

Mary paused a beat. "Yes. I thought he was fine at first. You know, he hasn't been close with his dad in so long."

I reflected back to my conversation with Shawn earlier that afternoon. Maybe I should invite Scott to our sibling support group.

Mary had gone silent, and I thought I lost the connection, but a peek at my phone screen told me the call timer was still ticking along.

"Mary?"

"I'm here."

"Are you alright?"

"You know what I've been thinking?"

I barely know what I'm thinking most of the time. "No, what's that?"

"Walker. Maybe I haven't let go quite as much as I thought I had. Talking to Scott today, we were reminiscing about the good stuff, you know? Scott's held on to all these great memories of his dad. He remembers so much more than I thought he did. He's never talked much to me about it these last several years." I heard her draw in a steadying breath. "Don't misunderstand. I love Harry. He's perfect for me. He's what I was trying to find all those years with the others."

"The others?" I burrowed deeper into quilt-covered cushions. She seemed to be warming to her story, with the point somewhere in the far distance.

"The other relationships I had after Walker. There were, well, let's just say there were more than a few."

"Sometimes it takes a while to find our prince, right?" I'd rubbed gills with a few frogs myself along the way. Who was I to judge?

"I went through a dozen before I found Harry."

"Dates?"

"Relationships."

Oh. Evidently, I was one to judge. If Mary could sense it, though, she hid it well. Or maybe she was used to it, because she went on without further response from moi.

"Harry put me together in the best way I could be mended. I wanted so badly for Walker to grow up, to grow with me, but he just wouldn't. Couldn't, maybe, would be more accurate. I always told Scott that we were better off without Walker, that we'd find a good man to be his daddy, and we did. I thought that Scott was okay with it, but I've realized being here with him that maybe that was me sugar-coating the memory. You know, to help with my guilt, I guess. I played a good game of moving on and letting go after each of my relationships failed, and I guess I convinced myself Scott was letting go when I was."

"Have you explained all this to Scott?"

"Some of it." Mary paused and I waited her out. "No, that's a lie. I want to, though. I really do."

"It might help him."

I heard Mary's breath hitch and let her have a moment to cry. She composed herself quickly, but her voice trembled when she spoke.

"I just hope it's not too late."

"Tell him now."

"He's in class. I can talk to him tonight."

"When do you plan on coming home?"

"As soon as I know he's okay. Maybe another day or two."

"I know this is hard on a lot of levels right now, but do you mind if I ask you a few more questions about Walker's past?"

"I guess so. What do you want to know?"

"Do you know much about any of his relationships after you two split up?"

Mary pushed out a breath. "God, not really. He um, let's see. He was with a woman named Sara for a long while. Just a girl, really. Another playmate to replace me, but I think she moved on to someone who was more responsible than Walker."

"Was their split amicable?"

"I think so. It was a long time ago and I got most of my information from Scott's nine or ten-year-old perspective."

"Anyone besides Sara?"

"One or two women I heard about through the grapevine, but when I got together with Harry I really tried to not look back. And by that time, Walker had stopped reaching out to Scott and Scott stopped caring. Or acted like it, at least. Have the police talked to any of them?"

"I don't know. I know you said you didn't think anyone from his acting circles would wish him bad, but what about any other friends you can think of? Has he had any fights or bad fallouts with anyone in the past that could have come up as an issue again?"

"No, I told you, no one. But we didn't talk enough for him to tell me if something like that had. I've been thinking about this a lot and I really think whoever did this must have been a stranger. Downtown can be dangerous and on the weekend, who knows what riffraff could have been lingering around looking for opportunity."

"The police don't think it was a stranger, Mary."

She went on as if she hadn't heard me, talking rapidly. "What do they know? There are homeless everywhere down there. Maybe the police are saying that because they don't want to admit how much of a homeless problem exists there."

"Mary, they have evidence."

"What kind of evidence?"

I made a two-second assessment and decided to zip my lip. I didn't get the info about the note on Walker's shirt directly from the police, and it wasn't like I'd been sworn to secrecy by Malik, but I still felt being prudent was the way to go. Mary was sounding increasingly hyper, and I didn't relish the thought of her running her mouth around about the note.

"I can't say, but it's specific. There's no way a stranger would have left behind what was left behind."

Mary's breathing hiked up a notch, but she didn't say anything.

"Mary, I can't imagine how hard this is, and I get that it might be easier to get your head around Walker's death if we knew it was random, but it couldn't have been. That's why I'm asking you to think back to anything or anyone who could have wished him ill."

"What about his boss?"

"Malik? Did Walker tell you they were having problems?"

Mary paused. "Not exactly. But Walker wasn't happy with that job."

"I thought that was because he wanted to be an actor. I heard he was stuck in the scavenger gig until he got his big break."

"Yeah, but maybe Malik was giving him a hard time, too."

"I think we might be stretching here, Mary." I tried to soften the message by smiling into my words.

"But are the police looking at him? They have to have some idea, right?" Desperation leeched into Mary's voice.

"They're working on it, but I don't know how much they have to go on."

"They need to hurry. I'm worried about Scott. I don't know if he can put this behind him until they find out who did it."

I racked my brain for comforting words, but I knew the police investigation could go on for months, and that was assuming the police identified any suspects at all. "At least Scott has you with him for now. I'm sure that's helping him more than you think."

"He's broken. I can tell."

My rational side wondered how broken he could be if he was already back in class, but my compassionate side reminded me that people grieve in different ways. Still, it seemed Mary was the one who was fighting to cope. I wondered again how infrequent her chats with Walker really had been. Especially if her husband isn't passing messages, and she's conveniently forgetting to take along her phone.

ΩΩΩ

I hung up with Mary and dialed Detective Barnes. I unsurprisingly got his voicemail and left a short message recapping my convo with Steve and Janie from that morning, and asked for an update on Ernest's arrest. I didn't know how long the police could keep him before he bailed out, assuming he had someone to bail him out. No sooner had I ended the call than my phone buzzed again.

"Of all the detectives in the world, it had to be you."

"Cute," Roman said.

"Not really, I was hoping for Detective Barnes to call back."

"Way to bring a guy to his knees. He running a plate for you, too?"

"He's running this scavenger hunt murder case."

"Ah, well, you still want this plate info?"

"Pretty please."

"Car's registered to a kid named Lionel Skidmore."

"What a name."

"Maybe dad was into trains."

"Or ensuring his kid got beat up in school."

"Twenty-eight-years-old. Born in Berea, and it looks like he never left, outside of a short stint in Morrow County Jail for breaking and entering and selling stolen goods online."

"Smart kid. Looks like he's trying to get caught again."

"Smart enough to take two tries at his senior year in high school. Works part-time for a quickie oil change joint down on Bagley Road and even less part-time off the books at an adult toy store on Brookpark."

"If it's off the books, how'd you find out?"

"Really?"

"I know, I know, you're a detective. You have mad skills. Mind helping a newbie out with your trade secrets?"

"If I did that, you wouldn't have a reason to call me anymore."

"Are you fishing?"

"I got your message about being hungry for a burger. I'm going to take a flyer and assume I'm getting a yes on a date?"

"I think so."

"It's not a difficult decision."

"Are you this aggressive in all your relationships?"

"Is this going to be a relationship?"

"Remind me never to get into an interrogation room with you."

"It could be more fun than you might think."

"Hey, Detective Barnes is calling me back," I lied. "Thanks for the info on this Skidmore kid."

"Do you avoid real conversation with Johnny like this, too?"

Shit. Yes.

I hung up and my phone immediately vibrated in my hand. Barnes. Thanks to whichever saint looks over fibbers, I could chalk my lie to Roman up to a halfsies.

"Hi, Detective."

"Samantha, gotta make this quick, we got a doozy of a case on our hands today."

"Don't need any details."

"This one's bloody."

My stomach flipped. "Really, no need to share. Tell me about Ernest."

"Mr. Brown was released to the care of his mother last night."

"His mother? She doesn't even care for herself. She's in assisted living."

"She was able-bodied enough to show up with cash to bail him out. Let's not argue semantics."

"So, he just gets to go home? What about what he did to Shawn?"

"Shawn's declined to press charges."

"He was on a bunch of pain pills last night. He may have a different answer today. I saw him a couple hours ago and he's not in the best frame of mind right now."

"He has my number and knows he can change his mind."

"Can't you talk to him again? Or charge Ernest anyway?"

"I'd love to, and I will, but it won't be for assault. It'll be for murder."

"Wait, with what proof?"

"Some of the forensics have come back and Mr. Brown has done us the grand favor of leaving a couple of his paw prints on the clue card we found in Walker's shirt pocket."

I shook my head for a long time before realizing Barnes couldn't see me.

"Is it possible Ernest was just the one messing with the clues? Why does it have to mean he murdered Walker?" I ran the idea through my head as I said it aloud and wondered why I was trying to defend the guy.

"Why are you trying to defend this guy?"

I pulled the phone from my ear and looked at it. "I'm asking myself the same thing. I just don't see him killing someone. What's his motive?"

"This guy's chain is missing a couple links. Sometimes that's motive enough."

"I don't buy it. Walker was Ernest's only friend. And yes, I'm aware it was one-sided and I use the term 'friend' loosely, but Ernest really thinks he was critical to the hunts and to helping Walker. Why would he kill his one connection that made him feel valuable?"

"His 'one connection that made him feel valuable'? Where the hell you getting this Dr. Phil crap from?"

"It's not crap. Think about it. Ernest doesn't have a job. He averages at least two hunts every week. It's not hard math to figure out that the sum of his life lives in these hunts. He's gotten heated with Walker about the clues, and he brokered a deal to stay involved. There's no indication that he's this passionate about anything else in his world. It doesn't take Dr. Phil or even Dr. Pepper to figure out that the hunts mean a lot to him. And Walker was at the core of that."

"Lick your pencil tip and try that math again. What all that adds up to for me is that Ernest wanted Walker out of the way so he could become the main man on campus."

"Come on! You saw him. Ernest is socially awkward on his best day. He doesn't want to be the main anything."

Barnes grunted at the other end of the line. "I got a dead host who says otherwise."

"Does Ernest know you have his fingerprints on the card?"

"Would you run tell him if I said 'no'?"

"Of course not. I want to figure out the truth of what's happened as much as you do. I'd just like to know how he'd explain it."

"Well, it's your lucky day, Because we asked him."

"And? What did he say?"

I heard a rustling of paper in the background and pictured the tiny notebook nestled in Barnes' palm. I waited patiently and stared at Gino's ceiling. A stain directly overhead caught my eye, and I shifted down to the other end of the sofa. The rustling on the other end of the line stopped.

"He said he picked up the card after he found Walker's body."

I closed my eyes and pictured Ernest discovering Walker's body. I thought at the time that he'd called out to us as soon as he discovered the body but in reeling back my memory film, I realized there could have been a short gap of time where he could have done some recon before calling for our attention. Maybe the shaky, stunned Ernest I'd initially seen was in fact a post-mortem snooper. Or, I thought with resignation, a murderer after all.

"I want to give you the direct quote here. Maybe it'll change your mind about whether Ernest has it in him to kill or not." I heard the flip of paper again. "When we asked him why he would take a card sticking out of the pocket of a dead man who he had just found, he said 'I had to know how it ended.'"

"How what ended?"

"The hunt. He needed to know the last two stops on the tour."

"But he's been on two dozen of these things. And has supposedly had input on creating a bunch of the clues."

"Yeah, and yet he couldn't walk away without the two bits to his shave and a haircut."

I rested my head against the back of the sofa and wrapped my free hand across my temples. "Ernest doesn't need to go to jail, Detective, he needs mental health care."

"Fortunately for him, the Cuyahoga County Department of Corrections can provide him with both. Plus three squares a day and a library where he can dig up as much history about Cleveland as he could possibly want."

"He may not be the straightest duck in the pond, but his story could be legit. Just because he couldn't control his curiosity doesn't mean he killed Walker."

"Woman, you're dreaming. I don't understand why you're on such a mission to help a man who means nothing to you."

"And I don't understand why you have such a hard-on for nailing him."

"The only thing I have a hard-on for is for you to back away from this. You are dangerously close to impeding an active police investigation."

I slapped the quilt in my lap. "At least tell me what you're planning to do next. Are you even looking at other suspects?"

"Last I checked, I'm not required to whiteboard my case progress with the unlicensed baby sister of a dime store private eye."

Be a lady, be a lady, be a lady. "Dime store, my ass. Paul's agency may be small, but he's damned accurate. As opposed to a lazy-ass detective I know whose sole focus is to slide into retirement and avoid expending so much as a thimbleful of energy toward solving his last case."

"Let me tell you a little something, Ms. Carter. All that extra energy you think I'm sitting on I can easily focus toward making your life as inconvenient as possible. Stay out of this case. Stay out of my way. And make sure to pass that message on to your brother."

Detective Barnes disconnected and I threw my phone to the other end of the sofa. I yanked on the edge of the quilt and pressed it to the hot tears that were flooding my eyes. Shit.

Paul was going to be pissed. I'd lost the one tenuous connection we had to the police investigation into Walker's death. Technically, we'd been hired to find out who was sabotaging the scavenger hunts, but Walker's death had to be tied to the clues. Losing access to Detective Barnes wasn't going to get us any closer to the answers we needed. I had to do some creative investigating and I had to do it fast. Barnes told me to stay away from him and his case, but that didn't mean I couldn't keep pursuing mine.

Chapter Seventeen

I put a pin in my self-pity party as I pulled into Ernest Brown's mother's assisted living center. I wasn't convinced Barnes had the right man, and I hoped Mrs. Brown could add a few corner pieces to my shapeless puzzle. Barnes would undoubtedly have a mini conniption fit if he knew I was there, but if I had to pull a story out of my caboose, I'd say I was here doing recon for my Nonni. Always good to keep a competitive eye out for a better facility, right? I knew it was a bad cover, but I desperately wanted to make some headway in the case before I told Paul that I'd killed our connection to Barnes.

I wound my way through the property, which proved to be no easy feat. I suspected an aerial view of the lot would look a lot like one of those magnetic table maze games at Cracker Barrel. I parked in front of the one-story gray building that boasted a "Sundown Village Welcome Center" sign across the front awning and scooped up the box of pastries I'd stopped for on the way. I'd made it to the bakery two minutes before closing and pickings were slim. I had a choice of anise stars or peach kolache. I'd hedged my bets and gotten a dozen of each.

I balanced the boxes on top of each other and wedged open the front door of the welcome center with the toe of my Puma. A man older than my Nonni who was leaning on the receptionist counter smiled a mouthful of perfect dentures at me. He pushed his weight off the counter and onto the carved, wooden walker to his left. He started a slow but energetic shuffle in my direction and I lengthened my stride to meet him.

"Let me help you with that, dear." He held out a shaky hand for one of the boxes, and I didn't have the heart to wave him off. I passed him the anise stars and signed them off as the sacrificial lamb, but the old man took the box and secured it successfully between the wooden slats that horizontally braced the top of the walker.

"Thank you. That's very kind." I smiled back at the man, strangely embarrassed that his teeth were prettier than mine.

"Of course, my dear. There are still a few of us gentlemen left in the world, and we need to set an example for the rest of them." He looked sideways at the receptionist at the counter, a heavy young man whose face was badly pockmarked from acne. The receptionist cast a baleful look at the old man, who sighed heavily and looked back at me with an eye roll.

I smothered a laugh and bent to whisper to him. "Your example is very much appreciated by me, if not by him."

The old man blushed heartily and tucked his chin to his chest. I shot a quick wink at the receptionist over the old man's head. Didn't want to completely alienate the man I was about to butter up for confidential info. I was playing both ends in a retirement village. I mentally patted myself on the back and made a note to tell Paul to add that to my PI performance review.

The old man kept his chin tucked and shuffled at double speed back to the receptionist's counter, where he unloaded the treat box and held out his palm. I tucked my fingers into his and accepted the dry kiss to my knuckles. I hadn't been treated that well in more months than I could count on all my piggies and toes. So what if I could divide my age into his three times over? Maybe I'd just found a creative solution to my Johnny and Roman dilemma.

A small chime sounded around us and the old man straightened. "Well, my dear, that's the dessert bell. Normally, I'd not let a sweet little bippy like you have a moment unescorted, but Friday is mousse day, and there's always the dickens of a line when they're serving something you don't need to take your teeth out for."

"That's quite alright. Thank you again for escorting me this far."

"My pleasure, dear, my pleasure."

I turned back to the receptionist, who had turned from baleful to annoyed.

"Visiting hours are over."

"I was told you didn't have visiting hours."

"That's for family only."

"How do you know I'm not family?"

"Who's your family?"

Deeyamn. "Mrs. Brown."

"Mmm-hmm. And her relationship to you?"

"Aunt."

"Do you call all your aunts by their last name?"

"It's a sign of respect."

"Is it a sign of respect to lie about an old woman who has no siblings and couldn't possibly have a niece?"

"It's more of an adoptive thing."

Bale Face raised an eyelid.

"A late in life sort of adoptive thing."

The eyelid raised higher, and Bale Face winced when a whitehead folded back into the crease of his lid. I winced at his wince and Bale Face reddened in embarrassment.

"I have pastry."

Bale Face slanted an eye toward the boxes.

"Whaddya got?"

"Kolaches and anise stars."

"Those are old people cookies."

"It's an old people's home."

"Gimme the kolaches."

I pushed the bottom box to him and said an internal thanks to my decision to get two boxes while Bale Face palmed the back of the box and pulled it toward him. He looked up at me, silent.

"Did you want me to wait while you count the cash?" Sometimes I just can't help myself.

He leisurely reached toward the cracked I Love Kittens mug that held an assortment of pens and chewed pencils, and pulled out a pair of scissors. He snipped the tape on the bakery box lid and peered inside. He nodded once, flicked me a look of approval, and closed the lid.

"Mrs. Brown lives in Suite 227 on Dolphin Cove."

"Could you point me in the general direction? This joint's more confusing than the hedges in The Shining."

Bale Face smiled at me, the gesture puckering the pimples around his lower lip. "I'm awful busy. Counting my kolache and all."

Damn my mouth. I spied a stack of property maps next to the day's cafeteria menu and snatched one just as Bale Face made a grab for the whole stack. I smiled sweetly, scooped up the cookie box, and made tracks.

ΩΩΩ

Dolphin Cove proved harder to find with the map than without. The names of the main arteries of the property were split among mammals, reptiles, and amphibians. From there, the offshoot side streets corresponded to one of the larger three categories. It took me ten minutes and one pilfered anise cookie to make the journey. I was banking that Mrs. Brown would neither bother to count that she was being gifted an even dozen, nor be partial to chocolate. As it turned out, neither mattered.

My knock on her gated door revealed a tall, thin woman who looked in every way possible different from her son. Where Ernest stood stout under his ginger curls, Mrs. Brown was lean with hair straight and gray as a steel I-beam. Her posture in the doorway was nearer to plum than the doorframe.

"Mrs. Brown?"

"Who are you?"

"I'm Sam Carter. I work with a private investigations agency that's helping to resolve an issue for a tourist company that Ernest is involved with."

"I may be old, but I'm not stupid. You're here to pick up where the cops left off with that murdered man business. Ernest had nothing to do with that."

"I don't think he did either, Mrs. Brown."

Two sturdy charcoal eyes glared at me. My gut told me none of the smiles in my arsenal were going to win me any points here, so I simply stared back.

"What's your angle, young lady?"

"I'd like to help prove Ernest didn't do this."

"Why do you care?"

"There's another young man who works for the scavenger hunt company who I'm trying to help. He's the one Ernest got into a scuffle with at the cemetery."

"That man's not pressing charges, and the police released Ernest."

"I know, but I need to understand why Ernest tried to hurt Shawn."

"Well, that's too bad. He's not here."

I believed her. During the brief time she'd hovered in her doorway, Mrs. Brown hadn't so much as twitched a shoulder, let alone looked over it or in any way acknowledged the existence of someone else in the home.

"I'm not here for him. I was hoping to talk to you. I want to help Ernest, but I need you to help me do that."

"Young lady, no one has ever wanted to help Ernest. I can't see how or why someone would want to start now."

"May I come in and explain it to you?"

Mrs. Brown looked to the bakery box in my hands. "There whiskey inside of that box?"

"No. But I have a credit card and a lead foot. And there's a Speedway down the street." Who knew I should have been choosing between Walker and Beam instead of peanut butter chunk and red velvet?

"Oh, never mind. Come on in. And you may as well bring the box."

I stepped inside the miniscule entryway and spied an equally small living room on the other side of a glass-block pony wall. Mrs. Brown had stuffed every square inch with furniture and accessories. All quality pieces, and enough of them to fill a three-thousand square foot home. She had shoved it all, or likely had a posse of young men who were good at geometry shove it all into what looked to be about eight hundred square feet.

"Go on and have a seat. I'll get this thing turned off."

I belatedly noticed the muted television set flickering images of *Weekend at Bernie's* and mused at the thought of Mrs. Brown kicked back in the well-worn blue plaid recliner that sat next to the sofa, watching a stiff getting dragged around a beach. I took in the amber filled tumbler on a doily-covered side table, the ice melted to near shards, and realized she may not have full control over her choice of programming. She thumbed a remote control resting on the arm of her recliner and sat down. I sat the bakery box down on the end table nearest her and flicked the tape off the edge of the lid.

"Can I get you a plate?" I asked, looking vaguely past the living room.

She waved me off. "Sit."

I tucked myself into a side chair opposite her. "Where's Ernest at now?"

"At home. I sent our doctor over to give him a little something to calm him down."

"Wow, I didn't know doctors made house calls these days."

Mrs. Brown watched me evenly. "He's an old family friend."

"Good to have. How much did Ernest tell you about what happened at the cemetery?"

"Not much. Just that he got in a tussle with someone who'd given him a hard time."

"Did the police give you any other detail?"

"The policeman told me it was unprovoked." Mrs. Brown stared at me as if waiting for confirmation and equally ready to defend.

"It was unprovoked. I was there."

Mrs. Brown nodded at her whiskey glass, which she'd shifted from end table to hand, without moving it to her lips.

"What was this boy Shawn doing or saying to Ernest?"

"He wasn't saying anything directly to Ernest. He was explaining Cleveland history to the people who had joined the scavenger hunt. Shawn was reading from a script, not singling Ernest out with any kind of confrontation."

The whiskey finally made its way to Mrs. Brown's lips. The glass stayed pressed there for a long beat before Mrs. Brown spoke again.

"Do you know how often Ernest goes on these hunts?" she asked in between sips.

I nodded. "We did some background research, yes."

"Did your research tell you how a grown man in his forties has the time and money to busy himself with a tourist trap multiple times a week?" Mrs. Brown sounded matter-of-fact, but I smelled a change in the air coming. Like Fall after the first of the leaves hits the firepit.

"We know he's not employed and receives disability, but we don't know what qualified him."

"Not 'what', but 'whom'. The whom is the government, Ms. Carter. Ernest is on disability for what they deem to be a mental health incapacitation."

"How exactly was he incapacitated?"

"I'd say by me and his father, and to some degree his brother."

"His older brother?"

"His only brother." She must have read the look on my face. "Yes, my dead son. Mitchell."

"I'm sorry. How did you all, um, incapacitate Ernest?"

She studied me for a few beats longer and the corners of her mouth turned down in the way they do when one is making a decision they don't like. She nestled the whiskey glass in her lap, wrapping bony fingers around its base.

"Mitchell was stellar at everything he did. In his studies. Athletics. Music. As a person, plain and simple. He was very much his granddaddy, my daddy, in every way. I hate to say he was a golden child, it's so cliché. But the halo was visible. And Ernest was drawn to him more than anyone."

"In a competitive way?"

"Not at all. It was very much adulation." The whiskey made its way back north and I watched as the last of the ice shards melted past Mrs. Brown's lips.

"It didn't bother him that Mitchell was the golden child?"

Mrs. Brown looked at the ceiling as she answered. "Ernest didn't want that attention. He just wanted to be a part of Mitchell's circle. It sounds weird even now, but I think he wanted somehow to feel like he was invited to the party, but he never wanted the party to be in his honor." She looked back at me. "Does that make sense to you?"

"Sort of. How did Mitchell feel about Ernest?"

"Oh, dear." Mrs. Brown blew out a whoosh of air, sending a trickle of whiskey scented wind in my direction. "That's complicated. Mitchell loved Ernest, he did. I think for a while even, Ernest's following him around all the time stroked Mitchell's young ego. But when he got to high school, the age difference between the two caught up and things changed."

"How?"

Mrs. Barnes squinted in my direction. "Do you have siblings, Ms. Carter?"

"Two brothers."

"Younger or older?"

"One of each."

"Did your younger brother ever try to hang out with you when you didn't want him to?"

"Sure, sometimes."

"He ever bribe you to play with him?"

I laughed and thought back to Vinnie giving me his allowance once to let him play with me and an early-maturing Mitzi Keptner. "He did, but I think it may had more to do with my playmates than with me."

Mrs. Barnes gave me a patient smile. "He ever black mail you?"

"Come again?"

"Black mail you. Threaten to tattle to your parents about something you'd done or tell your friends what's in your diary. That type of thing."

"No. Vinnie's not like that."

"Well, Ernest was. When Mitchell stopped letting Ernest tag along and the flattery of having a shadow wore off, Ernest threatened him. Not physically, mind you. But he would threaten to tell his father and me little secrets Mitchell had."

"What kind of secrets?"

"Childish ones. That Mitchell was holding hands with a girl. That Mitchell had seen an R rated movie when he told us he was going to see something PG. Silly things all teenagers do. Nothing that would get Mitchell in big trouble, but nothing he wanted to have to hear about from his parents either."

"So he let Ernest continue to tag along?"

"No, he sort of made deals with Ernest. He created special projects they could do together instead. He was quite sweet about it actually. He made up little treasure hunts for them on the back property. He'd hide things, those little green plastic army men, old trophies he'd won, and Ernest would have to follow a trail Mitchell built to find the toys. Then Mitchell let Ernest help hide the treasures and come up with maps for the neighborhood kids to follow. Ernest loved to build forts. They did that quite often as well."

"Mrs. Brown, have you ever gone on one of these scavenger hunts downtown with Ernest?"

"Don't be ridiculous. I'm holding well for my age, but I don't have any disillusions about being able to traipse around the streets downtown."

"Has Ernest ever talked to you about them in detail?"

"Not much. I know the gist of what happens on them, how they follow the clues and whatnot."

"Do you think these treasure hunts he did with Michell are the reason he likes doing the scavenger hunts?'

Mrs. Barnes stared into the bottom of her whiskey glass. The golden light from the lamp on her end table glinted against the heavily cut crystal of the glass. "I never really thought about it enough to make that connection, but I suppose so. Ernest has always liked puzzles and word games. I used to buy him those thick game books and he'd bury his face in them for hours at a time."

"Did he play sports or hang out with other kids besides Mitchell?"

"No, he was quite shy. I don't think he'd have done well on a sporting team."

I thought about Ernest's pudgy frame and wondered if it was a carryover from childhood. "Why not?"

"His father and I never could put a finger on it entirely, but it was like Ernest didn't believe he could win, or didn't want to somehow."

"At what?"

"At anything, really."

"Do you think he felt like if he tried, he'd have to live in Mitchell's shadow?"

"You know, in a weird way, I had the impression he didn't want to outshine Mitchell. I remember one day when the boys were coloring. They were, oh, they must have been five and three at the time. Ernest had been coloring inside the lines of his picture, and Mitchell was just sort of scribbling all over, drawing his own pictures in the margins of his coloring sheet. My husband complimented Ernest on how he drew so cleanly inside the lines, and Ernest looked at him in surprise, then put his crayon back to the page and squiggled right through all the lines."

Mrs. Brown shook her head at the memory and frowned in what appeared to be resignation or some long-suffering confusion.

"My husband and I decided early on that we wouldn't compare the boys in any way, whether it was their table manners, or grades, or physical abilities. It was obvious to us that Ernest had something internally driving that boat and we didn't want to make it worse."

"Sounds like it got worse anyway."

"That's true. By the time Mitchell died, Ernest had cemented a fan-club of one and he was destroyed. He's never been what you'd call mainstream, but Mitchell's death stunted him somehow. He lived his life in Mitchell's shadow when Mitchell was alive, and it's like he never wanted to crawl out of that afterward. Almost like—."

I watched Mrs. Brown fight for the right words, caution creeping across eyes that were just starting to take on the milkiness of age. She tipped her chin to her chest, and I wondered briefly if she'd fallen asleep.

"Mrs. Brown?"

She raised her chin slowly and looked at me.

"Almost like what?"

"Almost like he was chasing after something he could never finish. Mitchell died so suddenly, I don't think Ernest was able to ever really absorb it. That whole adage about closure is a reality for him."

"May I ask how Mitchell died? I heard only that he was sick."

"Yes," Mrs. Barnes whispered. Her chin trembled and she stilled it with a half-ounce of whiskey before speaking again. "He'd had a bad virus for a few days. Vomiting, diarrhea. He, uh, he choked on his own vomit."

"I'm so sorry."

"Thank you, dear. In some ways, we lost the whole family when we lost Mitchell. My husband and Ernest never really recovered from it," she said as she emptied her glass and turned her eyes toward the whiskey bottle on the end table. I followed her gaze and wondered if she realized she hadn't either.

Chapter Eighteen

I hit the foyer of Ernest's apartment building, a blocky brick affair wedged between a Convenient Mart and crumbling photo shop on Lorain Road. The foyer hit back with the pungent and unmistakable smell of boiled cabbage. Ernest's disability may have netted him a monthly check and the freedom to live without working, but the level of lifestyle may have left a little to be desired. Box air conditioners tilted haphazardly from the upper windows of the three-story building and the mailboxes in the lobby sported doors that hung crookedly in their frames. There were twelve boxes, four per row, in a mock outline of the building itself. Two had been relieved of their doors entirely, leaving me to wonder if their corresponding units had renters. Other than the mailboxes, the lobby was bare. No plants, benches, or otherwise. I walked the length of the short hallway and counted five doors. Flaky paint marked three as apartments, one as a laundry room that smelled strongly of mold through the closed door, and one as

"Manager". Someone had helpfully re-painted the manager's door, using blue spray paint to spell "Ogre" over the top of "Manager".

I walked back toward the front door and the foot of the staircase that led to the two floors above. This was not an elevator establishment, but despite my recent emotion-fueled buffet diet, thought I could manage a couple flights.

I navigated the stairs to the third floor and found unit 304 at the end of the hallway. I peered out the one window in the exterior wall of the hallway and found myself looking down on a small rear parking lot that must have formally served as a backyard. Patches of grass and dirt revealed tire tracks that had worn impressions in the ground that acted as parking spot markers for six cars.

Turning away from the window, I pressed my ear up to the door of unit 304 and heard a TV and what sounded like scraping. I rapped on the wooden door and found it soft to my knuckles' touch. The scraping stopped, but the TV volume stayed the same and after a moment, the scraping sound resumed. I knocked again.

"Ernest, it's Sam Carter."

The scraping picked up speed. I knocked again.

"Ernest?"

The scraping stopped, and I backed away from the door in anticipation of it opening. It didn't.

I stepped back up to the door and leaned in close. And banged.

"Go away." The scraping and the TV came to an abrupt silence.

"Come on, Ernest, open the door."

"I didn't mean to hurt Shawn." Ernest's voice came weary through the thin wood.

"That's not why I'm here."

"What do you want?"

"I'm not going to keep shouting through the door," I said, though the cheapness of the door kept me from having to talk much above my normal voice.

Silence.

"I just came from your mom's."

I heard Ernest breathing. He must have been standing as close to his side of the door as I was to mine. The door opened two inches, caught on a chain, and I clenched my muscles in an attempt not to jump back. Ernest's face peered out, bloodshot eyes bright in his furrowed face. Whatever drug that family doctor had given him looked like it had either worn off or been spit out.

"Why did you go to my mother's?"

"Because I wanted to understand why you hurt Shawn."

"I told you I didn't mean to do that."

"Your mom didn't think so either." I looked him squarely in the eye. "She told me about your brother."

Ernest stared at me with wide eyes for a long beat, then yanked his head back and shut the door. I heard the scrabble of the chain against the wood and the door opened again. Ernest pulled it to his belly, and stood back from the two-foot gap he'd created. I slid through it before he could change his mind, took a couple steps past him, and heard the door close behind me. There was no foyer, no entryway of any kind. I had stepped straight into what in other units would be the living room, but what in Ernest's place appeared to be a shrine.

Pooled on the floor near my feet was a mound of brown fabric that upon closer inspection I could see were bedsheets. These must have been what the detectives told Malik they had seen covering the walls on their previous visit to the apartment. The remains of what the sheets had covered were hanging in various stages of disarray on every wall. Pictures, newspaper clippings, certificates, awards, ribbons, and drawings papered the drywall. The wall to my left had been stripped of all but one long row of studio-produced, grade-school pictures. I took it all in. The walls, the portion of floor littered with torn and crumpled memorabilia, and the weathered sofa were blanketed by much of the same. Everywhere I looked, the Brown brothers stared back at me. Mitchell's eight-year-old eyes shining brightly in his little league uniform, his high school chin stubble underscoring a wet grin as he crawled out of the gym pool, his tanned muscular arms raising a massive trophy above the four heads of a golf quartet.

I gingerly stepped forward and around the nest of brown sheets. Ernest stayed rooted to his spot near the door. I peered back at his face. His head was tilted toward the floor, but I could see he was tracking me, waiting for a reaction. I ran through and rejected the first dozen thoughts that tumbled through my brain.

Two walls contained pictures solely of Mitchell Brown, but the center wall had been papered with pictures where the two brothers smiled out in every shot. Where Mitchell mostly beamed his smile at the camera, Ernest beamed at Mitchell. The adoration was tangible. Ernest smiling at Mitchell as he accepted awards, his diploma, even a shot of Mitchell and his corsage-pinned date for a school dance revealed Ernest in the corner, sitting on the sofa, a look of respect and admiration on his face.

I was looking at easily hundreds of pieces of proof that Mitchell was everything his mother described him to be. The athlete, the sweet son, the scholar, the patient older brother.

I also noticed in every picture from what must have been the last years of Mitchell's short life one very important thing Mrs. Brown hadn't told me. How could she? She'd never been on a hunt, the police wouldn't have any need to show her pictures, and Ernest would most certainly not have offered up this one glaring detail.

How could she possibly know that the man her baby boy had found dead, the man whose murder the police believed that baby boy to have committed, was the spitting image of her beloved and dead eldest son?

I stood as rooted to my spot as Ernest was to his, eyes riveted on the center wall, conjuring up the image of Walker's headshot sitting on Paul's desk. Mitchell and Walker could have passed themselves off as fraternal twins. My heartbeat ticked up, the sound of pounding blood engulfing my ears. I inhaled a long, slow stream and focused on keeping my face neutral while I did the math.

How had Detective Barnes not bothered to mention this to me? Did he know? Certainly, if he knew, he would tell me to stay away from Ernest more harshly than he had. I chalked his warnings up to a possessive ego, but he couldn't be so peeved by me that he'd let me unwittingly walk into a lunatic's lair, could he?

Ernest remained near the front door, but he hadn't replaced the chain or otherwise locked it from what I could see. That had to be a good sign. I took in another breath and screamed inside my head to think.

My gaze fell momentarily to the floor in front of the sofa, where just under the rim of the coffee table a half dozen bowls sat in a row, each with cereal crusted up their sides and pools of yellowed milk resting in their centers. Tucked up against the table leg were two boxes of cereal. I turned and looked fully at Ernest, who was watching me with about as little expression as one could muster without being asleep or dead.

"Have you had anything to eat besides cereal lately?"

A shrug in response.

"You wanna go down to the diner on the corner? My treat."

"I'm not hungry."

"How about we go for a walk?"

Ernest pointed to the wall. "I didn't do anything."

The shock must have still been visible in my eyes.

"The police don't believe me, either."

"Do they know about this?" I gestured toward the walls.

Ernest hung his head and shook it. He picked at a crusty fleck on his tee shirt and looked back up at a spot on the center wall. "They came the other day, but I wouldn't let them in. That detective talked to me at the police station yesterday after—. After I—."

"After what happened with Shawn?"

"Yes. That detective yelled at me for a long time. He said I killed Walker. He told me he had proof, and he was going to get me."

"What proof did he say he had?"

"There was a card. A card in Walker's pocket. I touched it." Ernest shot me a sideways glance, then adjusted his gaze back onto the center wall. "Just real quick, just to see. But he said that was enough to prove I killed Walker."

"But you didn't. Right?"

"No, I needed him."

"What for?"

"I told you before. I helped him with the clues."

"But you said you needed him. He needed you to help with the clues, but what did you need him for?"

Ernest looked confused. "I needed him to need my help."

"Like you helped your brother when you two were kids?"

"No, don't say that!" Ernest pressed the heels of his hands into his forehead and threaded his fingers into his orange locks. He curled his fingers in tight and yanked on his bangs before releasing them and turning to me with bright eyes. "That detective tried to say that, too."

"Okay, I'm sorry." I held up both hands. "Tell me what he said."

"He said that I latched onto Walker and tried to make him be Mitchell and that I must have killed him because—. Because—." Ernest bent forward slightly at the waist, as if he was preparing to sit, but there wasn't a chair in spitting distance.

"Here, come here." I pointed behind him to the end of the sofa not covered in crumpled pictures. Ernest watched me, wariness shining in his eyes.

"Come on, I'll sit, too." I stepped to the end of the sofa, careful not to nick a cereal bowl on the way while putting added distance between us.

I moved the stacks of pictures toward the center of the sofa, creating a mini barricade of printed memories between us. If he wanted to get at me fast, Ernest would have to risk damaging pieces of Mitchell's memory to do it. He watched me as I carefully constructed the barricade. When I had finished and lowered myself casually onto the edge of the sofa cushion, one foot planted firmly beneath me on the floor, Ernest eased over and took a seat.

"Tell me what else the detective said. Why does he think you did this?"

"He said I probably killed Walker because he wouldn't—. He wouldn't give me the time of day just like Mitchell wouldn't." The words finally out, Ernest deflated like a pricked balloon, curling in on himself, working his fingers back into his curls. He sobbed in six-year-old fashion, mouth wide and neck bobbing in a painful looking way. His already bloodshot eyes turned into beady red orbs. I looked around for tissues and found none.

I eased up from my post on the sofa and looked through the living room to the hallway. Both bathroom and kitchen were recessed into the rear of the apartment and I didn't want to risk burying myself further into the unit in case Ernest decided I was a threat, but his face was quickly becoming a snot factory of epic proportions, the neck of his tee shirt already soaked. I searched the room again and my eyes came to rest on the sheets laying in a heap on the floor. I didn't know why Ernest had covered his shrine to Mitchell and hoped fervently as I fingered one of the sheets up onto the sofa that I wasn't about to hand Ernest the equivalent of holy water with which to blow his nose. I balled the sheet, leaving a tail of fabric out, and stretched over the stacks of memorabilia in the center of the sofa to place the ball next to Ernest. Ernest snatched it before I had let go and I nearly knocked over the stacks of pictures taking my hand back. He pressed the fabric into his face and rubbed it back and forth before shoving it down between his legs, where it partially unraveled to the floor.

"But the detective was wrong about your brother, wasn't he? Mitchell did give you the time of day."

Ernest nodded vigorously and pursed his lips tight, tears

spilling down into channels on either side of his nose. He swiped the sheet up at his face, further unfurling the ball. The sheet draped like a blanket now across his knees.

"Mitchell always played with me and taught me stuff. We had projects together."

"What kind of projects?"

"All kinds." His face lit up and I could see remnants of the little boy on the wall. "We built model cars and ships, and made forts out behind the house. We had this little grove in the back and we tied sheets together and strung them up between the trees so we could hide from everybody and read our comics. Dad got so mad, but Mom just went to the Kmart and bought us a whole bunch more."

I glanced down at the sheet draping Ernest's knees, and swung my eyes around to the mound on the floor.

"After Mitchell went to high school, we didn't have so many projects anymore. He went to a new school and had new friends and we didn't do the fort so much anymore. But we were going to build a time capsule. But not a regular one, not one to find later but one the other kids on our block could find."

Ernest's eyes turned feverish as he spoke and I wondered if the doctor who'd stopped by had left behind extra doses of whatever he'd supposedly given Ernest the night before.

"A time capsule sounds pretty cool."

Ernest rubbed a dribble of snot into the side of his cheek and nodded vigorously. "We had all sorts of stuff to put into it. Mitchell let me make all the clues. But he never got to see them."

"I'm very sorry about your brother, Ernest."

I'm not sure if he heard me. "They were really good. I did really good."

"Making the clues?"

"Mmm-hmm. Really good. I'm good at that. Puzzles. Games."

"Is that how you found City Scavengers? Were you looking for a game to play?"

Ernest folded his hands in his lap and some of the shine left his eyes. "I saw an ad for it in the Money Saver."

"Was Walker the host the first time you went?"

Ernest's face stiffened and my quads tightened in response.

"I'm not accusing you, Ernest. I just want to understand."

"Yes."

"When did you first start helping him with the clues?"

"I don't remember the day exactly. I knew the clue, though. It was obvious. You'd have to be an idiot not to figure out he was pointing us to the Guardians at the bridge."

"Malik told me Walker didn't want your help at first."

Ernest blushed, patches of burnt umber spreading up through his temples and into his hairline.

"Walker thought I was trying to embarrass him. I just had to help him see I was there to help him be better. That it would all be better if we built the hunts together."

"Did you think if you could help Walker, it would be like you and your brother finishing the time capsule?"

Ernest's shoulders shook and anguish washed over his face. "I tried to tell him."

"Walker? What did you try to tell him?"

"I tried so hard. I tried so hard. He wouldn't listen. I swear, I tried so hard."

"Ernest?" I leaned forward, forcing myself into his periphery, but he lifted his head back and rolled it side to side. "What did you try to tell Walker?"

"Not Walker." He was sobbing again, mouth gaping open, squeaking as he ran out of air.

"Who? Who did you try to tell?"

I nearly missed the knock on the door for the wailing coming out of Ernest's mouth. I didn't miss the boom of the voice coming through the front door, though.

"POLICE. Ernest Brown, open the door. We have a warrant for your arrest."

Chapter Nineteen

Ernest didn't miss the knock or the voice. His head snapped forward and he sucked in a sharp breath that choked him. Phlegm gurgled in his throat and his eyes turned wild with fear. I pushed forward to stand at the same time Ernest threw himself toward me with his arms outstretched. He caught his foot in the sheet that was now twisted around one of his legs and knocked over the stacks of pictures between us, catching my wrist in his pale hand. I stepped back, directly into one of the milky cereal bowls, and yanked against him.

"Come here!" Ernest righted himself and gripped me harder. I spun to the left and buckled my knee, forcing him forward and into the coffee table. His shins rammed into the table and he loosened his grip with a yelp. I crab-walked backward until I cleared the edge of the sofa and flipped over onto all fours, using the spare seconds to scuttle closer to the front door. The baritone voice repeated its command from the other side of the door.

"No!" Ernest's desperate stage-whisper reached me from above. I looked up in time to see he had climbed over the sofa and was swinging his pudgy body across the top. I moved faster, but he landed with his torso on my lower legs and wrapped his arms around my knees.

"Don't do this, Ernest."

"Don't worry, I won't let them hurt you."

"Ernest, open the door." This time it was my voice doing the commanding.

"Hide with me. We'll get in the closet."

I flipped over, leaving Ernest's face dangerously close to my lovely lady spot. It did the trick. I could immediately see the look of frantic retreat in Ernest's face. The blush returned, engulfing his face and it was there that Detective Barnes and his cronies found us when they busted through the unanswered door.

To rub salt in the wound, Detective Barnes ordered one of his patrolman to handcuff Ernest before standing him up. Without hands free to brace himself, he was smashed face-first into the carpet in the V of my legs. Detective Barnes stared at me as he read Ernest his rights and the officer slapped on the bracelets. I met Barnes' stare and refused to flinch. The patrolman, sensing finally both the awkwardness of my position and the hostility emanating between the detective and me, yanked aggressively on Ernest to get him to his knees.

I pulled in my legs and raised up to a sitting position, slowly, in case Barnes got any cute ideas in his head about finding a reason to take me in, too. He read Ernest his rights and told two of the patrolmen to take him down to the station, then turned his back to me and stepped up to the far left wall of pictures. The remaining officer picked up a plastic box from the floor near the front door and disappeared toward the back of the apartment.

I got to my feet, watching Barnes' face. I saw annoyance, fatigue, and stubbornness. What I didn't see is what set me off. Not an ounce of surprise.

"You knew."

Barnes didn't bother to look at me. Instead, I watched his shoulders rise and fall, a shrug that felt like I'd been flipped the bird.

"How long have you known about Mitchell?" I asked his back.

"Not any longer than you. It was part of the background info we gathered on Ernest from the beginning."

"Godamnit, you know what I'm talking about. When did you find out about the resemblance between Mitchell and Walker?"

Barnes walked the length of the left wall and stopped in front of the center wall, blocking my view of his face. I walked around the sofa and stopped two feet from him. "When?"

"I don't think you're in a position to be demanding information from me. The better question is why are you over here, after I specifically told you to stay away from my case?"

"I'm not here about your case. And even if I were, you should have told me about his brother. How could you just let me walk in here? I thought your job was to protect the public, not send them into the lion's den."

"Now it's a lion's den?" Barnes turned around, a shitty grin uglifying the bottom half of his face. "Aren't you the one who was trying to convince me mere hours ago that your Ernest Brown is an angel?"

"What the hell is your problem? You couldn't know whether I knew about the resemblance. Don't you think telling me that would have given me the slightest pause?"

"When did it become your right to know the inner workings of a police investigation? I told you to stay out of it. You think I did that out of spite? Oh wait, no. Let me guess, out of laziness? Isn't that what you so eagerly accused me of earlier? You got no clue, Carter. This isn't a game. Maybe this will teach you something about listening."

I reeled back as if I'd been slapped. "Are you kidding—? Oh

my god." I took a step forward as Barnes diverted his attention back to the wall. He was staring too hard to be doing anything other than avoiding me. "You don't think he did it."

The patrolmen who'd escorted Ernest downstairs appeared in the apartment doorway. "Sir," said the shorter of the two. "Bakeman and Hines are taking the perp down to the station. You want us to help Torteri?" He looked toward the rear of the apartment.

"Yeah, you guys split up the bed, bath, and kitchen. Meet me back out here when you're done." Barnes pointed a thumb at me and jerked it toward the front door. "You're out."

The patrolmen hadn't moved from the entryway, and now flicked a synchronized look at Barnes. Barnes turned down the corners of his mouth and the patrolmen took a last look at me before joining their co-worker in the back of the unit.

I stepped closer to Barnes, who looked at me through hooded lids. "You don't buy it either, do you?"

"Either?" he echoed. "In the span of ten seconds you've gone from lion's den back to protecting your boy? You got a weird penchant for gingers, Carter?"

"Chew soap, Barnes. This guy just tried to protect me from you and your boys."

"We got a solid case, Carter."

"Admit it. If you really thought this guy killed Walker, you wouldn't have let me waltz in here."

"I didn't know you'd come running over here. I assumed you would follow my instructions and stay out of the way."

"Bullshit."

"Watch your mouth. We've got this clown's fingerprints on the victim and direct witness to multiple verbal altercations between him and the victim. Throw in a dead brother who's a ringer for our vic, and we've got plenty to run with."

"Back up a sec. His prints aren't on Walker's body, they're on a card. And saying he had 'multiple verbal altercations' is a bit of a stretch, no? Malik said they had one big blow-up and resolved it. They weren't exactly sparring."

"And that's why you and your brother are small-time, Carter. If you had dug beyond just talking to Malik, you'd know about the other altercations."

"Who's your supposed direct witness?"

Barnes blinked at me twice before answering. "Shawn Easton."

I pulled a confused face, and Barnes smirked. "You didn't think to ask him, did you?"

I couldn't answer him, because I didn't have an answer. I thought back to our first meeting with Malik at the laundromat. Shawn had said that Walker wasn't doing his fair share on setting out the clues and Malik was surprised that it was still an issue. Was it possible that Shawn also knew the fights were still going on, and was hiding that from Malik as well?

"What exactly did he say?"

Barnes lifted his arm and examined his wristwatch. "Time's up, Carter. I've got a warrant to execute. Do you think you can find your way down to your car, or do I need to send one of my men to show you the way?"

I held up two fingers in a peace sign, then crossed them and nodded at his wrist. "Here's hoping they get you a decent watch for your retirement."

Chapter Twenty

"Come on, come on, answer already."

I hit the End Call button on my phone and redialed Mrs. Brown's number. I sat outside the gate of the circular drive in front of Sundown Village. The guard shack was closed up tight and based on the unanswered ringing on the other end of the line, so was Mrs. Brown. When I'd left her earlier in the evening, she'd reluctantly handed over her phone number with the admonition not to call her between the hours of nine p.m. and eight a.m. I figured her son's second arrest in as many days would be an excusable reason to break the rule, but Mrs. Brown had probably hedged her bets by either turning off the ringer or finishing the last of the whiskey bottle.

I hung up and dialed again, trying one more time in vain. I willed the ringing of the phone to crack her consciousness. I didn't have contact info for anyone else who knew or could help Ernest, and from my earlier visit with Mrs. Brown, didn't think anyone else even existed.

I needed Mrs. Brown to tell Detective Barnes about Ernest's

relationship with Mitchell to convince him that it was doting and not jealous, but mostly I needed her to get Ernest a lawyer. He was a mess and I didn't trust Barnes and his merry crew not to try to throw every ounce of their strength into getting Ernest to admit to something he hadn't done.

I ended the call and tapped my phone against the steering wheel. I dialed Paul's number and the call went straight to voicemail. Damnit. I left a message with a Reader's Digest update, told him to call me right away, and hung up. I dropped the phone in my lap and played Eeny Meeny Miny Moe on two fingers. Johnny, Roman. PI or cop. I counted the last Moe, cringed, and dialed.

"Detective Stavros."

"Roman, I need your help."

"I'm finishing up at a scene. What's going on?"

I gave him the rundown on the last few hours with Ernest.

"Sam, I'm not going to force my way into a retirement home for you to hassle an old woman."

"I'm not hassling. I'm trying to help the woman protect her son. And besides, that's not what I'm asking. I need you to help me get Ernest some protection."

"And how do you expect me to do that?"

"Can't you talk to Barnes and get him to act rationally?"

Roman barked a laugh, and I pictured his head tilted back from his barrel chest.

"He is acting rationally, based on the evidence he has."

"You can't seriously agree with him. He's basing all this on super flimsy evidence, and he doesn't even have the story about Ernest's brother straight—."

"Stop, I don't need you to run your case down again. Look, Barnes may be stretching slightly, but he's also got a lot of good basis to go on. He's not coloring so far out of the lines that I have any room to try to convince him otherwise."

"But couldn't you ask him as a favor?"

"In return for what? I don't know this guy."

"But doesn't the brotherhood help the brotherhood?"

"You really gotta stop watching *Cops.*"

"I'm serious."

"Yes, we help each other time to time, but I've only met this guy a couple times."

"Roman, please. I know I'm asking a lot, but I need help."

Silence. I began to count to ten and got to six before I heard a sigh.

"Tell me why you're so convinced this guy is innocent."

I blinked up at the roof of my car and tried to compose my thoughts into something halfway articulate. And failed. "It's a feeling."

"Sam—"

"No, wait. It's a feeling based on a lot of small things. Listen, Ernest is not dumb, but he's not emotionally the sharpest knife in the drawer."

"Which only supports Barnes' view of things, Sam. He has a suspect who was unnaturally close to his dead brother and has now latched onto the brother's doppelganger. Said doppelganger doesn't respond to Ernest's brotherly advances and throws a fit. I've seen worse motives."

"Or, Ernest has such a love for the dead brother that transplanting that love onto someone else would only make him fight to protect the person. That's the other piece of it. Ernest thinks that Shawn had something to do with Walker's death, even if it's only the fact that he wasn't there when he should have been, and goes after him for it. In a way, he was avenging Walker. And tonight when the police showed up, Roman, I'm telling you. In some weird way, I think Ernest was trying to protect me. He wanted to hide me. He said he wouldn't let them hurt me."

"Sam, I'm not saying it can't cut both ways. But right now, it cuts equally. There's just not enough of an opening for me to question Barnes' approach. And I don't want to burn a bridge here unless I've got real good cause to do so. And our personal situation notwithstanding, I don't have that."

I rubbed my frustration into the top of the steering wheel. "I'm worried that the cops will try to trick him into saying something before his mom can get him a lawyer. Is our personal situation good enough to get you to change your mind about harassing a little old lady with me?"

I heard him swear softly, and I began to count to ten. I got to nine.

"Gimme the address."

ΩΩΩ

Three calls and fifty minutes later, Roman was able to rouse the security chief of Mrs. Brown's retirement home, but not Mrs. Brown herself. I'd busied myself with a trip to the liquor store, toting back a fifth of whiskey for the old lady and a 5th Avenue bar for me. I polished off the candy bar and then took my sugar-high for a walk back and forth across the parking pad in front of the retirement home gate. I called Paul again and got voicemail, skipped the message option and called Johnny. It rang five times and went to voicemail, and I briefly wondered if he was alone before aggressively telling myself not to care.

Roman showed up in his off-duty car, a worn but cared for sedan, and slowed to a stop next to me. I waved him to a spot next to my car before he could roll down his window. Less than a minute later, a silver haired man pulled up on the other side of the gate in a golf cart. He squeezed himself out of the cart and I took in his brown coat, vest, and pants. He reminded me of a 1980's country sheriff.

I walked to the middle of the gate and waited for Roman.

"Ma'am." The security guard nodded at me as he worked the gate mechanism and the doors slid back.

"Hi, I'm Sam Carter. I'm with Detective Stavros."

"He said as much on the phone. Name's Milo. Come on through. We'll take you on the cart."

Roman sauntered over and we piled into the cart while Milo and Roman introduced themselves.

We puttered faster than I would have believed a golf cart could carry us through the maze of the retirement village, and pulled up to Mrs. Brown's unit within a few minutes. On the drive, Milo spat twice as much as he talked, simply nodding a sleepy head at Roman's thank-you. He waved a hand at us after putting on the foot brake.

"Go on up. I'll wait for ya' here to make sure you get on back out okay."

Roman and I made our way up the path, whiskey bottle cradled in the crook of my arm. I was hoping to grease my return appearance and soften the blow of our midnight knock.

Roman took the honors of the actual knocking, but five minutes later with no response, we shared shoulder shrugs and headed back down to Milo. He was resting in the small cart, leaned back against the padded bench, arms crossed over his belly.

"Any luck?"

Roman shook his head.

"You try calling her?"

Roman and I looked at Milo like he was a dimwit. "She won't answer her cell. That was the whole point of dragging you out here."

Milo waved a hand in front of his face and scowled. "Aw, hell. I's assumed you was calling her landline."

Roman spoke with patience I didn't have enough money to buy. "You happen to have that number on you, Milo?"

Milo pulled a flip phone from the breast pocket of his vest and punched his way through the keypad. Either there were a lot of As and Bs at Sundown Village or Milo's thumb was a slow one.

"Here ya' go." Milo rattled off a number and Roman scribbled it into his notebook. I punched it into my cell and hit the Send button as I walked back up the path to the condo.

I heard ringing when I approached the front door, but Mrs. Brown didn't answer. I tried again twice more, the jangling coming loud and clear through the exterior wall.

"Damn, I wish I could sleep like that," Roman said.

"Amen. Melatonin and a hammer couldn't put me down that hard."

A faint smile crossed Roman's mouth as he nodded at the phone in my hand. "Again."

I hit the dial button on my cell once more and waited to hear the bleat of the phone from the other side of the wall. The second bleat cut off midway through and I heard a croaky voice come through my cell phone.

"Hello?" The grogginess in that single word made me consider the possibility that Mrs. Brown may be throwing Ambien into the bottom of her whiskey tumbler like worms in a tequila bottle.

Mrs. Brown may have been old and nearly catatonic with sleep, but she wasn't dull by any stretch, so I cut through the preamble. "Mrs. Brown, it's Sam Carter. I'm outside your front door. Can you let me in? Ernest has been arrested again and needs your help."

I waited through a short raspy pause while the wheels clicked in Mrs. Brown's head. "Let me get my robe."

Four minutes later, Mrs. Brown appeared at the door in said robe, hair set in tight rods I hadn't seen since the days of Ogilvy home perms, and slippers worn through at each pinkie toe.

"What is this?" Mrs. Brown took in Roman. She cast rheumy eyes over his thick body and I saw a flash of distrust cross her face.

"This is Detective Roman Stavros. He's my friend, and he came to help me get a hold of you."

Mrs. Brown looked doubtful, but stayed silent and cocked her head at me, listening.

"The Cleveland police brought a warrant to Ernest's apartment and arrested him for Walker's murder. I'm afraid if we don't get him a lawyer fast, the police will try to twist anything he says."

"They'll do that anyway." She cut her eyes at Roman, who simply smiled politely back at her.

"You can't just leave him there," I pleaded. "You said yourself he didn't kill Walker. Didn't you tell police he was with you the whole week?"

Mrs. Brown frowned at me, telling me with one look that she knew I was calling her a liar.

"You have to help your son with more than just a bogus story that you know they'll discredit later anyway. Do you really think he's guilty after all?"

"Absolutely not."

"I asked you earlier if you'd been on a hunt and you said no. Are you sure about that?"

"Yes, I'm sure. Why would I lie?"

"Did you ever meet Walker or see a picture of him?"

"No, why?"

"Mitchell and Walker could have been twins."

Mrs. Barnes looked at me sharply and the remaining dregs of sleep fell from her eyes. "What are you talking about?"

"I saw Mitchell's pictures at Ernest's apartment."

"The walls."

"You know about them?"

"I do."

"And you don't think it's disturbing?"

"Of course, I do," she snapped. Anger burst across her face, then resignation. She stepped back from the entryway and motioned us in. Roman put a hand at her elbow as we trekked through the front hall to the living room. He sat her in the chair I'd left her in earlier that night and we settled on the adjacent sofa.

"Mrs. Brown, Walker looks very much like an older Mitchell," I pressed on. "There's no getting around the fact that Ernest's fixation on the hunts is tied up in his relationship with his brother."

"Ernest would never hurt Mitchell or whatever surrogate you think Walker may have been to him."

"I agree with you, Mrs. Brown. That's why you need to explain that to the police. And get Ernest a lawyer who can back you up and fight for Ernest."

Mrs. Brown stared at the carpet, seemingly seeking answers within the Berber.

Roman brought her back to us. "Mrs. Brown, did Ernest ever talk to you about Walker's life in any kind of detail?"

"I don't think so, though really I can't say I would have paid much attention."

"Do you remember Ernest saying anything about Walker having enemies, or if anyone was a nuisance to Walker during the hunts?"

Mrs. Brown gave Roman a wry smile. "You mean besides my son?"

Roman acknowledged her attempt at humor with a sympathetic nod. "Did he mention anyone else giving Walker a hard time? Any disagreements, any other personal detail about any strife in his life?"

"No, not that I can think of."

"What about other people in his life? Did he tell you he thought any of his friends or family were in danger?"

"Detective, my son doesn't have anyone else in his life."

"Sam told me that just before the police showed up tonight, Ernest told her he'd been trying to warn someone. Sam thought he meant Walker, but he said it wasn't Walker. We're trying to figure out who Ernest would have been warning and what about."

Mrs. Brown began shaking her head before Roman finished, but suddenly stopped. She looked thoughtfully at me. "What did he say? Do you remember his exact words?"

I closed my eyes and thought. "He said he tried so hard and whoever he was warning wouldn't listen. He kept repeating how hard he tried."

Mrs. Brown's eyes glistened and she swept her tongue across her trembling bottom lip. "Mitchell," she whispered.

Roman and I exchanged a look, and he nodded at me to take the lead.

"What do you mean?"

Mrs. Brown rolled both lips inward and wiped the back of one spotted hand across them. "He was talking about Mitchell. Before he drowned in that pool."

"Wait, what? I thought Mitchell died from the flu. He choked."

"He did." Mrs. Brown swiped both hands across her face. "He choked in the community pool."

Gee-zuss. The pool Ernest destroyed. He killed the pool that killed his brother.

"Mrs. Brown, I'm so sorry to ask, but can you start from the beginning and tell us how Mitchell died exactly?"

Mrs. Brown looked at Roman, then me, then at the cold fireplace. "Mitchell had been sick from something that had been going around. He never missed a swim practice, even informal ones at the public pool, and he went as usual, despite my saying he shouldn't. He wasn't so much stubborn as he was disciplined and I knew he wouldn't be talked out of it. The best they could tell, he threw up in the water and couldn't catch his breath. The life guard spotted him and got him out of the pool and Mitchell laid down on one of the chaise lounges. He told the life guard he was fine and wanted to rest for a while, then he would pack up and go home. The life guard let him be, and then Mitchell threw up again and choked on his own vomit."

"And the lifeguard didn't see that?"

"A little girl on the other side of the pool had climbed over the toddler barrier into the deep end and the life guard was helping to get her out and calm down the mother. It all happened within just a few minutes. The doctors told us later that Mitchell had been severely dehydrated and likely didn't have the strength to cough up the vomit or even motion for help."

"Was Ernest there that day?" I asked.

"No. He wanted to go, but he had a test the next day and his father and I made him stay home to study. But Ernest had a bee in his bonnet that day and wouldn't let up, telling Mitchell over and over he should stay home, that it was dangerous. He was beside himself that Mitchell was going to get hurt."

"Was he usually that dramatic?"

"No. At the time I remember thinking he was just pouting because we wouldn't let him go watch Mitchell and he was using Mitchell's illness as an excuse to keep him at home, but later we couldn't help but wonder—." Mrs. Brown stopped and draped her hand across her eyes. "My husband and I were never hippie dippy or very religious, but we both wondered if there wasn't some unexplainable reason why Ernest was so adamant that day. How could he have possibly known, but it's like somehow he felt something bad was coming."

I turned my head and fought to control the tears threatening my eyelids. I couldn't imagine the horror a helpless Mitchell must have felt, to be so near help and so far from it. What got to me, though, was the thought of Mrs. Brown having to relive that in her head for the last two decades. And of Ernest thinking he could have saved his brother.

What I couldn't reconcile in my head was the thought of Ernest killing a man who reminded him of his brother. Wouldn't he want to save Walker, not kill him? Could Ernest have somehow reached out to Walker trying to connect, and Walker shut him down? In some way, had Walker acted so unlike Mitchell that it woke Ernest up to the fact that the two men were completely different and Ernest would never get what he was after from the relationship? Could that have sent him into a tailspin?

Mrs. Brown's stare stayed trained on the fireplace, but her gaze was obviously inward. She'd placed her fingertips over her eyes, patting first one then the other. Roman remained stoic, his gaze on Mrs. Brown soft but steady. He turned to look at me and raised his eyebrow, and I took in a slow breath to steady myself.

"Mrs. Brown." Roman shifted forward in his seat. "Sam believes strongly that Ernest didn't harm Walker. And I want to help her, regardless of whether that's true. But part of helping may be learning a truth we don't want to learn."

Roman paused and turned his soft look on me. I shrugged back in acknowledgment and swallowed the growing knot in my throat. Mrs. Barnes leveled her gaze on Roman.

"Detective, I've spent a lifetime accepting truths I haven't wanted to see. About Ernest, my husband, and many others in my life. I'm not trying to cover up anything Ernest has done. For all his faults, I simply cannot see Ernest hurting anyone or anything tied to Mitchell's memory."

Roman opened his mouth and Mrs. Brown raised a hand to stop him. Her voice was wet when she spoke. "But what I can and cannot see does not determine whether something is fact or fiction. Ernest was here the night Walker died, but he left right after supper. I assumed he was going back to his apartment, and I do believe in my heart that he did, but the truth is I don't know for sure."

During Mrs. Brown's speech, she'd leaned forward inch by inch in her chair, but now sank back into the cushion as the last words left her mouth.

"Mrs. Brown, do you have a lawyer you can call?"

She looked longingly at the whiskey bottle I'd set on the table between us. "I'll call now."

Chapter Twenty-One

I bid Roman adieu in the parking lot of the retirement home. I thanked him profusely and briefly considered giving him a hug, but Milo sat propped gut to wheel in the golf cart, watching us like a housewife glued to a telenovela. I opted for a firm handshake and several thank-you's before turning my car in the direction of downtown. Twenty minutes later, I rolled into the parking lot of the police station and parked against the fence corralling a line of cop cars that looked like dominoes in the dead-of-the-night sky.

I found my way to the public entrance and opened double doors into a brightly lit hallway. Benches lined either side of the hall and ended at a glassed-in booth, in which sat an officer looking oddly awake for the advanced time of night. Both his shave and shirt looked fresh and I surreptitiously looked down at my disheveled outfit. I swore I could smell the faint reek of old milk from where my sock had soaked up the detritus in Ernest's cereal bowl. It felt like three days ago, but it had been mere hours.

The officer looked up at me from behind the glass and gave me a chipper smile set against cautious eyes. "Ma'am?"

"Hi, I'm looking for Detective Barnes. Is he in?"

"Name?"

"Sam Carter, I'm here about the Walker Atwill case."

"Is he expecting you?"

I blew out a sigh. "Who knows at this point."

"Ma'am?"

"I don't think he'll be surprised to see me, but no, he's not expecting me."

The officer dropped the chipper, and I watched as his eyes assessed me. I imagined he was gauging whether he had a mental health case in front him, or just an overly-tired smart-ass.

"Is he here? I'm not a nut job. I'm positive he's got a lot of other names for me, but he'll at least vouch for that, I'm sure."

The officer laughed at that and picked up the phone on his end. He pointed the receiver down the line of benches toward the front door. "Have a seat at the far end, please."

I gave him a weak thumbs-up and planted my hiney where I was told. The last of my adrenaline had faded away with Mrs. Brown's commitment to call in reinforcements for Ernest, and I melted my back into the cement wall that the bench was bolted into.

Forty-five minutes later, I found myself laying with my back up against the cement, legs tucked into the bench, and Barnes was shouting my name. I ran a pinkie across the dot of drool pooled in the corner of my mouth as I pushed up into a sitting position. Barnes stepped back, but stood towering over me, arms crossed. I held up my palm in an effort to convey he was in my personal space, but he remained unmoved. I turned my palm around and flipped him off, raising my head to stare straight up at him. He surprised me by uncrossing his arms and holding up both palms. He backed up two paces and took a seat on the opposite bench. I pinched the corners of my eyes and straightened my back.

"What are you doing here, Carter?"

"Mrs. Brown is getting a lawyer for Ernest."

"And you came here to tell me that?"

"I came here to try one more time to get you to see things from my perspective."

"I do. But I get paid to see them from all possible angles." Hardness returned to Barnes' voice, and I took my turn to show my palms. I didn't have the energy for the fight.

"Look, I know I don't have any room to ask for favors here." Barnes snorted.

"For the sake of justice, can you just consider the idea that Ernest is innocent? You say you get paid to look at every angle, so why not try one more?"

Barnes looked at me thoughtfully. "Do you know something you haven't shared?"

"I wish I did. I really do. I don't know where else to dig, and I can't even fully explain why I don't think Ernest could have done this, but I don't. There has to be more."

Barnes rolled his forearms onto his quads and hung his head. He ran his hands across the crown of his head and cocked it back up, looking at me from under bushy brows gone haywire from the length of the day. He squinted at me, suspicion strong in his eyes.

"You sure you're not telling me something, Carter? Maybe you know something, but you don't want it coming from you?"

It was my turn for suspicion. "What are you getting at?"

"When was the last time you talked to Mary Abrams?"

"Walker's ex-wife?"

"When?"

I frowned and thought back. The last day had felt like a week and it took me a minute to place our last conversation.

"Don't hedge. When?"

"Shit, Barnes, I'm not hedging. I'm thinking. Um, day before yesterday? No, yesterday."

"What'd you two talk about?"

"I had called her house earlier that day, but she wasn't there. When she called me later, I thought she was returning my message, but she said she hadn't gotten it yet. She was up in Michigan visiting her son Scott."

"Why did she call you?"

"She wanted to see if you'd made any progress with the case. Scott's having a hard time with Walker's death and she thinks getting some closure on who killed his dad might help."

"Did she say she was with Scott?"

"Yes, at his school."

"Did you talk to Scott?"

"What? No. I think she said he was in class when we were talking. I remember thinking it odd that Mary said he was devastated but he was okay enough to go to class."

Barnes sat silent, staring at me.

"What?"

Barnes searched my eyes. I waited. Silence. I began to count to ten. When I got to twenty, I asked again.

"What's going on, Barnes?"

Barnes stared at me, unblinking as he spoke. "Mary Abrams confessed three hours ago to killing Walker."

I moved my mouth, trying to form several words before only one came out. "Gee-zuss."

Barnes hadn't blinked. He watched my face as I tried to process. "Why?"

"She said she never got over her love for Walker and she tried to reconcile with him, but he turned her down."

"Fine, don't tell me."

"I'm not bullshitting you. But I do think Mary's bullshitting me."

"Why would she bullshit you on the reason? Unrequited love isn't exactly a sentence-reducer for murder, is it?"

"The reason it's bullshit is because her entire admission is bullshit."

I rested my head back against the concrete. "You're gonna need to run this past me from the beginning."

"First, tell me where she really was when you two talked."

I lifted my head back up, feeling suddenly like a suspect myself. "She said she was at Scott's school. How the hell am I supposed to know if that was true or not?"

"Did you hear any background noise? People, sirens, TVs, music, wind, anything?"

I thought back. "No, she could have been anywhere, I guess. I don't remember any background noise at all."

"Could she have been in a car?"

I shook my head. "No, there wasn't that hollow sound or rushing sound that you hear some—. Wait, why are you asking me where she was?"

Barnes didn't answer. He picked up his staring game again. I looked at the uniformed officer in the glass box and down the hallway beyond before looking back at Barnes.

"She's not here, is she?" I asked.

Barnes stared.

"Where did she make this alleged admission?" I asked.

"She called us."

"Us?"

"The police. She called a neighboring station and they transferred her here. She asked for me directly, but I was serving the warrant at Ernest's. They sent to her my voicemail and she left a message saying she killed Walker."

"Holy bells. Did she leave a number? Did you call back? Can you capture numbers going into your voicemail?"

"I'd tell you for the thousandth time that I know how to do my job, but I'm starting to get the impression you can't help yourself with the obvious questions."

I flashed him the bird again, but couldn't stop a small smile along with it. "Took you long enough. Some detective."

Barnes' cheek quirked upward, but his mouth remained rigid.

"The number she called from is a burner phone." So that's how Barnes knew she'd called me. He had a call log.

"When I called her house, her husband said she forgot her

phone when she went to see Scott and picked up a prepaid."

"Forgot?"

"That's what he says. Any chance he's in on this with her?"

"Hard for us to know until we talk to her."

"Did she say on the voicemail what her end-game is? Is she going to turn herself in?"

"She said she'd call me again to talk about what she referred to as 'next steps'. She didn't say when that might be, but something in her voice tells me it'll be soon."

"What makes you say that?"

Barnes pressed his shoulders into the cement and crossed his arms under his chest. "She sounded manic. It was a short message, so it's hard to tell, but I've heard a lot of people as they ramp up into mania and something in her voice sounded familiar."

"She did sound a bit all over the place when I talked to her. I chalked it up to distress over Scott's reaction, and thinking maybe there was a twinge of feeling left for Walker." I waved my hand back and forth. "Not to the degree that she sounded like she was all bunny-in-a-pot over him or anything. Just very sad."

Barnes continued to eye me.

"What now?"

"You could be helpful."

I cupped a palm around my ear and echoed his words back at him. "I'm sorry, in normal English, I think you just said that you need my help."

"Don't push it. I could still easily haul you behind that door for impeding a police investigation."

"And I'd be back out on the street before you could say the words 'early retirement'. What do you want?"

"Call Mary."

"Done."

"There's more. You need to convince her to meet you. In Cleveland, if you can. Or at her house."

"Why not at the school?"

"I doubt she was ever at the school. We pulled the records on that burner phone and it never once pinged against any tower anywhere near that school."

"Where did it ping?"

"Once about thirty miles from her house, and twice on the West side."

"Of Cleveland?"

Barnes nodded.

"When were those?"

"This morning."

"Do you think her husband is lying for her? Didn't he alibi her for the night Walker died?"

"He did, but so did twenty pictures from the charity event they went to together. We've got her on film until eleven p.m. the night of the murder, and her husband says they went home together, made love - his words, not mine - and were in bed by two. If she left him happy and asleep, made the trip to Cleveland in say two hours and change, she still doesn't quite make the window. M.E. says time of death was somewhere between two and four that morning."

"But those windows can be off right? That's a tight margin."

"I'll give you that. She could have made it, but that means the husband is lying. Or at least overstating his lovemaking prowess."

"Because that never happens."

Barnes cocked an eyebrow at me. I ignored him and combed my hair up into a ponytail, wound it into a bun, and let it fall loose again. Things were not making sense and my tired brain was signaling defeat.

"How am I going to get her to meet me?"

Barnes shrugged his shoulders. "You want to do this PI thing. You tell me."

I blew out a sigh. "How about I just tell her that Ernest has been arrested and I knew she'd want to know right away. Then I'll punt from there."

"Good as anything I got."

"When do you want me to call her?"

Two officers pushed through the front door, a duffel bag slung over each arm, both nodding at Barnes as they passed by and started to chat up the officer in the glass box. Barnes looked down at his watch and back up at me. His cheek did that muscle quirk thing again.

I rubbed my eyes and rolled my shoulders back. "Fine. You got a quiet place where we can do this?"

ΩΩΩ

"This is my fault," Paul said.

"I'm proud of you for holding your own with Barnes. He sounds like a Grade-A dick." Johnny gave me a sympathetic smile and rubbed a hand across my neck. Paul must have been more upset than I thought because he didn't so much as bat an eye at the neck rubbing.

The three of us stood in between Paul's and my office desks, Paul leaning against his and Johnny and I holding up mine.

I shrugged at Johnny. "He is, but I can see where I'm probably encouraging the dickiness."

"I can attest to your ability to encourage."

"I should have been holding your hand more on this," Paul said, ignoring our pre-pubescent chatter. "I didn't realize how far you'd run with Ernest."

"No, that's my fault," I said. "I should have called you before I went to see Mrs. Brown."

Paul scratched the stubble on his chin and frowned. I looked around at the three of us and took in our mutually disheveled states. By the time I'd called Mary, left her unanswered phone a voicemail, and finished with Barnes, both Paul and Johnny had returned my earlier messages. We'd rendezvoused back at the office, and we were all showing signs of a near twenty-four-hour day uninterrupted by sleep.

"What's Barnes' plan from here?" Paul asked. "You gonna wait for Mary to call back?"

"For a little while, yeah. If she hasn't called back in the next few hours, I'll call her again."

"How are you going to get her to meet you?"

"I'll tell her Ernest was arrested and go on like I don't know about her admission, then see if she'll cop to it. If she does, I'll tell her I don't believe her and want to talk in person to help her. If she doesn't cop to it, I'll tell her there's more about Ernest she needs to know and that her safety might be in jeopardy."

Johnny shook his head. "I don't like it."

"I don't either," Paul said.

"There are too many ways for her to say no to meeting," Johnny said. "But more than that, what if she says yes? How is Barnes going to protect you?"

"If Mary's admission is B.S., I may not need protection. If she's lying about killing Walker, I doubt she's going to come after me."

"But what if she's not?" Johnny shook his head again. "And even if she is lying, she's lying for a reason. My guess is she's covering for someone."

"What if she's covering for Ernest?" Paul asked.

We all chewed on that.

"The big question is why?" Johnny asked. "Did you guys find any link between Mary and Ernest in your background research?"

"No," I said. "Not that we were looking for one. But I think it's worth looking at again. When I talked to her at Walker's funeral, Mary looked past me toward the gravesite at one point and turned completely pale. When I looked back, she was staring at Ernest. I asked her if she knew him and she just said she couldn't be there anymore and took off."

Paul threw his hands in the air. "Shit, Sam, that kind of information would have been helpful to know earlier."

"Paul—," Johnny started, but Paul cut him off.

"She has to learn."

"You don't have to swear at her to teach her."

"I'm not trying to get into her pants. I can use whatever language I want."

Johnny leaned his weight off the desk and stood straight up. Paul remained butt to desk, folded his arms across his chest and lifted his chin at Johnny.

"You guys," I jumped in. "I honestly didn't make any connection at the time, but I get what you're saying. Let's just focus on where we go from here. We don't have time to get sidetracked with this right now."

Paul pointed a finger at me, eyes still on Johnny. "Start digging. See if you can find any connection between Ernest and Mary. As soon as we hit a more humane hour, we'll start working the phones to see if any friends or family know of any connection."

"On it," I said in what I hoped was a confident tone.

"Did you circle back to Shawn to find out why he told Barnes that Ernest and Walker were fighting more than he let on to us?"

"No, it was too late to call him last night, but he's at Vinnie's. I'll run by there later."

"Who'd you get the info from on Ernest's brother's death?" Johnny asked. "I say we look back and see if Walker could have had any connection to either of the Brown brothers."

I couldn't hide my surprise. "You think Mary could have known the Browns?"

"No, but what if Walker had something to do with Mitchell's death and Ernest used Mary to satisfy a revenge plot?"

"Negative. Mitchell Brown died because he had the flu and choked on his own vomit during swim practice."

"Do we know for sure it was the flu?" Johnny countered.

"I'll get with Malik to find out who shared the case info with him. See if I can talk to someone," Paul said.

"That was twenty-some years ago," I said. "You think

anyone's still around?"

"Worth a shot."

"What do you want me to do?" Johnny asked Paul.

Paul considered him for a minute before responding. "Why don't you go home and get some sleep."

"Come on, man. Don't shut me out on this 'cause your pissed."

"I'm not shutting you out. But one of us has to get some sleep. I'll take first shift watching this one," Paul pointed at me. "You grab some shut-eye and you can relieve me in a few hours."

"Hey, wait a minute," I said. "What do you mean by 'watching' me? I may have flubbed a bit here, but don't I get credit for all the other progress I've made?"

"You're doing fine." Paul shook his head at me. "I'm just pissed at myself for letting you too far out on the leash."

"The dog analogies aren't helping."

"Let's resume the pissing contest later." Paul pushed off the desk and circled around to his computer. Johnny shot us a peace sign as he walked past our desks and out through the front door. I headed for the kitchen to put on a pot of coffee and by the time I returned, Paul was buried in his keyboard. I made it a full twenty minutes before I cried uncle and headed up to the storage room to take a snoozer on the futon.

Chapter Twenty-Two

When I woke up three hours later, I came downstairs to find Paul's chair empty and a note on my desk saying he'd gone out to grab breakfast. He'd gotten the name of a responding officer involved in Mitchell Brown's death who was still on the job, and was waiting a return call.

I reheated a cup of coffee from my middle of the night pot, jumped online, and two hours later I'd exhausted any accessible connection between Walker and Ernest, and Ernest and Mary. I hoped Paul would have better luck with the cop he was waiting on, or we were going to be near out of options. I checked my watch and decided it was late enough to bother Barnes.

"Any word from Mary?" I asked when he answered.

"I was about to ring you with the same question."

"You ready for me to call her again?"

"Let's give it another hour. Y guys are working on a possible connection between her and Ernest."

"Paul and I have been over here trying to do the same. Whaddaya got?"

"Not sure yet, but it looks like Ernest and Walker went to the same college for a short period of time."

"How did you find that? I came up with zilch in my search."

"Because neither of them were actually students. They both took a summer course offering that was open to the public. You didn't have to be a registered student, just pay the fee and it was first come, first serve."

"What was the course?"

"Photography."

I frowned and reached for the lid of the Red Vine tub on my desk. "When was this?"

"Last year." I heard paper rustling on Barnes' end.

"Before or after Walker started working for City Scavengers?"

"Before."

"Huh. Did you ever ask Ernest when he met Walker?"

"I'm corroborating that with the other detective working the case. I haven't asked specifically. I take it you haven't either."

"Nuh-uh. Ernest told me he found about the scavenger service in the Money Saver and I just assumed that's where he first laid eyes on Walker."

"What are the odds of that coincidence?"

"I've got a better chance at hitting the Powerball."

"Starting to come around to my side on Ernest being involved?"

I laughed. "See how you said 'involved', not 'guilty'? You're not so sure either."

"Hard when you've got another woman admitting to the crime."

"Do you think they could have been in on it together?"

"It's possible, and if we confirm that Ernest knew Walker before meeting at the hunt, then I'd say it's highly likely, but I've got one huge problem."

"Are you going to share?"

"It doesn't go farther than you and me."

"I can't tell Paul?"

Silence. I heard Barnes make a sucking sound with his teeth

and pictured him thinking it through.

"Fine, yeah, but tell him to keep his trap shut."

"Deal."

"The autopsy results show Walker died from blunt force trauma to the head."

"So?"

"So, we have two problems. The first is we don't typically see bashing someone's head in as a premeditating murderer's weapon of choice."

"Maybe it's not common, but neither Mary or Ernest strike me as violent. Maybe their squeamish factor is too high for guns or knives. Maybe a baseball bat is as far as they were willing to go."

"That leads us to the second problem. Walker wasn't hit with a bat, or likely anything at all."

"Come again?"

"M.E. says Walker likely hit his head on the cement wall bordering the planter."

That stopped me. "Like he could have fallen into the planter?"

"No. The damage was too aggressive. Someone helped him – shoved him or threw him down is more likely."

"Who plans to murder someone with a push?"

"My point exactly." I heard shouting in the background and Barnes told me to hang on. He must have put the phone down because the background noise became a distant muffle. I took the opportunity to shove a Red Vine in my mouth and reach for another.

By the time Barnes came back, I'd polished off enough Vines to count as a complete breakfast.

"Carter, I gotta run."

"What do you want me to do if Mary calls me back?"

"Still try to get her to meet you and call me right away. I doubt she's dangerous to you, but we'll get you covered anyway."

"Are you going to let Ernest go?" But Barnes was already gone.

ΩΩΩ

I looked up from my computer at the sound of the agency's front door opening and was surprised to see Johnny crossing the threshold instead of Paul. My surprise must have showed.

"I miss the days when you looked like the happiest girl on Earth to see me. Can we go back to that?"

"You couldn't pay me to go back to high school."

Johnny tilted his head at me in mock hurt. "I was talking about a few months ago."

"That may have been more gas than happiness."

"Liar." He stopped at my desk, leaned across it, and planted a kiss on my forehead. My chi-chi shrieked in excitement and my ass cheeks clenched in fear of Paul walking through the door and catching us.

I needn't have worried. Johnny straightened and headed for the conference table we'd set up in the dining room area adjacent to our desks. He unpacked a laptop and notebook from his bag, and dumped a couple wax paper-wrapped squares from a plastic sack.

"Breakfast sandwich?" He held out a square.

I shook my head and went back to my own laptop. "No thanks. I just ate approximately three pounds of licorice."

"Your pancreas must hate you."

"Paul would have made a crack about my pants, not my pancreas."

"That's because Paul's not trying to get into said pants. As he pointed out last night."

I cocked my head at him.

"Hey bitter, tell me you're not letting Paul get to you."

Johnny unwrapped a sandwich and tucked in, shaking his head at me. I watched him chew, but realized after he'd swallowed the first bite and taken a second, he didn't plan on answering me.

Paul chose that moment to return, and I wasted no time in

catching him and Johnny up on my call with Barnes.

"The cause of death bothers me," Paul said.

"What if whoever killed Walker didn't mean to actually kill him?" I asked. "Is it conceivable they just wanted to threaten him or scare him?"

"It's possible. But that makes me question even more why Mary would cover for Ernest."

"Or whoever did it."

Paul cut me a look. "You're still on the Ernest didn't-do-it kick?"

"I'll admit, knowing Walker wasn't bludgeoned to death changes things a little. I could maybe see Ernest unintentionally killing him, but I still don't understand why he would want to threaten or scare Walker, either."

"Let's not forget he gave Shawn a nice hearty tackle in the cemetery," Johnny chimed in.

"Because he was upset about losing Walker," I retorted.

"According to your Sally Struthers online psychology degree?"

"Hey!" I shook my finger at him. "You're starting to sound like Paul. I can only handle one dick at a time."

"I'm out," Paul said, walking through the dining room toward the kitchen. "Sam, call me after you talk to Shawn."

Crikey, I'd forgotten about that. I grabbed my purse and headed for the door before Paul could yank out my demerits book.

"Hey, Sam?"

I turned back, hand on the door knob, and looked at Johnny. "Yeah?"

"No kiss good-bye?"

Chapter Twenty-Three

On my way to see Shawn, I made a pit stop at the Thai joint next to Dudek's and found two sixty-somethings dining on an early lunch. When I asked the woman behind the counter the name of the young man who'd been working two nights prior, she looked at me cautiously until I told her I wanted to compliment him on his service. Her pursed mouth turned up at the corners and she hollered for another woman who came out of the kitchen and told me I was talking about her grandson, Lee. I asked when Lee was working next and hinted at an unspecified tip I'd like to bring to him directly, and was rewarded with a blue slip of stained receipt paper with Lee's scheduled scribbled upon it. I squinted at the handwriting, confirmed with the woman that Lee was working the closing shift the next night, and bought two spring rolls in gratitude.

Checking Lee off my short list, I turned my attention to Shawn and made tracks over to Vinnie's condo. A call to Vinnie on the way over told me that I'd find Shawn exactly where he'd been hibernating in Vinnie's living room, glued to one ninja combat video game after another, eating Fruit Loops faster than the

Toucan could sniff them out. I rapped on the door, but got no answer. Peering in the slit between the curtains netted me nothing but glimpse of a darkened front room. The condo was walled on three sides and didn't get a ton of daylight. No lights shone overhead or from the adjacent hall.

I dug through my bag for my cell phone and dialed Shawn's cell number. It rang five times before allowing me the privilege of leaving a message, which I did. I took one last peek between the curtains before heading back to my car. I fired up the Jetta and motored the few miles over to Dazio's. Pushing through the glass door, my nose was assaulted by the smell of yeast at the same time my ears were assaulted by the whine of Jade, Vinnie's new assistant manager.

I waved at the young man covering the front register and walked through the swinging counter gate to investigate the cause of the whining. I was met with the sight of a twelve-pound commercial bag of yeast split wide open across the restaurant floor. Vinnie and Jade stood on either side of the mess, feet split in a V, as if they were in a face-off. A very yeasty face-off. Jade's face was crimson and her mouth was working on a decent impression of Mr. Bill. Vinnie's face was a mix of surprise, anger, and something else.

"Hey, kids," I stopped a few feet shy of the sour smelling mess. "What's new?"

Vinnie turned his look to me and I rewarded him with a shit-eating grin. Maybe this was why Paul was an asshole to me. Because I deserved it. Or, maybe it was a trickle-down effect. The oldest sibling harasses the middle one, and I turn around and take it out on the youngest in line.

"I'm so, so sorry," Jade stammered. Her blue eyes reflected purple against her red skin and made her look other-worldly. I stole a look back at Vinnie and belatedly realized what the "something" was that I saw mixed in with the anger. Lust. Well, what do you know. I quickly switched from smart-ass mode to protective big sister mode.

"Hey, Vin? I know you're in a bit of a spot here, but can I talk to you in the office right quick?"

Vinnie's eyes bulged at me in response, but I stepped across the mess and pushed him toward the back of the restaurant. I looked back as we rounded the corner into the office and saw Jade's gaze following us, blue eyes looking morose.

"Sam, I don't have time to talk. We got three huge orders for the Panetieri's spring fling, the mixer's down, and Jade just busted the last bag of yeast."

"We passed six racks of dough already resting back there and I know you. You over-plan these things, so relax. Besides, I just need to know where Shawn is."

"At my place. I told you."

"Nope. I was just there."

"Did you ring the bell?"

"No, Einstein, I stood out front and prayed real hard that he'd hear me breathing on the stoop."

"Alright, you ain't gotta be a dick about it."

There was an awful lot of dick going around today. Either our little crew had started cycling together and PMS was hitting us, or we were just a bunch of assholes. I had zero cramps and feared the worst.

"He's not answering his phone. I called him while I was at your place and again on the way here. Did he tell you he was going anywhere today? Is he hosting a hunt tonight?"

"Not that I know of. He said Malik gave him as much time off as he wanted. He thought he'd take off the weekend and go from there."

"Has he been sleeping during the day? Maybe he's holed up in the guest room and his phone's on vibrate?"

"Nah, he's been sleeping on the sofa. Said he'd prefer not to make a mess in more than one room and he's been glued to the TV with his video games."

"Huh."

"Why you trying to find him?"

"He told our client some info that doesn't jive with what he told me. We're kind of at a crossroads with this case and pulling at every loose string."

"Well, I don't know what the info is, but I can tell you to be careful how much weight you put into whatever he tells you. I don't know that I'd trust him to tell me the right time off his watch."

I leaned back against the door jamb. "Why do you say that?"

"Not any one thing. He just doesn't make sense a lot of the time. He talks in pieces. Remember Jeremy Lakin? That kid across the street from us growing up?"

"How could I forget? He was so focused on getting high on anything he could, he nearly burned up our backyard trying to light the dandelion patch."

"That's him. You remember how he talked?"

"Like his brain stopped short every four words and when it started up again, his mouth was on the tenth word?"

"That's how Shawn sounds."

"Maybe his concussion is worse than the doctors thought."

"I don't know, but between that and his crying every other hour, I don't know what to think."

"Why haven't you called me?"

"Because I made a big deal about trying to help someone and thought I'd look stupid telling you I couldn't hack it." He reached behind him and unpeeled a sticky note from the desk. "I was going to call this trauma survivor's helpline before I went home tonight. See if they could give me some tips for talking to him."

My heart pulled in my chest. "Aw, Vin."

Vinnie blushed and reached back again, taking his time laying the sticky note back in its place.

"Look," I said. "Why don't you still call the hotline, and I'll text you when I find Shawn. Maybe he just went home for fresh clothes or something."

"Cool."

I turned to go, then turned back. "Oh, and Vin. What's the deal with you and Jade?"

Vinnie shot his head up. "What are you talking about?"

"Is her crush on you as strong as yours is on her?"

"She doesn't have a crush on me." I'm sure he meant to sound defensive, but it came out as a question. A hopeful one.

"Vin, don't play with me. You're the master of spotting the come-on. That girl has eyes on you, and from what I could see out there, you like it."

"Nah."

"You know Paul's not going to like you doinking the help. I can't say I'm crazy about the idea either."

"Jade's not the kind of girl you doink."

"Holy bells," I said, laughing. "You have it bad."

Vinnie pushed me backward through the doorway. "Don't tell Paul jack. Nothing's going on."

"Okay, but make sure it stays that way."

"Yes, mother."

"Oh, please. If Mom saw this, she'd have you outfitted for a wedding tux by nightfall."

ΩΩΩ

After contributing five minutes of dustpan services to Vinnie's and Jade's efforts, I pilfered a fountain soda for the road and left them to finish yeast clean-up. When I hit the front door and looked back, Jade was pulling moony eyes at Vinnie, and he was studiously avoiding her gaze.

I got in my car and dialed Malik with one hand while I shoved a bit of spring roll in my mouth with the other. I was still chewing when Malik's voicemail picked up. What was the point of having a cell phone if no one ever answered the damned thing? We may as well have gone back to rotary.

I waited through Malik's thorough outgoing message, then the seven instruction prompts including my option to fax him, and finally got the electronic go ahead to leave my message. I let him know I was on the lookout for Shawn and needed his home address. I assumed Malik had personnel files with that sort of info, even for his tiny three-man operation.

My cell beeped through with another call as I finished my message, and I peeked down to see Paul's number.

"What's shakin'?" I answered.

"Where you at?"

"Waiting for Malik to call me back with an address for Shawn. He bailed out of Vinnie's with no note."

"Okay, let me know what he says. Wanted to let you know the cop who worked the scene of Mitchell Brown's death called back."

"And?"

"Guy says everything seemed straight forward, no sign of foul play. Lots of witnesses who saw Mitchell throw up in the pool and get dragged out by the lifeguard. Those same witnesses were focused on the little girl who climbed out of the kiddie pool while Mitchell asphyxiated on the other side of the pool deck."

"Did he say whether there was any connection between Walker and Mitchell?"

"Not a one. The cop pulled the files to refresh himself before he called me back and said there was nothing in there or in his memory bank about anyone named Walker, Ridley, or Atwill."

"What about Mitchell having the flu? Did you ask him if that jived?"

"Yup. They did an autopsy on the kid and his system was clean as a whistle. The vomit he choked on was pure chicken soup, fed to him earlier that day by his own mom."

I hit my blinker and merged onto I-71. I thought Malik said at some point that Shawn was staying in Middleburg or Strongsville, and I headed in that general direction. "Speaking of Mrs. Brown, I haven't heard anything from Barnes on whether they're going to release Ernest or if his mom got a lawyer down there. Can you call him?"

"Yeah, soon as we hang up. Oh, and Johnny tracked down an old friend in the admin office at Cleveland State. Mrs. Brown signed Ernest up and paid for that photography class, but he never actually went, so scratch that connection. Far as I can see, Ernest wouldn't have crossed paths with Walker prior to meeting him on the hunt."

"So, basically, we got bupkiss on any connection between Ernest and Mary. Unless Mary really off'ed Walker all by her lonesome and isn't covering for him at all. But it still doesn't tell us why."

"What if—?"

"Holy shit," I said as my phone beeped and got a glance at the screen. "That's Mary finally calling back. Maybe I'll ask her myself."

I hung up on Paul, the sound of him calling my name faint in the background.

"Hello?"

"Samantha? It's Mary Barnes."

Had she not said her name, I would have thought I programmed in the wrong number to her burner at the police station. She sounded like a two-pack-a-day, no-filter smoker who'd gone cold turkey. Her anxiety came at me in waves through the phone and I cut across two lanes to take the next exit, nearly taking out a silver two-door in the process. I ignored the blare of its horn as I coasted down the ramp.

"Hi, Mary. Thanks for call—."

"I need your help."

"What's going on?"

"My Scotty's not doing well."

"How so?"

"I'm worried he's going to try to hurt himself."

"Can you call campus security?"

"We're not at his school. I don't think they could help anyway. I need you. I trust you."

I'll admit, anywhere I went, strangers tended to tell me some pretty dark shit after just meeting me. But this was pushing it.

"Are you with him now?"

"Yes." Mary's voice sounded small. "And I'm afraid."

"For him or yourself?"

"What? No, no, he wouldn't hurt me." Her voice changed from small to unconvincing.

"Mary, where are you exactly?"

"I'm at Scotty's."

I slowed for a red light and tapped my steering wheel in frustration. "I'm confused. I thought Scotty was at school?"

"Not anymore. We're in Strongsville."

What the double hell?

"Mary, you're not making any sense. Do you mean Strongsville, like in Cleveland?"

"Yes, yes. I know how it sounds, but I'll explain later. Right now, I just need your help. He's going to hurt himself if I don't get him help."

"Listen, hang up and call the police."

"I can't. They'll take him away."

"Mary, maybe that's the best thing for him right now."

"No! They'll never let him go."

How messed up was this kid? "You don't know that. And wouldn't you rather have him alive in a hospital than have him—. Have him hurt?"

Mary wailed into the phone. "They won't put him in a hospital. They'll take him to jail."

"What? Why?" I turned my Jetta into a bank parking lot and cut the engine.

"Because—. Because he's done some bad things."

The butterflies in my stomach started warming up their wings. "What kind of bad things?"

I heard Mary breathing and I strained to hear background noises, but there were none.

"Mary, talk to me."

"He didn't mean to, he really didn't."

The wing kicking ramped up into a full-blown synchronized performance. Had Mary roped her own son into killing Walker?

"Mary, if he didn't mean to do the bad things, then maybe the police can get him help in a hospital. Do you think he did these bad things because he's sick?"

"I don't know," she whispered.

"Is Scotty there in the room with you?"

"No, I'm in the bathroom. He'd be upset if he knew I was calling anyone."

"Mary, will he hurt you if he finds out you're talking to me?"

"No, no, never."

"Does he have a weapon?"

Silence, then a throaty moan.

"Does he?"

"He has a gun. But I swear, he won't hurt me. Please, please help me."

Shit, shit, shit. "What's the address?"

I rustled up a napkin from the console and scratched out the info as Mary read it to me. I recognized the section of town, a few miles away from where I'd pulled off the highway.

"Mary, listen. It'll take me close to ten minutes to get there. Go back out and sit with Scott, okay? And think about calling the police."

"I can't," she sobbed into my ear. "He's my son."

I hung up and dialed Barnes with a shaking finger, missing the right digits twice. Calm down, I told myself, but a wave of worry sloshed around in my belly. If Scott was involved in his dad's death and he was going mentally off the rails, Mary may or may not be able to calm him. But if Mary in any way pushed him to do it and now he was having buyer's remorse, Scott may see Mary as a threat. It didn't sound to me like Mary had entertained that thought yet, which meant she likely wasn't prepared to defend herself.

Taking another another deep breath to still my hands, I dialed again and silently begged him to answer, but was sent to Barnes' voicemail after five rings. I left a message that said I found Mary and to call me before he took his next breath, then ended the call and dialed Paul. To my everlasting relief, he answered. I gave him the fifteen-second rundown as I pulled my car onto the main road from the parking lot I'd been camping in.

"Where are you now?" Paul asked.

"I'm headed to the apartment complex."

"Hell no, you're not. Pull over and call 9-1-1."

"What if Scott hears the sirens and does something drastic to defend himself? Or his mom?"

"That's a risk you're going to have to take, Sam. Do not go over there. That's exactly what this woman wants. Call the police."

"I'll call, but I still have to go. I won't go in, I'll just see what I can see."

"Dammit, Sam. No, you won't. Stay away from there. I'm hanging up and calling the police. What's the address?"

"Paul—."

"Give it to me."

I read it out to him.

"Unit number?"

"Sixteen."

"Come back to the office. Now."

"Wait, Paul—." But Paul was gone.

I knocked my head against the seatback in frustration and the phone vibrated in my hand. I looked at the screen, expecting to see Paul calling back and was surprised to see Mary Abram's number come up. Not her burner number, but the number of the cell she'd left behind at home. I answered with a tentative hello.

"Ms. Carter?" A voice I'd heard before but couldn't place boomed in my ear.

"Yes?"

"Harry Abrams. Mary's husband?"

"Yes, of course."

"Have you heard from Mary?"

Unfortunately, yes. "I have. You haven't?"

"Where is she?" Harry shouted in my ear.

"In Cleveland."

"Where? Have you seen her?"

"Mr. Abrams, what's going on?"

"Is Scott with her?" He shouted at me again and I realized it was from fear.

"She says he is, but I don't really know. He may still be at school."

"No, he's not. He hasn't been there for months."

"What?" It was my turn to shout.

"I called. I called the school. Mary stopped answering my calls and I got worried. I tried to call Scott at his dorm, then the administration office. They told me Scott was expelled."

"Why?"

"Grades. He stopped going to class."

I shook my head in an attempt to clear my confusion. "This doesn't make any sense. Mary told me she was at school with him."

"She told me the same thing. I doubt now that she was ever there." He sucked in a deep breath that gurgled over the phone line. "I knew it. I freaking knew it."

"Knew what?"

"He's messed up."

"Scott?"

"He's been messed up since I met Mary."

"Mr. Abrams, did Mary ever say if Walker hurt Scott?"

212

"Walker didn't pay the least bit of attention to Scott."

"Did he abuse him in any way?"

"You mean, like, did he hit him? I don't think so. Mary never said anything about abuse."

I didn't know how Harry Abrams tied into this, but he seemed sincere in his confusion. "Do you—? Do you think it's possible that Mary would have harmed Walker in order to protect Scott?"

"What? From what?"

"From Walker."

"Walker hasn't seen Scott in years. What the hell would she be protecting him from?"

"Maybe not protecting, but maybe payback?"

"After all this time? What are you getting at? Don't try to pin this thing on Mary."

I kept my voice level and braced my hand against the steering wheel. "Are you aware that she confessed to Walker's murder?"

"What the hell are you talking about?"

"The police haven't reached out to you in the last couple days?"

Silence. "There's a couple messages on my machine for me to call a Detective Barnes. I haven't called back. I thought maybe they were just checking to see if Mary had come home yet."

"Did you know she'd been talking to Walker off and on?"

More silence. "She wouldn't hurt a soul."

"Did you know?"

"Maybe it's time for me to call the police back."

Chapter Twenty-Four

I covered the four miles to the apartment complex at a mind-numbingly slow pace and was so overwrought by the time I hit the right block, I missed the entrance and had to double-back. The complex sat on an acre of land, the units themselves all garden style and fashioned into a U around a kidney shaped pool. Yellowed curtains hung in various states of level in most of the windows, and I spotted an assortment of towels and sheets hanging in the windows of the end unit.

I parked in the farthest open spot to the left of the U and scoped out the parking lot. One long strip of asphalt bordered the street-side of the lot, with grass running around the sides. I counted eighteen sparsely-decorated front doors facing the pool. Large wooden numbers were set next to each door and I could make out a twelve and thirteen on the unit doors at the northwest corner of the U. That meant sixteen had to be three doors in from the arm of the U where I sat.

Craning my head around, I saw a young mom with a stroller crossing the far end of the lot toward the tree lawn, and an older man working a footed cane a good twenty feet behind her. The place was otherwise deserted. I heard strains of competing televisions through my cracked window, and somewhere on my end of the complex a child was not happy with the world. No police in the lot, no reassuring ring of sirens in the air. I knew, though, that Paul would have followed through on making the call.

Sweat worked its way into my hairline as I dialed Barnes again. Straight to voicemail this time. I skipped the message-leaving and looked around a final time before working up the nerve to pop open my car door. I eased out and looked back at the curtains of the units closest to me. Seeing no movement, I closed my car door and strode to the grassy area adjacent to the end unit, crossing behind it and taking a look along the back. A patchy field ran as far as I could see. The units all had what amounted to a tiny backyard. A six-by-six cement patch butted up to a screened back door, with a shared pony fence running four feet high around three sides of the cement patch. Beyond the second unit, a full-height fence separated unit seventeen from sixteen. No movement in either of the two end units.

I trampled through the grass to the end of the full-height fence. Squatting low, I peeked around the edge of the fence and found the identical layout separating the backyards between unit sixteen and its neighbor. Screened back doors, pony fence, cement pads. The screen door of unit sixteen was closed, but the slash of light told me the solid door behind it was ajar. I heard the faint sound of clinking dishes just beyond the unit and surmised the back walls supported the kitchen in each apartment.

I backed up a few feet past the fence and trotted back out to the edge of the parking lot. Glancing up and down, I saw the same old man hovering at the far edge of the lot, the young woman and her baby were gone, and no one else was around. Had Paul changed his mind about calling the police?

I ran back around the side of the building, slowing as I neared the fence bordering the apartment again, and crouched back down. Another peek around the fence told me nothing had changed in the thirty seconds I was gone. I squinted first one eye then the other, but couldn't see much beyond the screen door. The light didn't shift the way it might if someone was crossing through its beam and I decided to take my chances. Staying low, I quickly crossed the patch of grass to the edge of the cement pad bordering the screen door and pressed myself up against the wall the right of the doorframe. I held my breath and listened.

The kitchen window above me was closed, but bare of any coverings. I shifted my head a few inches toward the screen door and could see that the solid door behind it was three-quarters of the way open, the screen bent an inch off the track. The light I had seen was coming from the adjacent room, the kitchen itself dark. I slipped my finger between the screen door and the frame to hold it still and pressed my face lightly into the screen to cut the shadows. I made out a pair of jean-clad legs in the space between a living room and the kitchen wall. They looked vaguely male, but otherwise told me nothing. I'd seen a couple pictures of Scott when I'd visited Mary's home in Pittsburgh, but they were school portraits that showed only his upper half.

The denim legs crossed the space again, and were followed by a petite, bare pair topped with yellow shorts. I recognized the length of leg as belonging to Mary. I waited, but neither set of legs passed back through. Pulling my face away from the screen, I looked up at the window above me, then glanced behind me. Where the hell was the cavalry?

I pushed up from my position and tentatively raised my head above the window sill. Through the window, I saw the back of what must have been Scott's head on the other side of a pass-through cut into the kitchen wall. I startled, but held my position when I realized he was facing away from me. I could see a fraction of Mary's head where she stood near the front door, blanch-faced, her hands crossed over her heart the way a four-year-old makes a promise. She said something to Scott that came to me as a muffled murmur. I couldn't see his face, but he must not have liked what he heard because he swung his arms up near his head. I choked on my own spit when I realized one arm held a gun. Mary had warned me, but the reality grabbed me by the throat.

I pressed up on my tippy toes to get a better look at Mary. I couldn't see below her breastbone. Where were the freaking police?

Mary shifted her position from the door. I saw her hands briefly as she pressed them to her chest. They were empty, confirming my fear that she wasn't prepared to defend herself. I watched the back of Scott's head bob and heard the faint reediness of his voice through the window. Mary's face crumpled. We were out of time. I slipped my cell from my pocket and unlocked the screen to dial 9-1-1, but a text came through that stopped my thumb cold.

Malik's name and message filled the screen. He'd sent me Shawn's address from my earlier request. There had to be a mistake. My brain felt fuzzy, and I closed my eyes and took a deep breath to shake my neurons back into working order. I read the numbers on the phone again. I was standing outside of Shawn's apartment.

I hadn't heard Shawn in the background when I talked to Mary on the phone. I hadn't heard anything. I only had Mary's word for it that her son was with her. Had she and Scott somehow overtaken Shawn and she was luring me in to get more leverage against giving Scott up to Barnes? Shawn was a scrawny kid, but Mary was gymnast-petite. From the small glimpses I'd had of Scott, he looked roughly the same size as Shawn. I flashed back to Mary working the rolling pin at her house, man-handling the dough bowl. Between her, Scott, and a gun, Shawn may not have had a chance. Shit. I didn't know who was holding whom at this point, but I had no doubt Scott was becoming erratic.

I dialed 9-1-1, turned the volume down to zero bars, and set it on the edge of the cement pad, the tinny voice of an operator barely making its way up from the earpiece as I took the two steps toward the back door and peered around the edge.

Standing at full height, I could see neither Scott, Shawn, or Mary from the doorway, and fervently hoped it was mutual. Pinching the frame of the screen door between finger and thumb, I eased it open, one inch at a time, letting out a breath after each inch silently passed.

When the door was open wide enough for me to squeeze through, I placed one foot on the linoleum floor of the kitchen. I paused, then slipped the rest of the way into the room, keeping a tight hold on the screen door as I eased it back into place. Two inches from home, the door let out a squeak, but the stream of murmured voices from the next room only grew louder. I let go of the door and crossed the room in two strides.

"Please don't." I heard Mary's voice as a begging whisper. She said the words over and over, like a lullaby. I was hidden behind the eighteen inches of wall sandwiched between the opening of the kitchen to the living room, and the pass-through cut into the wall above the sink. I shifted a foot to my right and angled my head a few inches closer to the pass-through.

Scott stood rocking, his head shaking in sync with his torso, seemingly in response to Mary's plea. He locked his left arm around his torso and intermittently swung the arm holding the gun out in an arc and back to his waist as he twisted his torso side to side. To his right was a cramped bump-out meant to be a dining room, framed by a large window. Every time he swung his arm, I expected to see the window shatter. I still couldn't see the rest of Mary or the rest of the living room, but I stood stock still, not wanting my movement to draw either of their attention.

Scott turned his face to the side, allowing me my first good look at his face, but he was focused entirely on Mary. Had he not, he may have heard the gasp that escaped my mouth when I realized that I was looking at Shawn.

Shawn looked exactly like a kid who'd spent the last couple days playing non-stop video games and eating cereal. His skin was pasty and greasy, his hair lank. His eyes stared dully, blankly empty of life. His mouth hung partly open and he was working his tongue through the gap in his teeth in a slow push and pull. I wondered momentarily if he was high on top of whatever emotions he was dealing with. I wondered with more worry where Scott was. Was he on the other side of the wall? Did he still have a gun, or did Shawn somehow take it from him?

Mary lifted her hands to her chest again, before splaying them out in front of her in a pleading gesture. I prayed that Shawn would snap out of whatever trance had taken over, but I hoped he'd stay in it long enough to distract from me changing positions. I lowered myself to one knee and turned sideways to brace myself against the edge of the kitchen wall. I leaned my torso forward to look around the wall and felt my foot slip in a slick spot. I fell forward onto both hands and knees, my shoe squeaking against the linoleum. I held my breath. Mary never stopped murmuring to Shawn and I felt reasonably sure I remained undetected. A drip of sweat stung my eye, and I squeezed them both shut. I counted to five and, holding tight to the wall, pushed my face back around the corner.

Shawn and Mary remained in their same spots, but Shawn was now looking out the front window and Mary was staring at me. She shook her head once at me, and I combed my eyes over her, looking for any signs of injury. She was wearing slim fit shorts and a thin pink tee, but much of her lower half was hidden by the sofa. I scanned the floor around her, but didn't see any sign of Scott.

"Sweetie, you don't have to do this." Mary begged Shawn.

Sweetie?

"I don't have any other choice."

"Of course you do. I took care of everything." Mary took a step toward Shawn and he waved the gun in a sweeping arc in the general direction of her head. Mary took a step back and clutched her chest harder.

"You can't fix this." The sadness in Shawn's voice would have brought me to my knees if I hadn't already been resting on them.

"Baby, I did. I promise." Mary stepped forward again and this time, Shawn kept the gun loose at his side. Mary looked at him tentatively, then raised an open palm to cradle the side of his face. Shawn leaned into her touch and closed his eyes, but left his mouth ajar and I could see his tongue slowly pulsing in and out of the gap. Tears leaked between his lids as he pressed further into Mary's hand. She took another step until her chest was nearly touching his. She pressed a kiss to his opposite cheek.

I did some quick math in my head and after two tries, still came up with one hell of a Mrs. Robinson gap between the two. What on God's green earth was I watching here?

Shawn opened his eyes and looked curiously into Mary's. She smiled reassuringly back at him.

"How did you fix it?" Shawn asked.

"I told the police that I have proof you couldn't have killed Walker."

The curiosity fell away from Shawn's eyes and anger flared.

"What kind of proof?"

"Let me worry about that."

"Why did you lie?"

"For you. For us."

"What are you talking about? There hasn't been an us for years. Stop trying to make it better. You never made it better. Never."

Mary's hands flew from chest to mouth. "Please don't say that. Please, please."

"But it's true. What are you going to do this time? Tell me to act like nothing bad has happened? Tell me to think myself happy like you did when I was a kid?

"No, Scotty. That's not fair."

Chapter Twenty-Five

Holy hell, I was the dumbest PI-in-training alive. Mary hadn't turned white at the sight of Ernest at Walker's funeral. She had seen Shawn. Her son. Scott.

"Fair?" Scott yelled. "Was it fair when you jumped from guy to guy and left me to figure it out when I was left without a dad again?"

Scott flung his gun arm up again, wide to Mary's body but close enough to do some serious damage at that proximity. I fought between the desire to throw myself into the room to distract him and to hide in the kitchen until help arrived. I realized with a sinking stomach that any rescue might take longer than I had left before whatever climax was about to hit. Scott was back to shoving his tongue through his teeth at an alarming rate.

I heard a familiar squeak behind me and froze. The voices stopped on the other side of the wall and I thought I was made until I realized Mary was crying. I slowly twisted my head, expecting to see police, but instead saw Paul on his knees behind me.

Shuffling backward on my knees, I pivoted around and put a finger to my lips.

I peeked back around the wall and watched in horror as Scott smacked a cell phone out of Mary's hand with a sofa pillow and drove her backward to the dining room wall. Mary's eyes stayed glued to the gun in his hand, twisted against the pillow that was now braced on her chest at an alarming angle. She hit the wall with a whump and surprise brightened her eyes. I stuck my head partway through the door, but couldn't see Scott's face anymore. From its downward tilt and the hitch of his shoulders, he looked to be crying but didn't let go of the pillow pressed into Mary's chest.

"Scotty, please," Mary whimpered. "Let me get you help."

"It's too late."

"No, baby, no. It's not. Give me the gun." Mary raised one hand back to Scott's face, but he shook his head. He was close enough to Mary that his hair whipped her left eye and she twisted her head down to the side in response. Shawn took the opportunity to drop his head into the exposed crook of her neck and began to sob.

Mary had squeezed her eyes shut when she twisted her head and when she opened them, she caught sight of me again. I saw a mix of fear and anger, and she shot a hand up to Scott's head, palming the back of it and effectively keeping his head pinned into the crook of her neck. She cooed in his ear, something unintelligible, but soft. She begged me with her eyes, but I couldn't tell if she was pleading for me to help or leave. Leaving wasn't an option.

I didn't dare look back at Paul, for fear of tipping Mary off that I wasn't alone. I pushed from my knees into a crouch and maintained eye contact with Mary as I inched forward. When I cleared the door, I wove my way around it to the L end of the sofa, away from where Scott had Mary pinned to the wall.

When I made it to the curve of the L, Mary broke her gaze and curled her fingers into Scott's hair, murmuring steadily at him. I couldn't hear her words, but watched as Scott's head bobbed up and down against her neck. Either she was reassuring him or giving him an order to fire at me. Every nerve ending in my body screamed at me, as if I wasn't already aware that my only protection was pressed board and sofa batting.

I heard faint sirens in the background, and caught movement at the edge of the room the same time Mary did. Paul's head appeared, twisting around the door frame to find my location. When his eyes found me, I mouthed 'go back', but he crawled along the back of the sofa until he reached my heels. Mary murmured into Scott's ear again and my chest tightened when I saw his shoulders stiffen. He kept his head buried in her neck, but clearly said 'no.'

"Baby, you have to," Mary said. She lifted her head straight and lifted Scott's by his mane. "They're coming. Give me the gun."

"I just want it to be over."

"It is."

"All of it. I can't take it."

"It was an accident."

"Was it? Maybe it wasn't."

"Scotty, no. It's not your fault." Fear and denial stretched Mary's skin taught across her features.

Scott pulled his head back. "I pushed him. I pushed him so hard. I didn't mean—. I didn't know—." He began to blubber and I lifted my head above the sofa to look at him, but he wasn't saying words anymore so much as mewling.

"It was an accident, baby."

Scott sucked snot into his nose and jammed his tongue through the gap in his front teeth. "Maybe I knew, somewhere in the back of my head. That I could hurt him. I just wanted his attention. He wouldn't give it to me. Even then. Even when I told him who I was, that I was his."

"It's okay, baby, I understand."

"Stop it, Mom. I did it. It's over."

Scott lifted the gun from his side, but stopped as the sound of a siren whooping twice filled the air outside the front door. When it cut off, the silence in the room was deafening. Mary looked at Scott, then at me. Scott followed her gaze and his face showed confusion, then uncertainty. He looked back at Mary, then toward the front window, where a human shadow flitted past. A hard knock came at the door and a deep voice announcing themselves as Strongsville police, followed immediately by Detective Barnes' voice.

"Mary, it's Detective Barnes. Come on out, now."

Scott looked strangely at Mary. "Why is he asking for you?"

Mary hesitated and put up placating hands. "Baby, I told you it would be okay."

"What did you do?"

"Sweetie, trust me."

"Mary Abrams, put down your weapon and let Shawn go," Barnes boomed from the other side of the door. Time's up."

Scott's eyes widened, and he at last appeared to emerge from his fog.

"Mom," he whispered, wild-eyed. "What did you do?"

Mary smiled as sadness washed across her face. "I told them I killed Walker."

Scott's head swung down, and he raised both hands to his head. I pushed out of my crouch, but Paul yanked me down by my shoulders. I fell on my ass, still watching Scott's face. He looked back up at Mary, grief and pain written across his features.

"Why?"

"To protect you. I knew, baby. I knew as soon as I saw you at the funeral. Oh, Scotty." Mary placed a hand on either side of his gun hand. I watched as she slid forefinger and thumb around the barrel, and cringed as Scott's fingers tightened around the handle in response. He pushed her back with his free hand and screamed at the front door.

"I did it! It was me! I killed my dad. I killed him."

"No!" Mary screamed at Scott as he pulled his gun hand back

and pointed the gun at his head. She launched herself at him as two policemen busted through the front door, Barnes behind them.

Mary fell on Scott, slamming his head into the ground, the force of the fall knocking the gun from his hand. I watched as it slid underneath the sofa. Scott landed at the edge of the sofa, head lolled to the side, his eyes staring wide open, reminding me of the way he'd hit the ground in the cemetery. His gaze fell on mine and I felt hot tears course down my cheeks as I watched matching ones roll down his.

Chapter Twenty-Six

"Why don't you take tomorrow off? I can take Vinnie down to Wally's to help me." Paul placed a tissue box on my desk and settled into his chair across from me.

I mopped up my face with a wad of tissues and shook my head. "No, I'll go."

"I'm not trying to give you a hard time here, but I don't think you're in a position to focus."

"It's just an inventory. I can cry and count at the same time."

Paul leaned forward and braced his arms on his desk. "At the risk of sounding like an asshole—."

I raised my damp eyes at him.

"Ok, like more of an asshole than usual. Why has this kid gotten under your skin so much? I get he had a bad childhood, but millions of kids have shitty dads. They don't go around killing them."

I blew out a sigh. "I don't know. I honestly don't. It just feels like such a waste. He seemed like an okay kid, you know? And I feel bad for Vinnie. Speaking of, I need to call and check on him."

"I talked to him a couple hours ago, he'll be fine."

"What did he say?"

"Not much. He was with Jade. I've got a feeling she'll be doing her fair share of the consoling, so you should be off the hook for a while."

My mouth dropped open in surprise, and Paul smirked at me.

"I'm not blind."

"You don't care that he's got eyes for her? What if it goes south?"

"Irrelevant at this point. Jade gave her notice."

"Because of Vin?"

"Hell, no. Jade's a mess as far as the restaurant goes. She's been struggling through training, and her sister offered her a desk job at her husband's business this morning."

I plucked another tissue from the box as the office door opened, and Johnny walked in.

"Hey, kids." He walked between our desks, pulled a chair from the conference/dining table, and rolled it over to the edge of my desk. "How you holding up?"

"Okay." I shrugged. "Just wishing it had been a random stranger or some other jerk. I liked Shawn. Well, Scott, I guess."

Johnny reached over and patted my shoulder. "There's nothing wrong with that. You couldn't have known."

"That's the other problem. I didn't see it. It was right in front of me, and I didn't even stop to consider Shawn." I pointed at Paul. "I keep thinking how you said on the way to the first hunt that you were worried I'd miss information right in front of me. And I did."

Paul wrinkled his face and waved me off. "Jesus, I was just giving you shit about wanting to come up with a stupid back story. Any of us could have missed this."

"But I'm the one who did."

"That was largely my fault. I never should have let you run as far as you did with this." Paul looked uneasily at Johnny. "Which is why I asked Johnny to come over. We need to have a little family meeting."

"Maybe this isn't the best time after all, man," Johnny said, pointing his forehead in my direction.

"Can I tell you how much I freaking hate it when you two talk about me like I'm not here?" I threw a damp tissue at Johnny, who slid his chair sideways in time to deflect it.

"Listen," Paul said, placatingly. "It's my fault you got into the situation at Shawn's apartment."

"No, it's not. You told me not to go and I went anyway."

Paul shook his head and held up a hand. "No, it's deeper than that. You wouldn't have even been in the position to make a bad decision if I didn't have you working the case."

"Holy shit, are you firing me?" I looked from him to Johnny and back again.

"No, no." Paul sat back in his chair. "You have a job here as long as you want it. I just think – we think – that you'd be better suited to work more in the office. Go back to doing traces, admin, behind the scenes type of work."

"Because I messed up."

Paul and Johnny exchanged another look. I slammed my fist into the top of the desk, and Paul threw up both hands.

"Sam, give me a break here. I'm your brother. I'm not going to let you get hurt, let alone be the one to cause it."

"So this isn't about how I'm performing?"

Paul looked at me in surprise. "That's the problem you have with this?"

"Yes! I may be a screw-up at times, but I think I've been doing a pretty damned good job overall. And I thought you thought so, too. I thought that's why you've been letting me run on my own so much."

Paul stared at me, mouth tense, but silent. I looked at Johnny. "You feel the same way? Is that why Paul said 'we'? Does that mean you're taking the partnership?"

Johnny looked at me carefully, and I watched his pupils darken with emotion. "I don't want you to get hurt, either, Sam."

"And?"

"And nothing. I don't want you to get hurt. Period."

"And the partnership?"

Paul leaned back over his desk. "We've decided not to pursue the partnership at this point."

"Really?" I looked between the two of them, settling my eyes on Johnny. I wanted badly to ask why, but wasn't sure I wanted to hear the answer in front of my brother. Johnny searched my eyes and I knew he could sense my hesitance. Evidently, Paul could, too.

"The decision has nothing to do with you two wanting to bop each other. Or about you bopping each other before, or if you're going to do it again." Paul waved his hand as if confronted with a bad smell.

"We didn't bop," I said quietly.

"Whatever," Paul said. "I don't care. Bop away. I still don't want to know about it. Not as a boss, but as a grossed-out brother."

"No, nuh-uh. I'm not going to be the reason you two can't do business and be friends."

"You're not, and don't be so self-centered. Johnny and I are good enough friends to separate the two things. He just got a better offer."

I looked at Johnny. "What offer?"

"I'm going to contract with agencies and clients who have long-distance work that their local offices can't support."

"Like the North Carolina gig?"

He nodded. "Exactly. My old employer has thrown me a few more referrals for similar work, and I found out there's a good market for on-the-road PI work. I can pick up more than enough to make it my mainline, and still help out my old agency when they need it. And I'll contract with Paul here when you guys need it."

"So you'll be on the road?" I kept my voice steady.

Paul caught my eye and headed into the kitchen. When we were alone, Johnny rolled his chair behind the desk next to mine and took my hand in his. "Not all the time, and not for long stretches at a time. A few days here, a couple weeks there. I'll still live here."

I nodded and stared at my hand nestled in the bowl of his long fingers.

"What are you thinking?" Johnny squeezed my hand lightly.

"I'm thinking I'm pissed."

Johnny laughed. "That's not one of the top five reactions I thought you might have."

I took my hand from his and squared my chair to his. "What, did you think I'd throw myself at you and tell you not to go?"

Confusion crossed Johnny's face. "No, but I thought—. Hell, I thought you might be a little happy that we wouldn't have the partnership constraint. That we could see where this thing with us goes."

"Happy? I've just been demoted and lost you to an option I didn't even know existed."

"You haven't lost me."

"That's right," I said, pushing my chair back. "I never had you."

Chapter Twenty-Seven

I unrooted myself from my blankets Sunday morning with the mother of all headaches. I reached for my bleating cell phone and the voice on the other end did nothing for the pain in my head.

"Detective Barnes, to what do I owe the pleasure?"

"Carter, you sound like you just woke up. It's 10 a.m. Get your ass going."

"I give, I can't do this today. What's up?"

"Thought you'd like to know that we released Ernest yesterday afternoon."

I struggled to sit up against my headboard. "How is he?"

"Not great. But his mother told me she's arranging for intensive counseling. Somebody who can come to Ernest's place and help him work through his issues."

"Thank God for that." I hesitated. "What about Shawn? Will he get counseling?"

Barnes was silent and I heard him take a deep breath. "Scott. Scott will be arraigned tomorrow."

"For?"

"First-degree murder."

"And he'll plead guilty to that?" I thought back to Scott screaming his guilt through the door of the apartment. I guessed that three police personnel hearing a direct admission probably wouldn't help him any.

"No, he's pleading not guilty."

"Really?"

"For now, that's my understanding. His official story is that he invited Walker the night of the murder to set the clues with him, then told Walker who he really was. Walker hadn't recognized Scott and when he learned who he was, Scott says Walker blew him off. Didn't apologize for not being around when Scott was a kid, and went on and on about how it was his life that had been impacted by having a kid so young. He didn't acknowledge that Scott was the one who was hurt most of out the deal. Scott says he lost it in the moment and pushed his dad, but he didn't mean to kill him. He says Walker hit the edge of the planter and didn't move after that."

"Gee-zuss."

"Yeah, can't say as I believe the accidental bit, but we'll have trouble showing intent based on the physical evidence."

"Why don't you think it was accidental?"

"'Cause he copped to tracking down Walker on purpose. Kid drops out of school, lies to his parents, sets up a new life here and plays co-worker to his dad for months."

"Can't you believe that maybe Scott wanted to re-connect with his dad. In a real way?"

Barnes snorted. "And waits six months to say anything about who he really is?"

"Do you always to go to the worst possible scenario first?"

"Carter, I've been at this too long to do anything else. Wait another thirty years and your optimism will be for shit, too."

"I can't stand the thought of that."

"If you want to be an investigator, get used to it. By the way, speaking of you and your brother's two-bit show, you don't have to worry about those hunt clues being messed with anymore. Scott copped to doing that as payback for Walker making him set all the clues."

"I think that's the least of anyone's concern at this point, but I'll let Malik know. What about Mary? Do you think she was involved?"

"Not in Walker's death, but she definitely was trying to cover for Scott. After she saw him at Walker's funeral, she went back to Pittsburgh, packed a bag, made it look good for hubby, conveniently left her phone behind, and came straight back to Cleveland."

"Will she be charged?"

"Up to the district attorney's office, but unlikely. She technically didn't harbor or obstruct because she didn't know for sure if Scott had killed Walker, and we weren't looking at Shawn – Scott – for the murder."

"Do you think Scott will go to prison?"

"We'll see if he claims temporary insanity, or maybe they'll let him cop to murder two. Could be he'll see a manslaughter charge in the end, but that's not my preference nor my call."

I nodded into the phone but couldn't get any words out.

"Sam, I know you got the softies for him, but keep in mind the kid didn't call for help. He left his father to die alone in a flower bed."

"I know he has to be held responsible, but I want to see him get some help."

"And I want to see justice done."

"Why can't we have both?"

$$\Omega\Omega\Omega$$

I turned into the back alley behind Dudek's and coasted around the end of the building, braking when I saw all four slots were filled. Wally's car took up residence in one, but I didn't recognize the other three cars. We'd agreed to meet at ten o'clock after the shop was closed and I was surprised to see other vehicles. All the businesses in the strip were shuttered for the night.

Paul and Johnny stood next to Wally's open driver's side window. They both looked up as I drove around the corner and I rolled down my window as they trotted over to me. Paul leaned down and braced both forearms on the window frame.

"We having a party?" I asked.

"We were just wondering that ourselves." Paul leaned back and pointed toward the front of the building. "If you go out to the street and look through the window, you can see lights on in the rear of the shop."

"Who closed the store tonight?"

"Erin." He waved at the other cars parked on the side of the building. "These aren't ours. Johnny and I parked out on the street."

"Why don't we go take a look? Isn't it possible Erin just forgot to turn the lights off?"

Paul grinned. "See why I worry about you? Your first reaction is to go running into the fire."

I hit the auto feature on my window and moved to put my car in reverse.

"Wait, wait, shit." Paul gestured to me to put the window back down. I left it up and was working up some indignant mouth motions when he threw up his hands and I heard a muffled "you win" from the other side of the glass.

I motored down the window halfway. "Define 'win'."

Paul looked up at Johnny, who stood next to the hood and watched me through the windshield.

"Don't look at him," I said. "If he's not your partner, then you kicking me out of the agency is your decision."

Paul turned his head toward Johnny again before catching himself and looking back down at the window ledge. I watched his shoulders rise and fall, then he lifted his head back up to look at me.

"I'm not kicking you out. I'm watching out for your safety. You're my sister."

"Horseshit. You're making me a secretary. And doing that because I'm your sister is no different than you not wanting Johnny and me to work to together because we're—."

Johnny looked at me with interest and they both waited. I squeezed my eyes shut. "Whatever we were. You know what I mean."

Paul stared at me a few beats, then chewed the corner of his mouth. I bit back a smile. I knew from years of holidays playing Battleship with Paul on the floor of Nonni's den that I was about to sink his last carrier. I snuck a peek at Johnny and saw the smile in his eyes. He knew it, too.

"There will be rules." Paul gripped the window and gave me his school teacher glare. "That you will follow. And you will keep me better informed on your cases."

I raised my eyebrows and Paul held up a palm. "And I will be more involved. Especially now that this clown is deserting us."

We both looked at Johnny, then I met Paul's eye. "Do you promise to talk to *me* about me, instead of him?"

"How about I promise to talk to you first before anyone else?"

I wedged my hand out the window. "Deal."

Paul smacked the roof of my car. "Go park. We've got undies to count."

I gave the Jetta some gas and eased out onto the street. By the time I parked and ran back up into the side lot, Wally had gotten out of his car and all three stood at the back door to Dudek's.

Wally keyed the metal door and Paul held up a hand when Wally attempted to cross the threshold. He pushed past Wally and Johnny pushed passed both of us to follow Paul.

Wally looked at me with raised eyebrows. "I've never felt more like a 1950's housewife than I do right now."

My jaw dropped. "Wally, you have a sense of humor."

Wally ducked his head but not before I caught a glimpse of his grin. I swatted him on the back. "Come on, Wallster."

We crossed the threshold into the back hallway, walked past the familiar delivery squares marked on the concrete floor and stopped when we saw Paul and Johnny gawking through the opening to the showroom. I heard a faint trickle of music, with the kind of tinny quality you get from a cheap cell phone.

I stood on tiptoes to peer over Johnny's shoulder while Wally angled to look around Paul's torso.

Holy Ample Man. I squeezed my eyes shut and feared for a hot second that the one hit of acid I'd tried in high school had finally taken effect. I opened my eyes again and felt my mouth drop into the same gawking position as Paul and Johnny.

The tinny music I'd heard had amplified into what I recognized as The Weather Girls' *It's Raining Men*. Along the far side of the shop, streaming from the dressing rooms in one continuous parade line, were a half dozen male models adorned in nothing more than fuchsia bow ties and matching, polka-dotted silk boxers. An assortment of blondes and brunettes, peaches and cream and ebony skin, muscles and lean swimmer's bodies paraded in a loop onto the showroom floor. All wore white-on-white sneakers. And not a one measured over four feet tall.

I found my voice and whispered at Wally. "Ample Man?"

"Depends on your perspective, but I'd say so." Wally's eyes bugged in his sockets.

"No, Wally. The underwear. Are they from your Ample Man line?"

"Oh, yes. Yes, the fuchsia is new. Arrived this week."

The last model appeared from the dressing room and the group turned as one unit, high-kicked for three beats, and half the group collapsed to their knees, hands splayed out at their sides while the remaining half stayed on their feet with hands thrust above them into the air. They held their grand finale pose and the sound of weak clapping came from the dressing room.

"Well, gentlemen, what do you think? You want to do the fuchsia and the green this time?" The four of us hiding in the hallway simultaneously craned our necks around the wall to see Erin's greaser man-boy, Lionel, standing behind a clothing rack just outside the dressing room. Hovering behind him, misery written all over her face, was Erin.

One of the models broke his pose and pushed up from the floor. "We're going to need a better price if you want us to take both colors."

Lionel ran his forefinger and thumb under his nose, mimicking deep thought. He was a horrible actor, and I got the impression he bought into his own act. "The way I see it, where you gonna get better stock than what I can get you?"

The model straightened his back, thrusting his hips forward in the process. Johnny, Paul, Wally, and I sucked in a collective breath.

"Can you guarantee fifty sets by Friday?" the model asked Lionel. "You only delivered half last time and we had to dress half the boys with regular fit. Trust me when I tell you our guests do not appreciate a baggy fit."

"I'm giving you a helluva a deal as it is." Lionel looked at Erin. "And we've improved our, uh, ordering system. We'll get you everything by midweek."

The spokesmodel considered Lionel for a moment, then stuck out a tiny hand. "Alright, Dudek, we'll take both."

I felt a fist in my side as Wally pushed me to the side and squeezed between Johnny and Paul. He marched into the showroom and right up to the spokesmodel. Wally only had a foot on the man, but leveraged every inch of it to tower over him. Paul and Johnny automatically followed him, but stopped a couple feet short of the whole display.

Wally's face had turned crimson and he was shaking a finger first at the spokesmodel, then at Lionel. "He is not Dudek. I am Dudek!"

Lionel took two steps to the left and Johnny sidestepped to block him. "Hang tight, my friend." He wrapped one hand around Lionel's biceps and Lionel swallowed hard. He suddenly looked like the boy I initially thought he was.

The spokesmodel balled his fists and jammed one onto each petite hip. "I don't care who you are as long as I still get my deal."

"You're not getting any deal," Wally retorted.

"The hell I ain't. I dragged my boys all the way out here at this god forsaken hour to cater to him—." He pointed at Lionel. "And I'm getting the deal we agreed to."

"I didn't agree to any deal. And that joker's sure as heck ain't in a position to agree to squat. Who are you?"

Spokesmodel looked Wally up and down fully for the first time. Wally was taller by a negligible inch and the model seemed to acknowledge their commonality with a sly smile.

"We're Naughty in the Night." Spokesmodel waved a proud hand at the models still frozen in their finale positions.

"I beg your pardon?"

"Naughty in the Night. We're a professional dance troupe. For ladies."

"They're strippers. Midget strippers." We all looked at Lionel. "What can I say? You do business on Craig's List, you can find some unique business opportunities."

Wally shook his head at Lionel in disgust and took a half-step closer to the spokesmodel. "Listen, I don't care if you're putting on The Wiz for the Pope. The only deal you're getting from me is a trip to the police station. These are stolen goods you're trying to buy."

"Hey, man." Spokesmodel took a step back and started to unwrap the bowtie from his neck. "We didn't know that."

I piped up from the back and pointed a finger at Lionel. "You really thought this dude was the owner? He's like twelve."

Spokesmodel looked down the length of his own body and back. "I'm the last person who's gonna judge a book by its cover."

I shrugged in response. He had a point.

"You can't prove we knew this stuff was stolen," Spokesmodel said to Wally. He turned around and gestured to the rest of the models. "Boys, get it all off. We're outta here."

All five models began to unpeel their bow ties and I coughed hard when two of them slipped a finger into the waistband of their underwear. "Um, Wally?"

"Oh, no. No, no." Wally's angry crimson flared to a new level and his voice squeaked. "Leave it on. Just take it. Take what's on you. Just get your things and go."

The models formed a single line and wound their way back to the dressing rooms. Wally turned to Erin, who had inched her way toward the back wall by edging behind the cashiering counter.

Her face crumpled when she met Wally's eye. "I didn't want to do it, Mr. Dudek, I swear. He made me."

Wally looked over at me, then at a point behind my shoulder. I turned and saw two uniformed patrolmen standing in the entry to the showroom. Paul stood at their shoulder, filling them in on who was who.

Wally walked over to Erin and put his hands on her shoulders. With the height difference, it looked like they were slow dancing at the junior high jubilee.

"Erin, I know your auntie. Your people are good people. What are you doing with this hoodlum?"

Erin swiped at the teal mascara leaking to the tops of her cheeks. "I didn't know what he was going to do. We were going out and having a good time, and I was going to move in with him. He said we would do this just once to help with the rental deposit on our apartment." Erin's eyes widened in guilt at Wally. "Then my mom and auntie Marnie met him and hated him, and I tried to break up with him, but he said he'd tell the police what I'd done. He promised he'd let me go if I did just one more order with him."

Wally shook his Black and Tan hair and pulled a disappointed face. He looked over at the police, who were talking to Lionel.

"Listen, if you tell your family what you did and promise to say away from this loser, I'll see what I can do to help you with the police."

I tried to bite down on my smile, but Wally caught it. He squirmed and looked back at Erin.

"Really?" Erin clasped her hands over Wally's. "Oh, Mr. Dudek. I swear, I'll tell Ma as soon as I get home."

"I know you will. I'm driving you there to watch you do it."

I smelled Johnny's cologne and turned my cheek to find him standing behind my right shoulder.

"What are you smiling at?" he said into my ear.

I shrugged but couldn't wipe away the smile. "Wally might not be as much of a goober as Vinnie thinks. He should see this side of Wally."

"Somehow I don't think Vinnie's ever going to give this guy a second chance."

"Never say never." I nodded in Erin's direction. "If Wally can give her a pass, Vinnie can give it a try."

"Speaking of second chances." Johnny pressed one hand into the small of my back. "We need to talk."

I turned around and patted his arm. "I'll pass. I've seen enough dysfunctional relationships the last few days. I think I'm ready for something a little more straightforward."

Chapter Twenty-Eight

"This isn't working." Roman said.

"Want me to rub it some more?" I asked. He shook his head and I rolled off him to sit up straight on my sofa. "I've heard it happens to a lot of guys."

Roman let out a laugh that quickly turned into a moan. He tried to pull himself to a sitting position, and I held out both hands toward his. He looked at my hands, sighed, and waved me off.

"That's messed up. Don't be telling your friends I couldn't perform."

"But the truth is so boring," I said. "I'd think that telling them you pulled a muscle in your back before you even scored the first kiss would be more embarrassing than you not getting Roman Jr. to salute."

Roman cut me a look, but from his prone angle he came off looking more sleepy than disapproving. "You're obviously not a man."

"Thanks for noticing."

"You know what I mean." Roman's eyes softened and he waggled his eyebrows at me. "Oh, no. You're thinking. I can see it in your face."

I picked at the ticking creeping out of the corner of the sofa cushion. "Maybe you throwing your back out is the universe's way of telling us we shouldn't have started anything here."

Roman turned a pained look toward the ceiling. "If that were the case, why couldn't the universe have just jammed a nail into my tires on the way over here?"

My doorbell rang and I made for the front door, grateful for the interruption. I'd been mentally hemming and hawing since I agreed to the date. When Roman wrenched his back sitting down on my sofa, I wanted to boo and cheer at the same time.

I popped open the front door and found Johnny staring back from the other side of the glass.

Gee-zuss. I swallowed hard and forced myself not to look back at the sofa, which was aligned to the front wall of the house and out of sight from the front door. I prayed to every saint I could think of that Roman would stay quiet. Christopher, Michael, Paul. I threw in Ringo for good measure before Johnny started looking at me funny.

"You gonna let me in?" He reached for the handle on the storm door.

I reached out and held onto it from the other side. I flicked the lock with my thumbnail and Johnny registered the metal click with surprise.

"You can't still be that pissed at me," he said.

"I'm not pissed at you." I looked at him and he looked at the door handle.

"Samantha."

Peter, Paul, and Mary. I had run out of saints and was starting to panic. I heard the sofa squeak behind me and my stomach dropped to my bare feet. Johnny's eyes moved past me and I watched as the car crash of reactions played out on his face. Surprise, confusion, and then something that caught me completely off guard. Hurt.

"Sam?" Roman said from behind me.

"Uh-huh?" I couldn't take my eyes off Johnny's face. Roman put a hand on my shoulder and I turned to look back at him. The half-smile on his face faded away and he looked to Johnny and back to me.

"I'll get out of your way." Roman moved his arm past me to push on the door handle, then fidgeted with the lock until he was able to pop the door. I stood helpless, eyes locked back on Johnny's.

Roman pushed out the door and past Johnny without a word. Johnny had eyes only for me. We stared at each other until I heard Roman's engine turn over and accelerate down the street.

"It's not what you think," I said.

"That would be easier to believe if I couldn't see your hair."

I took a full step back from the door and leaned around it to peek in the foyer mirror. Shit. My head had been rubbing against the back of the sofa while I was rubbing the knot in Roman's back, and I looked like a groundhog had attacked me in the park. I leaned back around the front door.

"Okay, it's kind of what you think, but nothing happened."

Johnny took a step down off the stoop.

"Johnny, just come in and let me explain."

He held up a hand, turned, and headed down the walkway. "Not my business. Like you said, I never had you."

"That's not exactly what—."

"Close enough."

"That's not fair."

Johnny kept walking.

"Hey, you're the one taking a long-distance job," I called out to him. Johnny stopped at the curb and slowly spun around on one heel.

"That's what I wanted to tell you last night. I changed my mind.

ACKNOWLEDGMENTS

My endless gratitude goes to my insanely encouraging family and friends. Mamow, Jay, Ben, Brian, Junior, Tom Sr., Michele, Dee Dee, Tony, Neal, Carmen, and the entire Cleveland Office. For your ears, shoulders, suggestions, editing pens, and more…you're the collective reason this all got done.

Many thanks to my professional network at Desert Sleuths, Book Passages, Dog Eared Pages and independent bookstore family in Cleveland, Ohio.

An extra special thanks to Mel and Thom for introducing me to the "community".

Loving thanks to Jamie for allowing me to hijack every single Saturday.

A wink-and-a-nod thanks to Debbie Pullins for the inspiration she gave me that we can't talk about out loud.

Above all, as always, to the city of Cleveland and its many characters, both real and imagined. She is the muse of all muses, for both Sam and for me.

BOOKS IN THE SAMANTHA CARTER SERIES
CLUELESS IN CLEVELAND
CONNED IN CLEVELAND

ABOUT THE AUTHOR

Deborah "Nelle" Lewis is a fiction writer who splits her time between Phoenix, Arizona and Cleveland, Ohio. She has roamed all over the country, hopping lily pads coast-to-coast. Her eighteen-year stop in Ohio cemented the state forever in her heart as home.

She can be found online at dlwrites.com.